A Book of Two Halves

New Football Short Stories

A Book of
Two Halves

New Football
Short Stories

Edited by Nicholas Royle

VICTOR GOLLANCZ

LONDON

First published in Great Britain 1996
by Victor Gollancz
An imprint of the Cassell Group
Wellington House, 125 Strand, London WC2R 0BB

A Gollancz Paperback Original

A catalogue record for this book is
available from the British Library.

ISBN 0 575 06323 8

Typeset by Rowland Phototypesetting Ltd,
Bury St Edmunds, Suffolk.
Printed and bound by
Guernsey Press Co Ltd, Guernsey, Channel Isles.

96 97 98 99 10 9 8 7 6 5 4 3 2 1

For Fred Hardman

Contents

Acknowledgements

Thanks to Andrew Shields, Ivan Robinson and Brian Glanville; Mike, Ian, Lucy and Mic; Francis Lee, Georgi Kinkladze and everyone at Man City; Kate, Dave & Ruth, Nigel & Yuka, and my dad for taking me to Maine Road in the first place.

M John Harrison

I Did It

Chelsea lose two–nil at home to Portsmouth, and you want to go home and bury an axe in your face. You want to do it, there and then, bury it in your face. You tell your friends, they never believe you. Normally, you'd think twice. What sort of *sound* would it make? That puts you off. But this time, Two–nil, you think. Christ, that's it, I'm doing it. This time I really am. Chunk. Axe in the face.

It's easily done. Some people do that and it isn't even football.

Alex did it.

Alex did it and then phoned Nicola.

He said: 'I did it. I said I would, and I have.'

'Is that you, Alex?' she said.

'Don't you even recognize my voice any more?'

'I haven't got time for this,' she said.

She rang off.

Alex rang back. He said: 'You never believed I'd do it.'

'Wrong, Alex,' she said. 'I wished you would.'

'I'm coming to see you.'

'No you're not.'

'I'm coming for lunch,' he said. 'One o'clock.'

He got himself into the Audi and drove from Islington to Soho, where he waited outside her building. There was a sweet April wind. Alex breathed it deeply, feeling nothing he had expected to, only a delighted tranquillity. He did notice that he had quite an appetite. When Nicola came out of the building she stopped and stared at him.

'Still as beautiful as ever,' said Alex, though privately he thought she had put on weight.

'Christ, Alex, you sick fuck.'

'Good, isn't it?' said Alex. 'I hit myself in the face with it until it stuck. It was quite hard to do that.'

'Christ.'

'I had to use a mirror. I kept swinging it in the wrong direction.' He laughed rather wildly. 'And they call it the easy way out!'

'Well, I'm not coming to lunch with you like that,' she said.

Later, Alex saw her in a west London restaurant with Chris. They looked happy. Alex, who was less happy, had to turn his face sideways before he could press it up against the glass. Nicola and Chris, he saw, were eating respectively a layered sandwich of hand-rolled buffalo mozzarella with chargrilled vegetables; and bruschetta of seared baby squid. They were drinking red, but Alex couldn't make out the label. It was probably house red. Chris wiped his mouth on a napkin. He smiled. He leaned forward to lightly touch the inside of Nicola's arm above the wrist. Alex waited until they came out of the restaurant and then jumped in front of Nicola waving his arms.

'Like it? It's *your fault.*'

'It's a very female thing,' Nicola was explaining to Chris, 'like giving birth with wolves.'

She said: 'Alex, I'm not having this.'

Chris looked embarrassed.

I Did It

'Lost your tongue, Chris?' Alex asked him. 'I've lost mine.'

Alex wasn't one hundred per cent certain Chris's name was Chris. Everyone who lived in west London was called Chris, and that was the name he thought he remembered: but he did admit it could easily have been Sam, or Ben. He phoned Nicola up at one o'clock in the morning. 'Chris there with you?'

'Alex, leave me alone.'

'Is it Chris? I had the idea it might be Sam.'

'Alex, I'm getting an injunction.'

'I've had some photographs taken,' Alex said. 'Give one to Chris. It's his fault too.'

'Alex—'

'Is it Chris? They all have the kinds of names you give Border collies. Sam. Mick. Bill. Ben.'

'—for God's sake leave me alone.'

Alex said: 'Bill and Ben, eh?'

He said: 'I did it for you, Nicola.'

And he burst into tears.

Nicola did it next.

'You'll be pleased to know I've done it too,' she said. 'You made me, Alex. Chris couldn't bear you following us about.' It was her turn to burst into tears. 'Alex, he left me for some scrawny little twenty-year-old, and it's your fault. How does that make you feel, Alex?'

It made Alex feel annoyed.

'You've got no imagination of your own,' he said. 'Women never have.'

Nicola laughed nastily.

'I'm coming round to show you, Alex.'

'Show Chris,' said Alex, and hung up.

*　　*　　*

People all over London are walking about with axes buried in their faces. You see them on Tubes and buses, you never know why they did it. It might be that their whole family died in a nuclear incident on a visit to Poland. But it's more likely that they have recently been stood up, or that last night they had to talk to Igor the comics bore at the Academy Club:

'Nobody would ban *Lady Chatterley's Lover* these days. They just don't have time to read it. Visual images are a different thing.'

Chunk. Axe in the face.

The moment Nicola started following Chris, Alex stopped following Nicola.

It happened this way:

One morning he woke with a terrific headache. In the bathroom he was surprised by the thought: Is it a *good* axe? He also thought: Is an axe too much of a statement? Finally he thought: I'm not sure I ever liked this anyway. He examined his face, turning it right and then left, careful to stand back from the mirror. The axe was off-centre, and twisted a bit where it had bounced off his top gum. That had always spoilt it for him, as had the effect it gave of a hare-lip. He shaved round the axe and looked at it again.

'No. No good.'

Midday, he phoned Nicola.

'I've had it out,' he said.

'Why should I care?'

'They have to lever quite hard,' Alex told her, 'when they're loosening it. It's a very male, a very physical experience. How would I describe it?'

'I didn't ask.'

Alex thought for a minute.

'It's a bit like having your wisdom tooth done,' he explained. 'You know?'

He said: 'Now it's out, I feel great!'
Nicola put the phone down.

Chris told Nicola, as kindly as he could:
'Nicola, you need counselling.'
The very next time she phoned him, he hung up,
although not before she had heard her replacement in
the background, calling: 'Chris, is that the Mad Bitch?
Come and fuck me afterwards! Chris? Chris?'
She phoned Alex.
'Alex, I'm so miserable.'
'Get a life,' advised Alex.
He said: 'I have.'

That was the low point, they now agree. Shortly afterwards they were accepted for joint counselling at Islington Relate. As soon as they felt able to talk over their
differences without the help of a third party, they
arranged to meet in the Bar Italia on Frith Street. It
was a Saturday evening at the beginning of September.
Nicola wore her long, silver, one-sleeved dress from
Amanda Wakeley on Fulham Road, and carried an Anya
Hindmarch bag with a *diamanté* clasp. She was a little
late. She found Alex watching Italian football on the
Bar Italia TV: Juventus v AC Milan.
'Aren't you cold in that?' he asked Nicola. He said:
'You look very nice.'
The counselling service had persuaded Nicola to
have her axe out. She felt a little nervous, a little
exposed, without it; and she was shocked and upset to
see that Alex's was back. He had planted it squarely in
the middle of his face. This time he had thought about
it properly and gone for a good practical Stanley with
a black rubber grip. He looked tired.
'Alex! *Who is it?*'
'What?

M John Harrison

'Alex, *that*!'

'This? Oh, this is just United losing to City this afternoon,' laughed Alex. 'I'll get over it.'

M John Harrison was born in 1945. His first story, 'Marina', was published in *Science Fantasy* magazine in 1966 under the name John Harrison because the editor thought the M was short for Mister. He has since published three collections of stories and eight novels, of which *In Viriconium* was nominated for the *Guardian* Fiction Prize in 1982 and *Climbers* won the Boardman Tasker Memorial Award in 1989. His new novel, *Signs of Life*, will be published in the spring of 1997 by Victor Gollancz. He lives in London.

Christopher Kenworthy

Them Belgiums

Some people say there's beauty in everything, if you know how to look. But they've probably not spent much time in Belgium. I've driven through that country about two hundred times in the past few years, and managed to get through without stopping, not even for a piss. I'd slap the heater on full, and get the van to the ferry as fast as possible, not wanting to pause in such a hideous place. There are no seasons in Belgium, only changes in the severity of rainfall. The clouds let through a chilled, doughy light, which makes it feel like evening all the time. In England the leaves go yellow and glow at the end of the year; it's comforting, a little reward of colour before winter. In Belgium, the pine trees just get blacker the more it rains. They hold water in the air, so the country is swathed in a constant misty drizzle. When I was forced to stop south of Brussels last October, I thought I'd hate every frozen minute of being there. It was a surprise to see two beautiful things in one day.

Normally, I don't drive further than Wiesbaden, just an hour or so over the German border. There's a warehouse there, where I sell second-hand rock CDs for obscene prices. The Germans have a surprising amount of old jazz vinyl, and they're keen to trade it off, which is convenient. The journey's shorter than you'd think, if you get through Belgium quickly enough.

This time I went four hours further east, to Chemnitz,

because I'd heard about an auction where they were virtually giving away van loads of rarities. One Pres. Young record alone paid for the petrol. The auction was badly organized, though, and didn't finish until four o'clock. I hadn't accounted for the distance, or Friday traffic, and my eyelids thickened hours before I was due to reach the port. Exhaustion forced me to pull off at Tournelle, north of Spa. It looked more like a village than a town, apart from the massive football stadium, crowded with eight huge floodlight stacks, which illuminated the rain around them.

I knew I would have to find a cheap guest-house quickly, because I was too tired to drive safely, but I wanted a better look at the stadium. The road ran by the edge of a fenced-off car park, and I could make out signs which showed that the place had been funded by several EC grants. A nearby placard said there was a match tomorrow afternoon. Tournelle v Bruges. A vandal had spray-painted the word 'ballet' across this in red, which didn't make much sense at the time.

My sleep that night was deep, despite the fact that Mme Barrault insisted the heating be left off through-out the guest-house. 'We wait until November,' she said, in well-rehearsed English, 'for winter.' It wasn't the cold that bothered me, so much as the damp which made the duvet sticky. My need for sleep pushed me through discomfort, and I slept until after breakfast. I try to avoid sleeping in foreign hotels, because they make me homesick. There aren't many people to miss at home, but sleeping so far from home means hours and hours without a word to anyone. It makes me tearful, some-times. Having got through without a frown, I was proud of myself. The only thing that bothered me was the thought of my City season ticket. We were playing Bolton, and we'd probably slaughter them. I couldn't make it back in time, but it felt wrong to go a Saturday afternoon without football.

As I wandered out into the fresh, wet air, I could see the floodlights of the stadium between the trees of the park opposite. I could head straight through for a look, or I could find some food, a baguette, or the Belgian equivalent. I opted for the latter, which turned out to be a glazed loaf, dusted with purple-black poppy seeds. It was dry, but edible, and it gave me enough energy to walk over to the stadium. There was no real reason to go there, because I had no reason to watch their match, except that I might see some goals. I could even cheer on the local side. I wouldn't be missed if I didn't go back today, so there was nothing to stop me from staying.

That wouldn't have been the case three months ago. I tried not to think about Alice while abroad, but she was unavoidable now. We never exactly lived together, but she slept over at my flat so often we may as well have done. She came to one game with me a few weeks after we met, to show interest, which was good of her. Except that she picked her hands all the way through, and never looked up.

'Watch the match,' I kept saying, and she'd glance up, raise her eyebrows, then concentrate on her flaking cuticles. She missed two scorching goals, and I didn't enjoy them the same, because I knew she was bored. I felt silly jumping out of my seat, and she looked at me as though I was stupid.

Alice had no understanding of football, especially when it came to television.

'Look away now,' said Michael Buerk, part way through the news, 'if you don't want to know the scores.'

I covered my eyes, and begged Alice to do the same.

'I'm not covering my eyes,' she said, making a fluffing

sound after the last syllable, to show disapproval.

'Please.'

'I've seen them now.'

'Well, don't let me know,' I said, certain she'd give it away.

'It's only a game,' she cussed, leaning on to me, her body all sloppy, arms seeming far too long. I sat up trying to breathe more easily, wondering if she could possibly keep a secret until the highlights of the match were over. That was about two and a half hours from now. Unlikely.

'Stop worrying. You'll enjoy it.'

'Oh, so that means we won.'

She smirked. 'I'm not saying anything, but I can't wait to see your face.'

When *Match of the Day* came on, I spent more time trying to work out her body language than I did watching the game. Afterwards she went straight to bed, my bed, expecting me to follow. When I walked in she was curled up, face hidden. She didn't speak for about two minutes while I stripped off, then, as I was about to get in, she said, 'Well, your team won, I don't know what you're so bothered about.' And then a minute later, 'I don't know what you're sulking for.'

She was also prone to saying, 'You watch your football,' trying to sound all understanding. Which meant, *Don't you dare watch. If you have any interests other than me, you're a shit.*

Why do we waste our time with these people? It will never work out. Even if you stay together, she's going to piss you off like this every time there's a game on. Or any time she's not getting exactly her own way. That's no way to spend your life. But we're told to be considerate, to work at it, sort it out, say sorry. There's more to life than football. So you agree, calm things down, apologize.

Them Belgiums

But then you find yourself sitting in the bath, door locked, muttering, 'What's the fucking point?' while she's on your phone to her mates, making plans for the night. At that moment you should stop, because in all honesty you'd rather watch the match than spend more time with her. To shut you up, she says that's not the issue; it's not football. But you can guarantee that if you're going to make her happy, there won't be any talk of goals this afternoon.

Everybody has somebody they regret, my mate Colin used to say to me. It was just a phrase he liked repeating when things weren't going well for me, or when he was especially boxed. It always seemed fitting, and we'd both nod slowly. I regretted everybody I'd been out with, because I never really wanted to be with them.

My face was red, thinking about this, but it cooled as the air became frosty when I passed into the shadow of the Tournelle stadium. Getting a ticket for the match was no problem, because the population of the town could easily fit into the stadium. Even with a keen following and a strong appearance by the visitors, there were spaces. I had no intention of staying longer than that, and vacated my room, begging permission to leave my van on Mme Barrault's car park. I planned to come straight back and get the late ferry once the match was over.

The teams ran out to polite clapping, until Flensse trotted on to the pitch. He was built like a rugby player, but he also looked hollow, because his movements were so light. His skin was unaccountably brown, almost Asian in comparison to his countrymen. His nose was broken in two places, spread across a thick head. The crowd chanted: 'Ballet, Ballet.' I don't usually like football being compared to art, or dancing, or anything like that. It's just football. The way he moved, though, even when warming up, made me think his nickname didn't lose anything in translation. He was on tiptoes the whole time.

The crowd didn't throw bog rolls or bits of paper, like we used to, but flowers. Roses, carnations, even bushy chrysanthemums. Red and yellow, like the Tournelle strip. I couldn't imagine our lot chucking flowers. Too girlie for starters, and what's more, you can't nick them from the toilet. The plants didn't have quite the same travel as the soft-strong and long, but the effect was more pleasing.

Flensse never acknowledged the crowd, even though their shouts of praise were quite frantic at times. The closest he came to me was about twenty yards, and I saw him coughing up. He kept the gob in his mouth, concentrating on the ball, and just as I expected him to spit it out, his Adam's apple bulged. He swallowed his own gob. There was a tiny yet audible sigh from the crowd around me, admiring his restraint.

Tournelle had only one tactic. Pass to Flensse. He would do the rest. He was marked by half the Bruges team, but if the ball came near him, he just walked between them and took it away. His size made you expect him to lumber, but he minced, then moved with alarming, sharp strides and, with a tiny chipping movement, plopped it in the net time after time. You could say there was beauty in that, if you looked hard enough, but that might be distorting the truth. It was good to watch; impressive, skilful. The man was an original, but he held his moment of beauty back until the second half.

It was dark by half-time, and the air was becoming foggy. After a few minutes, I couldn't see the other side of the pitch. The floodlights didn't cut through the fog, but swelled in it, making the space in the stadium into a steady, cold flare. When the players emerged for the second half the mist was so thick they could hardly see each other. In any other country the match would probably have been called off. In Belgium they had to play on in these conditions or they'd never get through a game.

The silhouette of Flensse seemed more substantial than the rest, and where the fog slowed them like a syrup, he skipped on. At times, there were only a few players in sight, and I hardly saw the ball. It was probably the same for the players, and no goals were scored. The crowd went quiet, trying to hear where the ball was, listening for the dulled sound of the whistle, and the yelps of pain from secretive fouls.

Towards the end of the game it rained ferociously, and the fog was flattened away in seconds. The floodlights shone on the soaking grass, and the players resolved into focus. Flensse had the ball, and for a change he passed it across, ran forward, stalled to avoid offside. Then he began to run with a look of certainty that made me know he was going to score. Bruges saw it too, and ran at him from all sides. From his left the ball was lobbed clumsily across. It never hit the ground, but strummed off Flensse's right foot with a snap. It was as though two curved lines had been drawn to that exact point: the curve of the ball, and the arc of his foot. Sacred geometry. Perhaps it was the water and light on the ball, but it appeared to spark as his foot made contact. Everything about the day had led to that moment. The ball sank into the net at the same moment Flensse padded on to the ground, arms by his side, head down as though embarrassed. The others cheered and leapt, and although they danced around him, they knew better than to maul him.

When you see something beautiful, you don't celebrate or scream. You feel lonely. Beauty reminds you how much you are on your own, because there's nobody to share it with.

Afterwards, I felt quite strange and stayed in my seat until most of the crowd had gone. I had no memory of the goalies, because one had nothing to do, and the other could do nothing to stop the ball. It was only five o'clock, but so dark it felt later. I tried to pick out each spot he'd scored from; there were six patches in all, but my gaze kept returning to the place where he landed the last one.

It can only have been ten minutes later that I saw something else. Managing to get lost inside the stadium, I came out of the wrong exit, and walked round the perimeter to get back on track. I looked for a dark place in front of the lights, and guessed it would be the park. The road curved that way, so I followed, walking slowly, enjoying the rain cooling my skull.

On the corner of the main road and the park, I saw the florist's where Tournelle must have bought their flowers. It was closing for the night. The girl who worked there was taking flowers inside. She drew a bunch from its green pavement bucket, shook the sappy water off and went inside. She came back, eased the bucket over, its water sloshing into the gutter. She did this four times as I walked up. Light came from the shop windows, the pavement shining like ice. I could hear every drop, the squeak of stems as she gathered them together, and even from this distance, I saw every movement of her hair, her hands. The fifth time she came out, I saw her face.

When you see a good-looking person, what is it that stirs you, even if you've never spoken to them? Even if you stand no chance of ever smiling at them. I didn't realize at the time, but looking back, I think it was the simplicity of what she was doing, emptying water, taking in flowers. There was nothing to it, but the light and smell and the sound of her hands shaking that water. It made me feel sad for her, but I couldn't tell why. Perhaps it was the dark and cold, or the fact that I wanted to talk to her and knew I probably wouldn't.

I slowed down to get a better look. Inside, she put on a duffel coat and a satchel, turned off the light, and came out as I approached. Her hair glowed in the streetlight, and her eyelashes were stuck together with rain, making them look sparkly. She adjusted the straps on her satchel, wiped her face, and smiled.

It's easy to say that I was deluded about all this. A goal is a goal. A pretty person you've never spoken to is just that. But I don't think so. The point is, we both turned up at that moment. I was there by mistake, in the wrong country, a day late, walking back down the wrong road. She was leaving work. Meaningless coincidence, you could say. But I can't get Flensse's goal out of my head. The geometry going on, his leg, curving and arcing with exact mathematics to intersect the line of the ball at that one moment. I'm not sure who's responsible for that sort of precision.

I almost walked past her, but stopped and smiled. It was more like a grin, and I'm surprised she didn't walk away, thinking I was weird.

What did we share? She looked up at the stadium, still not knowing I was English.

'Flensse,' I said. 'Six–nil.'

It was only a starting point, I know that. And I was brought there by chance, not effort. But when so many things come together at once, you know that something good will follow. It's the moment of contact that counts.

Christopher Kenworthy ran an influential independent press, Barrington Books, until he could no longer accept the extent to which it ate into his writing time. His consistently surprising stories have been published in a

Christopher Kenworthy

wide variety of magazines and anthologies, from *The Third Alternative* to *Northern Lights*. His first collection, *Will You Hold Me?*, is published by The Do-Not Press.

Irvine Welsh

The Best Brand of Football

They were groovin down big time in Leith Walk; this
was a fuckin full-flight job and absolutely no half
measures, no prisoners taken. They were in total telepathic mode, the three of them all dressed in the same
green and purple striped away tops, Walkmans on their
heads, all listening to the same Lee Perry mix that
Martin had cooked up earlier when they headed back
to his to chill from the coke and amphetamine binging
the night before at Sublime. That one had been a
cracker all right, cause when all the other cunts were
loved up on quality E, the boys were strutting in the
middle of the floor giving it big time, patrolling that
section of the dance like three pre-heart attack Graeme
Sounesses ... but that was then and this is now; the
next morning and bubble bubble went Scratch as they
shouted at each other to the bewilderment of the Saturday shoppers in the Walk because they had necked
some Es at the same time and were coming up just as
the synchronized tapes had hit some particularly crazy
deep dub FX.

They were all thinking the same thing: what about
the poor cunts in the street who can't hear Lee Perry or
can't feel upward of a hundred and twenty milligrams
of MDMA coursing through their bodies? From the
perspective of Martin, Faz and Hendo, the resounding
answer was absolutely fuck all. This was their show, their
scene, their Saturday, and the rest of the world, its

shoppers, squads of casuals and auld cunts looking disapprovingly, were just a backdrop, all just part of the hologram they were walking through, a big computer-generated game for their entertainment.

They surged and floated and strutted up the street. They were going to see Hibernian play and this was the only fuckin way to do it.

—THIS IS MASHIN UP THE FUCKIN NUT GOOD-STYLE! Faz said, drawing a breath, only to get a thumbs-up from Hendo.

He felt Faz pulling him towards him,—SOME FUCKIN TRIP THIS, EH?

—NO HALF. AH'M TOTALLY CUNTED HERE, MAN.

They saw two elderly women with shopping bags and pseudo-punk bubble cuts who were mouthing something at them, but they could hear nothing, as they just watched those tight mouths moving soundlessly in disapproval while Lee Perry kept it frothing and sweeping and jet-propelled them down Albert Street towards the ground.

Struggling to keep it cool in the queue for the turnstiles, they got into the stadium easily enough, but were then confronted by a police officer who clocked their funky dance movements and the size of their pupils. They couldn't make out what he was saying but they flashed a telepathic agreement and gave each other the one-two-three finger count and switched OFF.

Our boys felt as if they had just dropped down into the stadium from the height of the gods.

—Hello, mortals, we have descended upon your planet from the skies. Our quest is to watch Hibernian FC play against Motherwell, Faz said.

—Well, if you're gaun intae the stands wi personal stereos oan, make sure ye keep them low, said the cop.—We get complaints fae other people tryin tae watch the match.

This irritated Martin. No cunt ever complained about anybody having a personal stereo on at the fitba, certainly not here, in the East Stand. Maybe some of the mumpy auld cunts in the old North Stand, aye, but no here. It was a joke to call this old fuckin cattle pen a stand anyway. Two gleaming state-of-the-art jobs at either end of the ground, but this side, the punters' side, where the hardcore support always stood before the seating, this would be the fuckin last place to get done up.—Ye cannae really call this place a stand, he said.

—If you're gaun intae the stands wi personal steros oan, make sure ye keep them low, the cop repeated.—Like ah sais, we get complaints.

—No problem, officer, we were unawares that our personalized high-fidelity systems were at such annoying volume. Many thanks for bringing this to our attention. Come on, boys, Hendo said.

—Keep them low in the stands, the cop reminded them,—they personal stereos.

They moved along the East Stand up towards the away end.—Moosey-faced cunt thon, eh? Martin complained.

—Ah thought he was a sexy fuckin bitch. Ah wanted tae shag the cunt, Hendo said.

—Never mind this boys, any cunt up for another pill? Faz asked.

—Aye, the rushes are runnin doon a wee bit, Hendo observed.

—You cunts are fuckin mad, Martin moaned.

—You dinnae need tae have one, Faz told him.

—That's easy for you tae say but ah want us aw tae stey oan the same wavelength, Martin complained.

—Right, c'moan, up the back, Faz said.

They headed to the back of the stand, clocking where the security cameras were, before passing the pills round and necking them. Faz seemed in distress.—Fuck, this is isnae gaun doon at aw, ma mooth's too dry. Ah'm gaunny have tae git a cup ay tea.

—No way, we've goat tae dae them at the same time, there's a queue up there, it'll take ages, Martin said,—open yir mooth.

Faz opened his mouth, and Martin could see the pill, intact on his dry tongue. He pulled Faz's face to his and gobbed in his mouth.—Get it doon yir neck.

Faz pulled away and smiled.—Thanks, man, it's away now. Hep B here ah come, but it wis worth it. This is the best brand of football the world's ever seen.

Martin looked round to the Ladbrokes kiosk at the back of the stand.—Lit's git a punt oan the first goal before they rushes come oan.

They made their bets.—Ah goat Keith Wright, twenty-two minutes, Martin said.

—Darren Jackson, twenty-seven, Faz smiled.

Hendo elbowed Martin and shouted:—The teams are oot! Synchronize your Walkmans! One-two-three . . .

ZOOOOMMMM . . .

They blasted into the other dimension as sounds and chemicals swept through their bodies. They kept a window on to the football stadium at planet Earth so they could observe the match.

Scratch and his crew were giving it big licks when the first huge rushes of the new E started kicking in and Martin, Hendo and Faz cheered massively when a throw-in was awarded to Motherwell on the far stand side. Half the East Stand crowd looked around at them.

Another cop came towards them. He made a gesture with his hand that they should sit down and take their seats. They reluctantly stopped dancing against the back

wall and sat rocking autistically in their seats. Scratch
set up a space-rocket war as Darren Jackson netted for
Hibs and the place went wild.

—THIS IS TOO FUCKIN MUCH, MAN! Hendo
roared.—The best brand of foot-bahl . . .

—Who goat it? Faz asked, lowering the sound on his
Walkman to hear the stadium announcer beam:—And
the scorer for Hibs . . . number ten . . . Darren Jackson!

—YES! WE'RE IN THE FUCKIN DOSH, BOYS! Faz
roared, cranking up the volume on his Walkman.

—FUCKIN PERTY TIME! Martin shouted.

Hibs went two up before half-time, and the trio went
for a pish, then necked another pill and spent most of
the second half vibing it up behind the stand. They
went back to their seats intermittently, but Motherwell
were getting back into it so they came back out to dance.
It was great looking over to the new stands, Martin
thought, but the one at the visitors' end shouldn't have
been built, because it spoiled the great view of Arthur's
Seat. That was what he liked about Easter Road, when
that end was open. It gave the illusion that you were
right on the edge of the country while you were in the
city. That had been spoiled a bit with the new stand's
construction, although you still see that extinct volcano,
one of the seven hills that Edinburgh, like Rome, was
built on and around.

After the game, the crew collected the cash winnings
from Faz's ticket for Darren Jackson's goal. He had put
twenty quid on it at five-to-one, so he was well chuffed.
Then they fired back up to Faz's flat in Montgomery
Street where they lay around smoking dope and watching football videos to come down a wee bit, before
deciding to go on to Smokey Robinson's party in East
London Street.

They hit a local off-licence and bought several

bottles of cheap, red Bulgarian wine which was on offer at one pound seventy-five a bottle.—Smokey's a sort ay cheese and wine cunt, Faz pontificated,—he'll lap this up.

—Bit cheapo though, man, Hendo remarked.

—Aye, but yir always better gaun fir quantity, Martin opined.

—Too true, Faz agreed.

When they got to Smokey's, they had to knock for ages before securing entry. There was loud, pumping music coming from the flat. All they could hear was the boom-boom-boom of a bass which seemed to shake the entire building.—Wish ah hud neighbours like his, Martin said.

Eventually a skinny young guy chewing rapidly at some gum opened the door. The loud, pumping hardcore almost drove them backwards as they advanced into the flat. The place was overrun with young crews who had obviously come there from Friday's Rezurrection. They didn't recognize any faces. None of Smokey's crowd seemed to be here yet.

—This is my flat and you will respect this flat, they had heard Smokey say to a guy who was being sick in the sink, which had a load of dirty dishes still piled up in it.

—Awright, Smokey ma man! Hendo shouted.

—Hello, boys ... how are you? Smokey turned round, his face igniting in a smile.

—Sound, Smokey, sound.

—Excuse me ... Smokey said slowly and urbanely nodding towards another room where the tartan techno music was blasting out from,—I have to check on my guests.

Faz looked around.—Doesnae seem tae be many cunts fae the Joy crowd here but, eh no?

—Naw ... it's a fuckin sin. Perr Smokey, Hendo said.

—He doesnae seem tae be bothered, Martin shrugged.

—Dinnae be fooled by that smile oan his face . . . Hendo said.

— . . . it's just thair tae fool the public, Faz observed.

Smokey came back out into the lounge. He looked in distress, but then Smokey usually did and it was difficult to tell whether it was real or theatrical.—That bedroom is a disaster. It's full of those wee bairns that hang around the Kirkgate. Honestly. That's Brendan, inviting them up. All they talk about is the blasted raves they attend at the weekend. I find that tedious. There has to be some sort of life beyond the psychoactive experience.

—Ah'll take your word for it, mate. When ye find it, tell ays aboot it, Martin smiled, wrapping a playful arm around the host with the most's shoulder.

Hendo put the carry-out down on the table.—We brought some wine along, Smokey. Tae be honest, man, we're no in the best ay shape right now. We've been cunted since last night at the club. Sublime, eh. We just went for it with Es and Lee Perry tapes the day and then headed off tae the fitba.

—Hibs' defence wis in better shape in the second half thin we are now, Hendo smiled.

—We hud a big win oan the first scorer. Darren Jackson. Thus aw the wine, Martin explained.—It's oan Jacko.

Smokey examined the labels on the bottles of the red wine and tried not to look too disappointed. The door went and some girls came in.—Whoa ho! Faz said under his breath,—Manto alert.

—We got here as soon as we could, one woman with long, dark red hair said, kissing Smokey's cheek.

—It's wonderful to see you, Smokey enthused, raising his eyes as a skinny young guy vibrated past him *en route* from the bedroom to the toilet.—We have a rather motley crew tonight, Emma.

—Mmmm . . . is that tartan techno I hear? Emma said,—I love that music. It's so . . .

— . . . Soulless? Smokey smiled.

—Oh, you . . . she pushed him gently in the chest.— Where's the gang? Brendan? Vincent?

Smokey waved his hands in the air and looked ceil-ingwards.—Oh them. I'm not speaking to them any more. That's just two of the names that are taboo in this house, strictly *verboten* and what have you.

—Oh? Emma widened her eyes.

—Let us just say that words were exchanged with certain parties.

—Tell me more, Emma said.

—In time and in drink, my darling, Smokey smiled, patting her on the arm.

—I didn't think they'd ever stay away. That must be sooo hurtful, another woman said.

—Not even a card, darling, not even a fucking card . . . Smokey's features contorted briefly in distress before opening up with inspiration.—But you haven't met my other friends. Emma, Jacqui, Louise and Jenni-fer, meet Martin, Fraser and Brian. You must call Brian 'Hendo', however, and Fraser's often known as 'Faz', aren't you, Fraser?

—Aye . . . Faz, Faz coughed.

—You never told me . . . how was the football? Did Hibernian win? Smokey asked, his eyes intense and his lips trembling.

—Four–two for Hibs. Mind you, we were cunted, Faz acknowledged.

—Mmmm . . . Smokey nodded thoughtfully.

—I love football, Emma announced.—It's one of those games I shouldn't love but somehow I do.

—It's sooo . . . tribal, Louise declared.—That's

the only term I'd use to describe it. Has anybody got any fucking coke? Oops, I can't believe I just said that!

Taking the cue, Jacqui took a seat on the couch and started chopping out lines on the coffee table with her credit card. Martin considered that he didn't like her but he fancied her toot and sat next to her.—We were coked up last night at Sublime, he said.

Jacqui had decided that she did not like this man and she was fucked if he was getting any of her coke.—Really? How ... sublime, she sneered. Emma and Louise laughed loudly. Faz smiled broadly, as did Hendo, in spite of himself. Smokey nodded in slow approval.

Emma was chatting to Faz.—So tell me all about this football game. What you boys get up to. It all sounds very intriguing, very male-bonding sort of stuff to me. I only ever follow it on the telly.

—You've never been to a live match before?

—No.

—You'll have to come along some time, Faz smiled. He liked this woman. He couldn't think why.

—I think I would rather like that, Emma smiled. She liked this man, but only hormonally, she considered. Then she looked at his Walkman.—What music have you had on?

—Lee 'Scratch' Perry.

—Really ... what is that?

—It's sort ay like dub. Dub reggae.

—Really! Oh, I love reggae!

The doorbell rang and some more tartan-techno pups vibrated into the flat and started taking more pills. Martin and Hendo scored some and necked them with the wine.—Looks like it's the two ay us now. Faz's pulled, Hendo observed.

—Did ye hear that fuckin cow, man? I love reggae!

Martin mocked.—Student fuckin cunts, man. Probably goat one Bob Marley and two Police albums.

—UB40 or something, Hendo nodded in acknowledgement.

—We love reggae, Martin mocked in a posh accent,—all this lovely music made by all those lovely black people, provided we don't actually have to see them dancing with us in our student clubs . . .

—Dinnae be too cruel. Anybody fortunate enough tae have both a fanny and a bag ay toot can never be written off completely, no matter what a fuckin twat they might seem tae be, Hendo nodded at Jacqui who was doing lines with Louise and Jennifer.

—That sow cut me oaf for deid, man, when ah went ower tae investigate the charlie situ. Cheeky fuckin cunt. As if ah wis intae her.

—You'd knob it but.

—Probably, Martin shrugged in weary concession. He was feeling a little bit rough and jaded and the E he'd scored from the Rez posse hadn't come on yet.

—I love Bob Marley . . . Emma said.

—No really into him, Faz shrugged.—A wee bit borin, eh. Sortay like a black Phil Collins.

At this point two younger girls came through from the bedroom and started hanging around Smokey, who had begun to chop up some more lines on the glass table.

—Fuck me, ah didnae ken thir wis any lassies in they hardcore posses, Faz said.

—Ken what really bugs me? Martin said,—Look at they lassies' skins. Same wi the guys; nane ay they wee cunts've goat spoats. Five years ago at least one ay they wee lassies would have hud a wee patch ay grease oan the foreheid wi some plukes oan it. Now thuv aw goat that porcelin skin.

—Better diet? Hendo speculated.

—Naw.

—Better drugs?

—Possible.

—Mind you, mibbee thir's as many young cunts wi spots, it's jist that they stey indoors, too scared tae go oot. The power ay advertisin. Stigmatize the perr cunts cause they dinnae live up tae this ideal.

—Aye, ah hud bad spoats as a teenager. It's nae fun.

—What dae ye mean as a teenager? You've still goat fuckin bad plukes. Look at that! Hendo pointed to a spot on Martin's cheek which he hadn't known had come up.

—Fuck off, Martin said, rubbing the spot.

Hendo laughed, then felt a shiver as the drugs coursed through him. The shiver seemed to settle in his eye. He held it with his warm hand until it stopped. Vulnerable scar tissue. He looked across at Smokey. It was Smokey who had saved his sight, four years ago, when they first met.

One of the young girls who'd been watching him do the lines spoke to the host while nodding to her friend.—She said that she would gie ye a blow-job for a line ay coke.

—Did ah fuck, you, ya cheeky cow! the other one said in mock outrage.

—My darlings, Smokey said, there's absolutely no need to prostitute yourselves in that way. A simple gaze into your eyes to watch those beautiful little ecstasied souls fluttering like butterflies is a more than sufficient reward for a line of coke. Suck my cock, by all means, but do it out of love, darling, or out of a spirit of adventure, not for simple mercenary gain. How are we to build our Learyesque psychic Utopia with such crass concentration on the cash nexus?

—Aye, right, one lassie said.

The other one looked at Smokey.—Ken somethin? You sound just like that posh guy fi Perth, eh Angie?

—Aw aye . . . him, Angie smiled.—Tell um the story, Kathy.

—Well, Kathy began,—we wir at this deck's perty in this cottage oan the grounds ay this big estate up near Perth. We were trippin so wi went tae look at these hoarses in this field. They were beautiful.

—Yes, the horse is a noble beast . . . if rather long in the face, Smokey smiled.

—Aye . . . well, at this field, this posh guy comes up tae us. Tell him what he said, Angie.

—He goes tae her, 'Do you ride?'

Kathy arched her eyebrows.—Ah just turned tae him 'n sais, 'Fuck off, ya cheeky prick.'

—The poor bastard wis mortified. He meant, do ye ride *hoarses.*

—Personally, Smokey smiled,—I prefer sheep. They're just the right height for me, and much more compliant, he gestured towards the lines of coke.— Ladies first.

Hendo felt a surge of goodwill towards Smokey. He was a generous man. He remembered when his sight had been saved by the host. Hendo had been living with a girl called Suzy who he was in love with but the chemistry wasn't right. Both of them could be quite hyper, they wound each other up constantly. They were just unable to chill with each other. It was partly to do with all the speed they took as well, he retrospectively considered. Their conversations were a hyperactive spiel and it was during one of them that his eye was injured. Suzy was eight months pregnant and her hormones were all over the place, and he was full of speed, trying to cut up some vegetables for a curry he didn't want but had decided to cook. She started on about something, he couldn't even remember what it was, then he became animated, talking with his hands. There was an itch in his face and as he went to scratch it he forgot he still had the kitchen knife in his hand; a small, razor-sharp vegetable knife which he accidentally stuck in his right eye. He did more than that: he nearly gouged the cunt out. They rushed him up in a taxi to the eye pavilion and only the skill of the surgeon, a certain Mister Robinson, saved Hendo's life. He was so grateful that he named his son after the surgeon, William Robinson Henderson. The surgeon was nick-named Smokey.

Hendo met up with him by chance at a gay club in Edinburgh when they were both Ed. Hendo and his mates had started going there because they sussed out that the most happening dance sounds were played there first and that the best-looking women in town went there to escape from the beer monsters who fre-quented most of the straight clubs, at the time when there had been a quality dip in the Es. Hendo and his mates became firm friends with Smokey.

—Pity the rest ay the Joy crew never showed up, Smokey, but, eh? Martin said.—Like, your mates 'n that.

—Fuck them, man, Smokey said.

—Or better still, dinnae, Martin smiled.

—They deserve only to have sex with each other, especially that Brendan and Vincent. In fact, they do, that's why they're so self-obsessed and miserable all the time. Do you know what Brendan said to me the other week?

—Nup, Martin shrugged.

—He went on about this supposed book he was writing about his life story. His life story! I ask you! Calum was rather droll. He said something about hav-ing a spare postage stamp, which went completely past Brendan. Then I started joking that I was thinking of writing my autobiography and that I already had a title, which was: *I Surgeon.* Of course, that went completely over his head.

—That's a good one, Smokey, Hendo laughed.—
Fuckin Cartesian. I-comma-surgeon.

—Thought you'd like it.

—You could also see it as affirmative, like *A-Y-E Sur-geon*. Yes, surgeon. Like that fuckin *Yes Minister* shite
that aw they straight middle-class cunts lap up.

—I never thought of it that way, Smokey admitted,
nodding thoughtfully.

Faz and Emma vanished together a few hours later, and
Martin was chatting to Angela and Kathy. Hendo spent
most of the night talking to Smokey and some tartan-
techno guys. In the morning only Hendo and Martin
were left. They were feeling very uncomfortable with
their comedowns. The dub seemed far away. They asked
Smokey if he could connect them up.

—Hendo. Do you know how much a saline drip costs?

—Goan, Smokey . . . ah widnae ask but wir Donald
Ducked, man. We need tae get this hangover oot the
road soas that we can go oot the night.

Smokey tutted, but set up the chairs and the stands.
Then he produced some saline bags and drips from the
fridge freezer and hooked the boys up.—I am totally
committed to the National Health Service, Smokey
shook his head.

—This is fuckin great, this, Martin observed, feeling
the drug and pish hangover recede as the fluid completely rehydrated his body. In an hour they'd be able
to go out again as if nothing had happened. The three
of them sat reading magazines like wifies under the
hairdresser's dryers.

For Smokey, as a surgeon, it was essential that he was
completely sober when it came to operating. Fortunately, many surgeons were alcoholics or drug addicts
and an old piss-head from the cardiovascular unit
showed him the ropes. Smokey resented wasting saline

drips in this way though; his pals were taking liberties somewhat. Still, what could you do?

—What are you reprobates going to do with this money you won at the football? he asked stiffly.

—Spend it on drugs, Hendo declared.

—You're as well to, Smokey conceded.—You'd only waste it otherwise.

—That's if Faz husnae spent it aw impressing that bird.

—It's possible . . . Smokey speculated,—Emma has expensive tastes.

—Ah fuckin bet, Martin groaned.

—Naw, we'll track the cunt doon, man, Hendo said.—We'll spend the lot oan charlie.

—Naw, Es and speed, Martin declared.

—Fuck it, man, we won it at the fitba and cocaine's the fitba players' drug. It doesnae stey in the system for long so ye can beat the random tests. So it has tae be charlie. It's only appropriate that the money should stey in the game.

Martin looked at the saline bag above him. It was empty. He felt good.—Right, Smokey, it's disconnection time, mate. It's the second half and we're shooting doon the slope this time! The best brand of foot-bahl the world's ever seen . . . goal!

If intelligent life exists on another planet circling another star on the far side of the universe, chances are they'll have heard of Irvine Welsh. In fact, there's almost certainly a moon orbiting that planet whose only notable geological feature is the regular pattern of publishers' dumpbins containing copies of *Trainspotting*, his first novel, recently made into a successful film. Welsh has also published a collection of short stories, a second novel and *Ecstasy: Three Chemical Romances*, a collection of novellas.

Tim Lawler

Villa

Mercedes always seemed a Latin sort of name; I was never under any illusions on that score. I knew from *Look and Learn* (and just from knowing what boys know before they know girls, i.e., sport and transport) why Herr Benz had called his cars that. And soon I knew for myself the multi-cylindered power of Hispanic females, and understood.

I met her in Zimbabwe, where Bruce is still the closest they get to a local hero, and she could have been Spanish, Chilean, anything. When she turned out Argentinian it was fine at first. In those days I still called her Evita rather than Diego.

It's almost two years since our opening encounter, a graceless game of three-and-in between piles of discarded clothes, and we've been getting more makeshift ever since. This time it's Thailand, but it's taking us more than a week to acclimatize.

As we fetched up with all our kit that warm and sullen Sunday – last Sunday, and already in a different league – there was little to suggest that this would be the place. That this place out of so many would choose itself as the last. Our final relegation battle, after almost two seasons gallantly (and sometimes shamelessly. Cravenly. Totally butterfly) avoiding the inevitable plunge.

Your squad's just not strong enough, mate, well-wishing spectators would opine from their African sheltered terraces, their Asian home stands, as we wandered the world deep in savage argument. *You just haven't the strength in depth.* Which even now is as capable as ever of hurting like missed penalties. But that's that word depth for you, especially in the context of girls.

At first it presented itself as just another in the long, long sequence of places together – the faraway kind, the kind that wove the entire shabby fabric of the, er, relationstrip. Our sporadically beautiful game. Wherever we started, the next was always far away, and far further away from anywhere we'd ever belonged. We only ever played away, only it never seemed like playing. You know how the Bari players arriving to inaugurate Middlesbrough's splendid new stadium loved it all except for not being able to plug in their hairdryers? Well, that. We knew how they felt.

As they swirled and dived and complicated themselves, these places, this sequence of unfamiliar undressing rooms still failed to create anything as majestic as a tapestry. More a tattered rug, spattered with intricate cigarette burns and the lingering aftershow of old wine as it mellows into vintage stains. The sort you can't design; the kind you don't bring home.

Who's we, then? There is no easy way. We is Mercedes and me. Me is David, and He is Ricky Villa, and the reason this place will be the last.

We were both just being nomads (Wanderers. Rovers. Casuals), a different home every week or so. She'd left her *rancho notorioso*, her *casa blanca*, when her gaucho wouldn't marry her with her nose ring and wouldn't not marry her. I have rings for my bulls, he'd say. Not for my wife. And she'd say I'm not your wife and they're not your bulls. They're my papa's. You can push them and prod them and make them do things, even tell them when to have sex, but you can't with me. Look. See how free I am. See my ticket. Hurrah. I'm off to sunny Spain.

And not six months later there she was in Bulawayo, drinking far too professionally and meeting strange boys like me. Not so strange, in reality, except in my devotion to Manchester's Other Association Football team, but so much for reality. The glut of recent Red achievements seems to have lent the patina of permanent melancholy to a mere geographical accident (*the English fellow*, ripe old topers will whisper over their palm wine as they steal respectfully sympathetic glances at the paleface in shorts at the corner table, *calls to mind Mr Rick in* Casablanca; *always under the downward thumb of a light variety of blues* . . . that class of thing, anyway) but not even a genuine Moss Side birth is enough to qualify me as an appropriate partner for one whom bus drivers the third world over would always favour with the best seat. They'd always let her smoke, too. She just looked so *special* with a cigarette dangling from her lips and the soft focus lent by smoke, as boys and men everywhere knew she would, recognizing true international class (Colin Bell! Bert Trautmann! Ed Cetera!) when it brushed haughtily and naughtily past them.

And now here we were in Bangkok, fetching up at this secluded guest-house and laughing at its name. Well, she was laughing at its name. I've never been able to see the funny side of places called Villa. Nor Ardiles, though you come upon those so seldom. Well, never, really. Look, it's not just me. I know other City fans who still feel it as keenly. Our lone FA Cup Final since the sixties, wheezing heroically through extra-time and all the way to the replay, and the hirsute gangler chooses that as the time to play his one decent match for Spurs. He'd been great in the World Cup, he and his pint-sized sidekick, and when Keith Burkinshaw invaded Argentina and returned with the Patagonian Pair, the Tierra del Fuego Twins, it seemed like something of a coup. Rejoice, we said. Latin flair come to

grace our dourly Anglo-Saxon league? Top idea, Keith.
A bit like getting R. Marsh back to play for us. Full
marks for inspiration, less sure about the work rate.
Still, that's Spurs all over, isn't it? Haven't been the
same since Danny's day. And all that.

We'd just come back from a night of pugilism, Thai-
style, and tucked straight into one of our own. It had
started with shouting. She'd said something at normal
volume, at that normal pitch of hers that's exactly the
same as three thousand people shouting over an excit-
able orchestra at strangers hitting each other, and I
hadn't heard and had said Eh? So she'd repeated it,
something about Why don't they just trip each other
up, but I couldn't be sure. So I leaned close and said
Why don't they just rip what? and she said Doesn't
matter and sat in that way that says Huff, and Hrrmmph,
or whatever the Spanish is for that.

So I said, at that pitch of mine that's precisely calcu-
lated to cut through the sound of three thousand, etc,
Are you cross about something? And do you want a
fight about it? I'm sure no one would notice. And after
three times of asking she said, Well, I just get fed up
have to repeating everything. Look, we just watch, OK?

I sat and watched her, with the scoreboard behind,
and fumed a bit. And during the fourth and most fren-
etic round as the seconds ticked down I thought of her
at all those ages. 29. That's her now, watching people
kicking each other, and cross about repeating things.
Seeming even crosser than those perfect leggy boys
seem with each other.

27, that's her at home on the range, kicking like a
wild thing and breaking corral. 26, 25, 24, and down
to the time she lived wild and free in Buenos Aires and
would sleep with no one unless they had a body just
like these boxers, but still seemed to find plenty. She's
shown me the kind of guy she'd seduce in her wild

years – 23, 22, 21 – and those sleek and flat-stomached heroes in the ring are the closest I've seen, and she's enraptured, and I find myself minding.

15, and she's entertaining the whole first team, upstairs at the party thrown by Papa in honour of their victory at the All South America Schools Cup Final. Five of them came to Wembley for a friendly once, grown up into full internationals and carrying somewhere in their elegant expensive heads the memory, or at least the knowledge, of my girl's body back when it was young and even harder to resist.

Then it all becomes too much and I go out for a cigarette. She comes and finds me and says That was best yet, there was knockout, why you didn't stay? And I say Why didn't I say what? And she says There is something wrong, no? and I say There's something wrong, yes, but I don't tell her what it really is. That it's minding that she's ever known anyone bare before me. I'd be too embarrassed, as I always get when I have no leg to stand on.

Instead I said If I said something and you couldn't hear I'd think What am I doing wrong? What can I do so it'll be easier? But you just think Cloth-eared idiot, what's wrong with his hearing? Is he getting old? Unlike those lovely boys down in the ring?

And she just said Cloth what? What this means?, so I dropped it, smiling at her and saying Hey, *comemos*. Let's go eat. But I still had the same taste in my mouth, and when we saw the sign again for this place we started Round Two.

Villa, Villa, Villa, she taunted. Look, who this? Who I am being?, as she dribbled and feinted with the key she'd dropped especially for the purpose. He passes one. He passes two. Will he pass? No, *no pasará*! He will score! Ricardo will defeat the Manchester City! Hurrah for Tottingham! Bravo Argentina! He will have hotel in Bangkok name after him. For ever he will live on, Señor Villa and this *día maravilloso.*

And I said, Guest-house. Not hotel. Grotty hostel, really. And how come I can hear you now?

Because now nobody cheering, she pouted. Only grouching. That was a word I'd taught her. We had a joke when she was annoyed, I'd call her Groucho and she me Gaucho and we'd laugh and it would be better. But it was always me who did the jollying out, and this time I didn't. I knew what I really minded but couldn't say, could hardly admit it or put my finger on it well enough to articulate, especially not to someone with her tenuous grasp of nuance, idiom and set-piece tactics, so instead I resurrected a familiar theme.

So, Maradona, I taunted back. Trick or cheat?

And she said, as she always did, *Mano de Dios.* Nothing do to with him. God, his hand. Miracle. But then she added a new bit. She said Like Ricardo Villa and *los pobres Azules de Manchester.* He cannot play like this. Miracle.

And this time I really minded. I'd thought I'd really minded about the boys she'd known, and how there were so many of them, and how she made me feel insecure even just after the sex we had with exhausting frequency and which no matter how Athletico Madrigal, how Dynamo Kievic, always carried the suspicion of being never quite enough. But that wasn't what I minded, after all.

I minded about Argentina, and how it always seemed to spell disaster for me, and I minded about minding. I minded feeling that way about a country. I felt draped in a Union Jack and I've always hated that. That's one of the reasons I'm not in England any more. But even here, six thousand miles and twenty-six months away, it's with me. And I tell myself it's only a corner of Manchester I'm carrying in my emotional luggage – not a whole foreign field, not forever England – and remember how I got my very drunkest on hearing of the sale of Garry, with me stuck in Zimbabwe and realizing I'd never see him score again and be happy for it, and how when that night I scored myself with Mercedes for the first time I couldn't care less whether he ever scored again.

Except for England. I'd still be glad if he ever knocked them in with three lions on his shirt. I'd still find bars – in Manila, in Melaka, in Mandalay – where they'd show my country's matches, and barmen would know Gascoigne and would still ask about Robson and even, bless them, in the more godforsaken dives, about Bobby Charlton. And I'd say Wilf Mannion, mate. Tom Finney. Stanley Matthews. And yes, one time in Cairo, Allah's honest truth, there was a flicker of recognition. Someone had seen Stan play. And I'd say Garry Flitcroft. He's the one to watch. He's one of ours. And they'd say Leeds United? Tottingham? And, far too often, Manchester United? And I'd just say City. He's one of ours.

I figured if it took that long for the news about Sir Stan to filter through, I had a fair chance of getting away with claiming Garry for a while. But meantime there's a stunning *chica* who wonders what she's done wrong and just wants me to be nice and I can't and I worry about why, and there's a niggle starting that whispers it might just be time to go home and find out.

So I turn to her now and say Where will you go next? and it's the first time I haven't said Where shall we, and when that night in the room next to the flickering sign that says V*lla we have our very best sex ever, all shimmies and feints and spectacular strikes and our best ever score, we both know that this will be the last place and silently agree it's for the best.

I know I'll never really escape Mercedes. I already suspect that before I finally go west I'll find myself in the tiny coastal village in the Philippines that bears her name, thinking of her as they bargain for fish at dawn. The bay there is called San Miguel, and I further suspect that of all the beers in all the towns in all the world I'll have to be careful of that one from now on. The same will go for taxis. I'll never be able to visit Jerusalem again, where they're all Mercedes too.

But it can't be helped. There are vehicles even more powerful, and I've just sadly seen what's driving us apart. It's that I'll never get her to be honest about Diego. And – saddest of all – that it matters to me, and always will.

Although he lives in north London, Tim Lawler's story was submitted by fax from Bangkok – it's certainly one way to get an editor's attention. Lawler has had two plays produced on the London stage, but this is the first time he has made the scoresheet in terms of fiction.

Stephen Baxter

Clods

Holt Academy, Wrexham
1887

H. G. Wells blew up for half-time.

Billy Williams followed the rest of the Holt boys off the pitch. It was already getting dark, and the iron-grey November clouds seemed to be sucking all the colour out of the world.

The Holt boys gathered in a huddle at the touchline. Wells handed out slices of orange. There wasn't enough to go round, and Wells always favoured his *samurai*, as he called them, his team within a team of 'keeper, a full-back, and Toddy Robbins, an inside-left.

Billy Griffiths, as a wing-half, didn't get any orange. The wind started to get into his bones, and he found himself shivering.

Wells was talking again. 'A football team should be a model of a Utopian community,' he was saying now, waving his arms around. 'All elements must work together to serve the Common Good. You are eleven men with a single objective. Like the parts of a body, you see, boys. And all co-ordinated by the operation of a central Brain – my *samurai*, the Platonic Guardians of my football team from Utopia. Eh, boys? Eh?'

Wells was a skinny man, only about twenty-two or twenty-three, Billy figured; he was shorter than Billy was, at fifteen. Wells had tiny girl's feet and a stupid straggling moustache. His eyes were pale blue, as empty as church windows. And he was always bloody talking, in his squeaky bloody Cockney voice.

Jimmy West nudged Billy. 'What the bloody hell's he going on about?'

'*Dained* if I know,' Billy said. 'Sounds like Geography to me.'

'So what's this U-topia, wherever *that* is, got to do with the price of fish, then? Not bloody much as far as I can see.'

'Not if we play the way we did in the first half,' Billy said.

'Aye,' Jimmy West agreed. 'We're lucky to be just the one down.'

The worst of it was, Billy thought bleakly, Wells's *samurai* weren't even supposed to tell the rest of them what the latest bloody plan was.

Billy looked across at the other team, from St Bride's. They were gathered around their own teacher. He was a fat, red-faced block of a man who was snapping at his team, making hard chopping gestures with his hands.

Wells blew his whistle – as Holt were at home Wells was refereeing today – and the team started to shamble back on to the pitch. The *samurai* threw their orange peel into a bucket.

The sky was low and hard, confining. Billy could hear the gurgle of the Dee, a couple of hundred yards away or so, and the old bridge to Farndon was a gaunt silhouette. On the far side of the pitch the school buildings loomed, black and oppressive, their square windows lamp-lit already, and from the chimneys the thin smoke of good Welsh anthracite curled up to the low clouds.

The pitch was just *dorrix*, really, Billy thought, riverside weeds and trash; it was roughly marked out with whitewash, and it had already cut up into clods.

He spotted Annie Budberg, hanging around behind one of the goals, wrapped up in her coat. Annie was only a cleaning girl, but she had a small, sweet face and a full figure. Visions of her round breasts and slim legs had warmed Billy in the isolation of his cold bed more than once.

But, maddeningly, it was Wells she chose, and she waved at him now.

Wells wanted the boys he favoured to call him by his initials, 'H.G.'. But to Annie he was Bertie, Bertie bloody Wells, with his fancy talk and empty eyes. Billy had even heard Wells talking to impress her, saying how, for now, he was forced to 'grind Euclid into these wretched apologies for immortal souls', but one day he would be a famous writer, and a Socialist Thinker too, by God.

To Billy, Wells was just a *floity* bastard.

Someone called his name.

It was old George Webb, who taught them History. He was over on the line, waving Billy over.

Billy trotted across.

Webbie used to be a fair sportsman himself, by all accounts. But he'd taken a bit of shell in the Crimea, a long time ago, and gradually that had slowed him up, until he was pretty much a *kroker* – he could hardly move at all. So now Webb had to stand on the line in his greatcoat, like a great grey fleshy pillar in the mud, while a *rodni* like Wells coached the football.

'Look over there,' Webb said. He pointed to the goal, where Annie was standing.

A bulky man in an expensive-looking coat had strolled over there. Silver hair shone in the fading light. He must have been sixty if he was a day, and he was chatting to Annie. It looked as if he was making her blush.

'Do you know who that is?' Webb asked.

'Who?'

'Only John bloody Houlding, that's all. King bloody John, of Everton. That's all.'

Billy stared at Houlding, as if he was Jesus Christ himself, walking on the *dorrix*.

Houlding had once been the Lord Mayor of Liverpool. And now he was putting all his passion into Everton Football Club, the club Billy's father, down in Saundersfoot, still called St Domingo's.

'What's he doing here, Webbie?'

Webb reached out a huge hand and patted Billy's shoulder. 'He's come to see you, boy. And one or two others.' He tapped the side of his nose. 'But you especially. A bit of scouting, you might say. At my advice. I hear they're looking for a good prospect for wing-half. Play well now, Billy boy, and who knows where it might get you. Who knows, eh?'

'Yes. Yes, thanks, Webbie. Thanks for—'

'Save your breath.' Webb's big, battered face creased up into a smile. 'Thank me by bagging a brace of goals, eh. Show him one of your cannonballs, eh.'

Billy trotted back on to the park.

Wells blew his whistle again, and Holt kicked off. Soon, the calls of the players drifted once more over the *dorrix*.

Ah, but if only Billy could catch the eye of John Houlding! *If only* . . . It was going to be easier said than done, in this bloody team.

Billy's family lived in Saundersfoot, a mining town down in Pembrokeshire. Billy's father and uncles were miners, and so had been his grandfathers, on both sides. And that was where Billy was going to end up – coughing up his lungs too – unless he could get out of the trap, as his mother called it. His mother had saved to send him here, to Holt. To give him a chance of some education.

The trouble was, Billy was finding he didn't have a brain in his head.

When George Webb talked about History, he could make some sense of that. But the likes of Wells with his Geometry and Science, and his spidery diagrams of Triangles and Pentagons and anecdotes about dead Greeks – well, that all passed by Billy's poor head without even ruffling his hair.

The irony was, Wells would spout on about how important education was in improving the lot of the Common Man. But, as Jimmy West would whisper, 'The idiot could improve the lot of *this* Common Man just by buggering off back to London, boys.'

The game developed. Now Toddy Robbins, the Holt captain, got possession of the ball. He ran forward tentatively.

Billy ran up on the left wing, shouting to Toddy. A big ape from St Bride's chased after Billy, but Billy had the legs to find a bit of space by the line.

Toddy was thirty yards away, but he could have tried the pass. If Billy got the ball, he could maybe reach Jimmy West, who was lurking in the centre. And then—

But there were two backs closing down on Toddy, and he was staring about uncertainly.

Toddy turned and started going backwards, for God's sake.

Billy screamed for the ball, and so did a couple of others. But now Toddy had passed the ball back, all the way to the Holt 'keeper, who had come off his line.

Billy saw it now. The 'keeper was another of the *samurai*. And there was the third of them, Freddy Fowler, a big centre-half, who had drifted up into St Bride's half.

The plan was as clear as day. All the Bride's backs were supposed to be lured forward by Toddy, and then the 'keeper was just going to punt the thing up to

Freddy, who would stroll through, and score. Just like that, a neat geometrical move, like one of Wells's bloody Triangles. And just the three of the *samurai* involved.

Billy stopped running, and rested, his hands on his hips, watching it all unravel.

The Holt 'keeper got to the ball. But so did Bride's centre-forward. He was a big lad with a frame like a door, and he just ran into the 'keeper and sent him into the mud, clods flying around him.

The Holt 'keeper flailed at the ball, and missed, and the centre-forward was through clear.

All he had to do was push the ball forward. The leather sphere rolled, slower than walking pace, between the sticks.

John Houlding was still there, behind the goal. He wasn't even watching the game. He was poking at Annie's waist, making her giggle.

Billy trooped back disconsolately into his own half.

Wells was shouting at his *samurai*. 'No, no, no. Can't you wretches grasp the most simple concept? Look here. A football match is an exercise in Geometry. In fact it is an exercise in Four-Dimensional Geometry – think of that! – with the Fourth Dimension being, of course, Time, superimposed on the Three of Space. You as a team comprise a sort of living Geometrical Theorem, embedded in the Four Dimensions of Space and Time – do you see – with goals as necessary Corollaries. All you must do is *demonstrate your proof...*'

On Wells talked, and talked. His high voice was like the cry of a gull, carrying across the *dorrix* to Billy.

Billy finished up close to the halfway line, facing the big Bride's centre-forward, who was grinning all over his face.

'Funny sort of a bloke, that,' the centre-forward said.

'Aye, well,' Billy said. He nodded to the fat, red-faced

teacher from St Bride's on the touchline. 'What does yours say to you?'

' "Kick the buggers," ' the centre-forward said.

'That's it?'

'Aye. Or he says, "If they're quick, knock them down and then kick them." '

Billy rubbed his hands together, trying to keep the blood flowing in his fingers. 'Well, we're a team with H. G. Wells as our manager. And that's why we get stuffed every bloody game we play.'

The centre-forward laughed, good-natured enough.

The game started again.

The play got bogged down in the churned-up mud in the middle of the park. The ball was soaked, and very heavy now, and Wells screamed at his players even as he refereed. At least, Billy thought, this time Holt were managing to pass the ball around a little bit. But Bride's were already two up, and all they had to do was hold Holt back.

Billy sneaked a glance at the touchline. Houlding was still there, and he was watching the game now, with a kind of distant interest. Annie had moved away from him, looking demure. Billy wondered if Houlding had suggested something improper to her.

Then, from the middle of a ruck of players, Toddy passed Billy the ball. For once Toddy had got his pass right – it was heading to Billy's feet, a few yards ahead of him – and it came to him, a great leather sphere coated with mud, rolling across twenty yards of sweet, empty turf.

Suddenly, the game opened up for Billy. With the ball at his feet, he surged up the left wing.

He glanced around sharply, envisaging the state of the game. Of Holt's players, only Jimmy West had the pace to keep up with him; good old Jimmy was charging like a bull up the middle of the park. There was the

Clods

Bride's 'keeper, and four backs, strung across the park ahead of Billy. He and Jimmy were outnumbered.

But two of the backs were pulling towards Billy, out of position.

He felt his mind working. He imagined passing the ball sharply to his right, to Jimmy. While the ball was in motion he, Billy, could hare off to the left and get behind the distracted backs. And then – if Jimmy had the wit to get the ball back to him – there he'd be, with only the 'keeper to beat, and the ball at his feet.

He could hear Webb shouting his name, encouraging him.

It would be a fine angle, but the 'keeper was off to the right, and Billy reckoned he could get in a good low shot at the near post. And if he made it one of his cannonballs, that 'keeper would have no bloody chance.

The manoeuvre unfolded in his head, a sort of light-filled diagram of movement and space and angles, even as the ball ran easily at his feet.

At moments like this – when he was in flight, when his head and his heart and his legs worked as one – Billy wondered if he was *feeling* some of what Wells was trying to communicate, with his endless words of Geometry and Four Dimensions.

He and Wells would never know what was lodged inside each other's heads, Billy supposed.

He was nearing the line. Jimmy was still with him, slowing a little as he tired. Billy swung his left leg, and hit the ball as sweet as a kiss towards Jimmy, and set off on his run.

But the Bride's right-back stuck out a hand, as brazen as you like, and palmed the ball to the ground. The ball landed neatly at the back's feet, and he started to lope clumsily down the field, towards Holt's half.

Billy's crystal vision of the move collapsed, like the surface of a burst soap bubble.

Jimmy West had doubled over, panting. 'Where's the bloody whistle?'

Billy turned and looked for Wells.

Wells wasn't on the pitch, he was behind the other goal, and he was talking to bloody Annie, laughing with her. He hadn't even watched the play.

A kind of mist filled Billy's head, driving out the geometric visions.

He sprinted after the right-back who had fouled, and quickly caught him up. The back was a big, ungainly lad, and Billy just pushed him off the ball.

Billy picked up the ball – literally picked it up with his hands, stopping the play – and stomped across the field through the mud and churned-up clods towards Wells. 'Mr Wells! Mr Wells!'

George Webb called. 'Now, Billy. Just you calm down.'

The other players stopped still, just watching Billy.

Billy was still thirty yards from Wells. 'What the bloody hell do you think you are doing? That was a foul! You had no *arrant* to be over here. No right, man.'

Wells looked a bit shocked at Billy's language. Annie giggled. Wells toyed with his whistle, and started talking. 'Ah, well, Billy, we must be philosophical about setbacks. We live in a *Universe Rigid*, after all, in which all our Trajectories – of footballs, of the remote stars, of our very lives – are laid out like specimens in a Kensington museum. And—'

The mist condensed in Billy's head. 'You're bloody tapped, man.' He threw the ball on to the ground ahead of him, and ran forward.

He kicked the ball while it was still rolling. He got it just right, with the outside of his foot.

It was one of his cannonballs: bending shots the like

Clods

of which nobody had ever seen, so Webbie had told him. The ball flew, just as it should have done into the goal.

The ball was a sodden leather missile that caromed into Wells, just above his right hip. Wells cried out, and clutched his kidney. He fell over.

Annie squealed and pressed her hands to her cheeks. Billy ran across the last bit of grass.

Other players had gathered, goggling and grinning. George Webb was here, holding Billy's arm.

The mist in Billy's head was dispersing.

Wells's small feet, embedded in muddy boots, were twisted up underneath him. Wells looked up at Billy, his mouth working. It occurred to Billy that this was the first time Wells had looked him straight in the eye.

'Oh, Billy,' George Webb said. 'Oh, Billy, Billy.'

Billy thought to look around. John Houlding had gone.

Wells, lying on the churned-up ground, coughed. It was a broken, ripping sound, and blood splashed from his mouth and over his shirt.

'He had no *arrant*,' Billy whispered. 'No *arrant*.'

. . . *One of the clods* [Wells] *taught, in an apparently deliberate act, fouled him with a kick to the kidneys. Wells began to spit blood* . . .
   H. G. Wells: Desperately Mortal, David Smith, 1986.

Wells produced . . . his early scientific romances . . . and the bulk of his short stories with astonishing swiftness. The intensity of this phase of his writing . . . [is] *the surest* [sign] *of literary genius. 'Consumption' was diagnosed after his footballing accident in 1887, and, like consumptive writers before and after him, he was impelled to write with such speed . . . because he thought he had little time.*
   Shadows of the Future, Patrick Parrinder, 1995.

Stephen Baxter

DEATH NOTICE: **William David Griffiths ('Billy'), at the age of forty-two, of bronchial ailments. Retired from the colliery at Bonville's Court, Saundersfoot, last year . . .** Western Mail, 1913.

Born in Liverpool in 1957, Stephen Baxter worked as a teacher and in computing before becoming a full-time writer in 1995. He has published over fifty science fiction short stories and six novels; his next, *Voyage,* is due in November 1996. A lifelong Liverpool supporter, he shook hands with Bill Shankly when the almost legendary Shanks presented him with a tie for playing the flute in the school orchestra. As a centre-back he was renowned as a tough tackler.

Maureen Freely

More Than Just a Game

You ask when I found out it was more than just a game. Well, it was during the junta – I must have been twenty at the time. I was travelling third class which, on most Greek ferries, was a large, crowded, and tediously safe open deck, but on this one for some reason was a tiny afterthought of a covered deck, and all of the other passengers were soldiers.

When I think back on that day now – when I remember how they all fell silent as I hauled my suitcase on to an empty bench, how they kept their eyes on me while they nudged each other and giggled and settled into mock heroic poses – my first thought is, why didn't I upgrade my ticket? My second thought is, how amazing it must have been to get that kind of attention.

At the time, I'm afraid, it was anything but welcome.

And so I wearily did all the usual things to fend it off. I took out a cardigan and draped it over my bare arms so as to look extra modest. I kept my sunglasses on and put on a hat. As the ferry edged along the shore from Piraeus to Sounion, I kept my eyes on my book and tried not to notice the football they kept rolling back and forth to each other, and occasionally kicking directly at me. I pretended not to understand their animated discussions in backwater Greek about my possible nationality. But then when we went around the cape and hit the open sea, the wind knocked the book out of my hands and slammed it against one of the lifeboats. One of the soldiers retrieved it for me and I made the mistake of saying thank you. I suppose I should explain that even saying thank you under those circumstances in those days was as good as pasting a message on your forehead that read: *I am a foreign woman of loose morals who has come to this country with the sole aim of being gangbanged.*

'Mees! What is your name? Your country? *Bitte schön, skol, mademoiselle, fräulein, voulez-vous coucher avec moi?*' First they were amused by my refusal to answer. Then they started getting annoyed. When one soldier walked across the deck to read the label on my suitcase, I told him in Greek that he and his friends ought to have worked out by now that I had no desire to speak to them.

I remember how stunned they were that I had spoken to them in Greek. After a long silence, one of the soldiers sitting directly opposite me turned to his friend and said, 'Why is this woman in Greece if she doesn't want to talk to Greeks?'

'We should teach her a lesson,' his friend said. He stood up, crossed the deck, and placed himself on my right. I picked up my suitcase, which was on my left, and put it between us. Then another soldier crossed the deck and sat down where the suitcase had been. I picked up my suitcase and moved to the bench closest to the hatch that connected us to the second-class snack bar. When one of the soldiers climbed underneath it to stare up at me through the slats, I stood up and told the soldiers that they were barbarians who were bringing shame to their country. Then I called for help through the hatch and eventually attracted the attention of the second-class steward.

He was a small, muscular man with the large black eyes of a cow. After berating the now silent and shifty-looking soldiers not just for being barbarians but peasants whose uncouth behaviour was threatening to destroy the nation's tourist industry, the steward offered to save me from their attentions by putting me into a second-class cabin. I thought he was trying to be kind, but no sooner had I walked into this cabin than he had followed me in and locked the door behind him. He pinned me against the wall, moaning, 'At last! At last!' When I told him there had been a misunderstanding, he said, 'You're lying, I can tell you're dying for it.'

Please excuse me if I sound callous but – as strange as it may seem to you now – I had been in this situation many times before so I knew what I had to do. I told him a big sob story about my Turkish fiancé who was going to be waiting on the pier in Naxos. 'What's a Turk doing on one of our islands?' was the steward's alarmed and outraged response. I explained that it was love. Love and an expert knowledge of the martial arts. We had been promised to each other since childhood, I said, but now that I had met *him*, I told the steward, it was clear to me that I was going to have to break off the engagement. Honour still compelled me to break the sad news to my fierce fiancé face to face. I begged the steward to tell me when his ferry would be paying its next visit to Naxos. I promised that I would come on board a free woman and give myself to him for ever. I appealed to his better nature and he fell for it.

He stood up, his chest positively rippling with manly forbearance. 'My darling,' he said as he opened the door. 'I can see you're tired. You'll need your strength for Naxos. Why don't you get some sleep?'

'No!' I said, plunging past him into the corridor. 'Our conversation has revived me and I am longing to breathe in the sea air!' In so doing, I must have betrayed my true feelings, because when we got back to civiliz-ation, he wouldn't let me anywhere near the sea air. He insisted on my staying with him on the wrong side of the counter in the smelly and steaming second-class snack bar. Whenever one of the soldiers came up to the hatch – not necessarily to stare, but also for a drink or a chocolate bar – the steward would hiss, 'Keep your eyes to yourself. The girl belongs to me.'

When we got to Naxos, he grabbed my arm and pushed me out on to the fast-emptying second-class deck and nodded to the agitated crowd that was wedged between the offloading traffic, the slabs of marble and the mountains of potato sacks, and said, 'Where is he?'

'I can't see him,' I said.

He tightened his grip on my arm and stared into the crowd as if he wished he were a rifle. 'No,' he finally said. 'No. I'm coming with you.' When I protested he said, 'Shut up, woman, and give me your suitcase.' I decided, the hell with it, why should I protect him? I followed him down the steps to the car-deck.

It was not my Turkish fiancé waiting for me on the pier but my father. He took stock of the steward, who had thrown my suitcase down in front of him, and folded his bare arms across his heaving chest. 'Who's this?' he asked me.

'He's the second-class steward,' I explained, 'and he just tried to rape me.'

My father was taller than the steward and had the advantage of surprise. He had the steward pinned to the ground in five seconds flat. Now the real fun began, and please don't raise your eyebrows at the word fun. I was being ironic.

The crowd that gathered around us was at first more curious than offended. 'Is it a Greek or a foreigner?' they asked each other. When they worked out that it was a foreigner on top, one man said to another man, 'What right does a foreigner have to sit on a Greek?'

'Mr Yannis is not any old foreigner,' said the second man. 'He brings his family here every summer and has a house in the Castro. This is his daughter and she is a good girl and used to play with my daughter.'

'I don't care if his daughter plays with Queen Frederika,' said a third man. 'It still doesn't give this German the right to sit on a Greek.'

'He's not a German!' I protested.

The steward cried out, 'He's a Turk!'

'He's not a Turk, you fool,' said the man who had been defending our honour.

'This woman lied to me!' the steward protested.

My father growled, 'Tell these idiots that this man is a rapist.'

'I can't remember the word for rapist.'

'Oh, for God's sake, *try.*'

I was still trying when my father's great drinking friend, the harbour master, pushed his way through the crowd.

'Oh, Mr Yannis! Mr Yannis! What has happened?'

Everyone in the crowd tried to explain to him at once. The story had got pretty twisted by now. The harbour master tried to talk my father into letting the steward get up so that the three men could go into the shack that was his office for a civilized discussion. My father said he was only letting the steward go if it was to release him into police custody. 'Mr Yannis,' the harbour master pleaded, 'for the love of the Virgin Mary, shouldn't we establish what actually happened before we involve the police?'

But even as he said this, the crowd was parting. The man who now planted himself in front of my father was not in uniform, but there was something about the way people deferred to him that left you in no doubt that he had already thrown a lot of their relatives into political prison. As I said, this was during the junta.

The off-duty policeman ordered my father to stand up. When my father did not oblige, and went on to accuse him (in English, thank God) of being a fascist, the off-duty policeman got the German standing next to him to explain that if my father did not obey his order at once, he would be charging him with resisting arrest as well as assault and battery.

At least that was according to the German. I couldn't make out exactly what the off-duty policeman said to him. I didn't and in fact still don't know the Greek for assault and battery. Although the German tried to mediate honestly, he complicated matters even further – first by telling my father in strained euphemisms that it was unwise to call an official of a military regime a fascist, then by trying to explain to the crowd that the steward was a rapist. 'How can you say such a thing?' one woman cried. 'He can't be a rapist. He's a Greek.' She turned to the off-duty policeman. 'How can you take this insult from a German?'

'This man may be a German,' another woman cried. 'But he is a good man. He comes here every summer. He rents a house from my brother.'

'Yes,' said an old man. 'And maybe you'd like to tell people how he met your brother, and what business it was that brought your brother and this good German man together in the winter of 1943.'

'What are you trying to say to me? That my brother was a collaborator?'

'No, I'm saying that this German of yours learned his Greek from the heroes he murdered during the occupation.'

'How can they say such things!' the German cried in English. 'In 1943 I was a mere thirteen years of age! Oh how much longer am I to bear the curse of my forefathers! What is it I must do to atone for their misdemeanours?' He was not much use as a mediator after that. In the end, the off-duty policeman got selected members of the crowd to lift my father off the

second-class steward, who was promptly dispatched
back to his ship, which set sail as soon as he had walked
on board. The crowd dispersed. The harbour master
tried to offer his sympathy while looking anxiously over
his shoulder to make sure the policeman wasn't noticing. I was anxious to get off the pier before my father
called the policeman a fascist again, so I picked up
my suitcase and started walking. My father eventually
caught up with me and grabbed the suitcase.

'Why are you angry at me?' I asked.

'I'm not angry at *you*,' he shouted. 'I'm angry at
those *fascists*.' But soon he was angry at my mother, too.
This was because she gasped when he used the word
fascist in his description of the events on the pier. 'You
can't call a fascist policeman fascist to his *face*!' she
said.

'If he doesn't want me to call him a fascist then he
shouldn't act like a fascist!'

My mother tried to head things off by suggesting he
sit down and relax with a drink and his newspaper. This
was when he remembered that he had forgotten to buy
a paper. My mother offered to pick one up for him
while she was down buying things for supper. When
she returned without a paper, and said that the news-
agent was shut, he accused her of being a liar. Off he
went into town again to prove her wrong. He came back
twenty minutes later without a newspaper and looking
spooked, but was unable to admit to my mother's face
that she had been telling the truth.

We sat down for a grim supper of tomatoes and Uncle
Ben's Rice. All the grocery stores had been shut, too.
'I wonder what's going on,' my father said in a thin
voice.

My mother, who had not yet forgiven him for calling
her a liar, said, 'Maybe you set off an international
incident.'

He said, 'Don't be preposterous,' but the punch had gone out of his delivery.

We fell into silence.

It must have been nine in the evening by now. We were sitting on the terrace, which looked down over the town and the harbour. Normally the waterfront would have been packed with evening strollers at this hour. Children would have been climbing over the marble slabs and potato sacks on the pier. A few boys would have been kicking a football around the little square directly beneath us. The first couples would have been making their way out along the causeway to the nightclub on the island where the tyrant's arch was. But tonight there was no one. 'I wish you'd remembered to buy the paper when it was still possible,' my father said to my mother. 'It's as if the place is on red alert.' After another long silence, he added, 'I wonder why no one told us.'

My mother said, 'What I think both of you forget is how easy it is to create misunderstandings in a foreign country and how dangerous these can be in the event of an emergency.'

'I wasn't implying there was a real emergency,' my father snapped. 'I was speaking hypothetically.' It was right after this hypothetical statement that we heard it for the first time.

It was a roar, the sort of roar that called to mind a distant battalion of helicopters. Except that it didn't come down to us from the sky. It came up to us from the town. But not from any particular place in the town. It came from everywhere.

'What's that?' my father asked.

'I don't know, dear,' my mother said.

'What a pity you didn't get that paper.'

My mother sighed, and then we heard the roar again.

'It sounds like it's coming from underneath the

town,' my father said. My mother said, 'I wonder if this means the junta's fallen.'

My father said, 'If you'd remembered the paper, we wouldn't have to guess.'

But before my mother could protest, there was a third roar – this one short and sharp, as if the whole town had been slapped by a giant hand. My father jumped to his feet and came back with his transistor. 'Let's find out what they're saying on the radio.'

We couldn't find the World Service or the Voice of America, or our usual fallback, Radio Tirana, so we tried the Greek stations. The commentators were too agitated for me to understand a word they were saying. 'That settles it,' my father said to me. 'You and I are going to have to go down there and locate this roar for ourselves.'

'Oh darling,' my mother said. 'Haven't you courted enough trouble for one day? Couldn't you wait until tomorrow?'

'It doesn't seem to have occurred to you,' my father told her grimly, 'that tomorrow may be too late.'

We left the Castro through the front gate and made our way to the agora. At nine o'clock on a normal evening, these alleyways were full of children and mothers and grandmothers. But the only person we saw was the harbour master's wife. When my father asked her where her husband was, she shrugged her shoulders in an unusually unfriendly way and said he was in the café. As we continued down the alleyway in the direction of the café, my father said, 'I wish you hadn't worn those shorts. They really aren't appropriate for evening wear.'

'You know,' I said, 'even if I wrap myself up in a sheet, they're still going to stare at me.'

'All I'm saying is, don't make life harder than it already is. I'm tired of playing the goon.'

By now we had arrived at the café.

There was not a single person sitting at an outside table. All the chairs were missing, too. Everyone was inside – everyone we didn't want to see. The off-duty policeman was there. All the men who had taken offence at my father sitting on a Greek were there. So were at least ten of the soldiers, not to mention the misunderstood German. When they all roared, I thought at first it was because they had noticed our arrival. But no, their eyes were all fixed on the tiny television the café owner had placed over the glass refrigerator where he kept his rice puddings. It was the first television I had ever seen on the island of Naxos.

A muffled voice was commentating wildly but the screen itself was all black and white zigzags. The absence of a picture did not stop the men in the audience from craning their necks and trying to look around my father and me as we made our way to the back of the café to join the harbour master.

If they did this now, I would think of it as normal. Or else not even pause to think about it at all. But at the time it was something of a jolt to be treated like an obstruction. I hate to admit it but I do remember asking myself, what could they possibly be seeing on that screen that could be more interesting than me?

My father must have noticed my annoyance because after the harbour master's friends had seated us and bought us drinks, he put a firm hand on my shoulder and said, 'I am expecting you to do your best to pretend to enjoy this. After what you put us all through today, it's the least you could do.'

And so I pretended to be captivated by the zigzags and the wild commentator. In the beginning, and in my usual way, I betrayed the spirit of his instructions by obeying them to the letter. I shook my head when the men around me shook their heads, pounded the table when they pounded the table, leaned forward in dismay when they leaned forward in dismay. Out of the corner of my eye I watched my father watch me anxiously out of the corner of his eye. And I watched the clock, which seemed to be frozen at nine twenty-seven.

Three more minutes, I said to myself as I watched the minute hand struggle to release itself. Three more minutes and I don't care what they say, it's the longest I can sit here going through these motions and pretending to enjoy this. But that was when it happened, when I was at my lowest ebb and had run through all my defences. The zigzags suddenly disappeared to reveal a cannonball of a football player burst out of a huddle of adversaries, to kick a blur of a football into a perfect arc that went between the outstretched arms of a vaulting goalkeeper and into the top right-hand corner of the net. And I couldn't help it. It rose up in a warm and intoxicating wave from my deepest inner recesses without my willing or understanding it.

The roar.

Newspaper columns, almost without exception, are irritating beyond belief. Those bearing Maureen Freely's byline are the exception. It was an *Observer* column in which she wrote about her male friends' endless appetite for childish games which put her at the top of the acquisitions list for this book. Born in New Jersey and now living in Bath, Maureen Freely writes regularly for the *Guardian* and the *Observer*. She has published four novels and two non-fiction books.

Tim Pears

Ebony International

It's said life can be seen as either a race or a dance. But it's more: it's a game.

I went to a rugby-playing grammar school. Every year a majority of pupils petitioned the headmaster to let us play soccer, in vain. So we made do with a kick-around every break-time. At home, in the Devon village I grew up in, my friends and I cobbled goals out of fencing posts and raspberry netting and played on every sloping field and winding lane.

We moved to a larger village, Christow, where the shopkeeper Terry Atwill ran a club. When he started a second team I scraped into it. One thinks of football as an urban sport, but we were crazy about the game, and there were teams in all the villages around Exeter.

Football's played at a series of levels, from Premier League to where it's barely worth wearing kit or marking out pitches. What separates successful professionals from those they leave behind – to scatter their dreams across council playing fields up and down the country – is not so much talent as a crucial difference in temperament.

There was a lad in the Christow team, Terry Millins, who came from Hennock. A winger with speed, skill, courage and wiry strength, he had an athletic exuberance for the game: he would push the ball over-optimistically past the full-back and, with a huge rush of energy, burst forward to reach it first. You'd sometimes hear a squeal of laughter at the sheer joy it gave him. And sometimes he'd come back just to beat the guy again.

Word got round, and one Saturday afternoon I watched our first team, top of their division, play the bottom club on an Exeter council pitch. It was known that scouts were coming to take a look at Terry, and they ambled over in a group, in long overcoats, hunting in a pack. It was the worst we ever played, couldn't put two passes together, and as for Terry, he went into hiding out wide on the left wing, retreated into a shell. The ball reached him once, and he fell over it. Eventually, a quarter of an hour from the end, the scouts had a word with our manager, shrugged their wide shoulders, and walked away. We were 1–0 down. In the last ten minutes we hit five goals, and Terry scored four of them. That's the truth. I guess we all realized then that our star would never make it as a professional.

Back then, as a teenager, I assumed my passion for football was part of my youth. Most teams we played had one or two ageing veterans. I despised them for failing to outgrow their adolescent fantasies, for not relinquishing this punishing activity and settling into less gruelling pursuits. I despised their pot-bellies and their slow turns, their lung-racked breathing; for refusing to accept they'd grown old.

So soon, I became one of them. So soon. In the summer of 1994 I quit, aged thirty-seven. Now I only play five-a-side, kick-arounds, odd friendlies ... Football's harder to give up than smoking.

I was a useless player. English football at its professional best is exhilarating, but at anything less it's invariably a dismal game. I played for a couple of Sunday-morning sides composed of thugs with hangovers, in games where the ball was merely a hurtling cushion for the legitimized violence of our national aggression; and for a couple of other teams with players even more inept than myself. But I was privileged to play in one team with men from whom I learned about football and about life.

Wilfrid de Baise was a charismatic six-foot-six black Frenchman who hated Paris and fell in love with Oxford; so he stayed, DJing in the crummy nightclubs of this town and hiring out his own mobile disco, Ebony International. We used to kick around in the local park on Sunday afternoons and, gradually, recruiting players from the dance floor, Willy put together a team and organized friendlies against Bangladeshi waiters, Libyan trainee pilots and tutorial colleges of European students.

Ebony won them all – as the team improved, by increasingly embarrassing margins. Instead of entering a local league, Willy, being an original, went and organized a whole new one of his own. Articles appeared in the *Oxford Star* and rumours circulated in clubs and bars. The league started in 1985, with two divisions made up of new teams from banks, pubs and company social clubs.

Often I was the only Englishman in Ebony International. There were so many languages spread amongst our illegal immigrants and transient visitors that to avoid confusion we played in silence, our small North African midfielders passing in triangles around opponents yelling at each other: 'I can't hear you! Fucking SHOUT!'

We played everywhere: in the mudbath behind Botley Allotments; on the winter windswept wastes at Horspath; the college lawn on Mansfield Road; at Marston where the only spectators were seagulls lined up on the crossbar; at Lucy's, on a single pitch marked out in the middle of a vast field of grass, so that more time was spent retrieving the ball than kicking it; on the top pitch at Cutteslowe surrounded by a play-park, aviary and steam train, and hundreds of fleeting watchers.

The first goalkeeper was my best friend Philip, who began playing at 38 and retired at 40 with a nervous breakdown, vanishing from the team and the town. He was succeeded by Eric, an American at Oxford University writing a graduate thesis on Renaissance theatre. Eric had the reckless courage and the morbid psyche necessary for a keeper, but he also possessed both astonishing agility and American naïvety. He was worth a goal a game: one for us and one for them.

Eric had the positional sense of a moth. When an attacker broke through one-on-one Eric came out widening the angle – the opponent stroked the ball past him into a yawning goal. When Eric turned and saw where the goalposts had been moved to he did a double-take of paranoid disbelief, threw off his gloves and stalked after the ball. He retrieved it from the net and punted it as high into the air as possible, venting his anger and despair upon it.

It took us weeks to persuade Eric not to hoof the ball upfield for clearances but rather to throw it to a defender so we could play out from the back; and it took months to teach him to call for the ball on crosses. Unfortunately this demanded so much of his concentration that he lost his already flimsy grasp of the ball's flight. Over it came from the wing, this stentorian American accent roared: 'KEEPER!' stunning colleagues and opposition alike into startled immobility, and in slow motion Eric rose and flapped in mid-air as the ball sailed over his head.

He could be a liability, Eric; but more often he was an inspiration. Every game there came an instance when the ball was headed for the net, opposition players already celebrating, only for Eric to soar like a salmon and miraculously scoop the ball over the bar; you could feel their will being sucked out of them, and ours energized. Or he'd hurl himself head first into a blurred mêlée of frantic boots like a blind man in search of the slithery ball, and clutch it like a baby. Afterwards, with grimacing pride, he would display that week's broken finger or loosened tooth.

Goalkeepers are oddballs, outsiders, peculiarly masochistic, brave and vulnerable. When the ball's upfield they lose interest – they make lousy managers. When we scored at the other end Eric felt as sorry for his opposite number as jubilant for us: his perfect score was 0–0. And we *never* had a 0–0 draw.

Radko and Ramon were Slovak brothers. Whenever we scored, Ramon yelled: 'Ebony! Ebony! Ebony!' Radko was always the last of our team to arrive, traipsing across Cutteslowe Park trailing a line of kids and dogs, like Yosser Hughes. Their father was a dancer and Radko had inherited a whiplash body: when we were lined up ready for kick-off he did a standing back-flip for good luck.

Radko was a full-back, and a mercurial defender. If a winger ever dribbled past him he recovered so quickly the man would have to beat him again; and no one beat him twice. The sad thing was he wanted to play in goal – if Eric was away, Radko filled in – and unfortunately he wasn't very good. During one memorable defeat he watched the ball trickle over the line for goal number six and, in one of those weird silences, his voice croaked: 'I'm 'avin' a nightmare.'

When Eric returned, Willy put Radko back outfield, and Radko played wearing his goalkeeper's gloves, whether in silent protest or simply as protection against the cold it was hard to tell.

Sean was our Scottish central defender. He lived on

the estate overlooking Cutteslowe, where we played our home games, but Willy always had to dispatch someone to drag him out of bed and a drunken stupor. He stumbled over, paint-splattered from his latest moonlighting job, and began games bleary-eyed, beer thick and sweet on his breath as he shouted, 'Sean's ball!' crunching into an only slightly mistimed tackle.

We had our share of violent players. Like Sam, a skilful full-back who when he was made to look stupid – by an opponent's trickery or his own error – flew off the handle and kicked out at the nearest opposing player like a petulant child. Eventually he had one temper tantrum too many and Willy came rushing on to the pitch, trenchcoat flapping, and hauled him off for good. Or Martin, a gentle giant, who once on a pitch in the grounds of Blenheim Palace inexplicably stamped on an opponent who happened to be lying on the ground at the time. Without waiting for the referee, Martin walked off the pitch, collected his clothes, drove away and was neither seen nor heard of again.

And there were the two attackers – Jay, a Central African, and Ali from the North – with equally extravagant talent and egos, whom Willy made the mistake of playing together up front. Once. They ignored each other throughout the entire game, while a silent, palpable animosity grew between them, and as we walked off at the end they suddenly started trading blows.

Like road rage, violence lurks just below the surface of contact sport. And, sadly, winning too often makes you mean, and brittle, both as a team and as men.

Sean was never violent, he was a true hard man. He made every tackle with equal vigour, whether against a spindly seventeen-year-old or a sixteen-stone bruiser. Uncompromising and fair. When he'd won the ball he gave it to someone else to do the fancy stuff, like passing it.

Once, playing against a police team, Sean and the player he was marking turned in a crowded penalty area and ran, face to face, smack into each other. A freak accident. Sean's nose flattened against the other guy's forehead; the sound of bone and gristle snapping and tearing made my knees go, never mind theirs. They both dropped poleaxed to the ground. There was blood everywhere. I knelt beside Sean thinking: *Phone, 999, ambulance, casualty*, while registering amazement that he appeared to still be conscious, his hands over his face. Blood pouring. Then this Scottish-accented voice emerging from under the mess: 'Ah'm goin' tae register a complaint against police brutality.'

My best days were behind me ('About twenty years behind ye, grandad,' I hear Sean's voice) and when Willy first put the team together I dropped back from midfield to partner him in central defence. I was over six foot myself and was almost as bad a header as he was (Willy didn't like to mess his hair up, nor to muddy his long legs with so uncouth an act as a sliding tackle). But it rarely mattered, since when opponents booted the ball up the middle we just dropped off their centre-forward, who flicked it on. We said: 'Thank you very much,' collected the ball and played it on the ground the way we liked.

Soon, though, we came up against better teams and so Willy moved us out to the full-back positions (there was nowhere left to move after this, except over the touchline, as Willy soon did in his trenchcoat and scarf).

In came Mark, a cussed Yorkshireman, now a BBC film-maker, and the most immaculate defender I ever played with. He not only won fifty–fifty tackles and headers but made passes out of them; under the most extreme pressure he never simply cleared the ball but cleared it to a colleague. When he joined Ebony it became possible to play out from the back because there were now two of us who wanted the ball off the keeper, dropping back for Eric to roll it out.

A regular, depressing sight in English football is that of a goalkeeper gathering the ball and his defenders cantering away from him. They dash off, pretending that they're implementing the masterly tactic of leaving attackers stranded in an offside position should their keeper's aimless punt upfield be swiftly returned. It's a sham. They're merely trying to cover up the fact that they don't want the ball. Sure, they'd like to rob an opponent of it, preferably in a bone-jangling tackle, but they don't want it played to their feet, to be obliged to bring it under control and then pass it accurately on.

Does the globe come from nature, or do we impose the mathematical notion of a perfect circle upon nature? Is the moon round, or is there a human aspiration towards the ideal that makes us see it so? Searching a beach for one round pebble, we imagine the elements combining in artistic endeavour. Our pathetic illusion.

The football is a symbol of the game's simplicity and of our striving for the ideal (and this is why rugby is intrinsically inferior to soccer, its essential component an erratic oval, wayward and imperfect).

Salim played central midfield; Salim was our playmaker. A stocky Algerian in his thirties, he was past his best, but his best must have been something to see. He'd played semi-professionally back home (here he was a chef in a Greek taverna and was just beginning to work as a youth coach with Oxford United). Salim roamed around the middle of the pitch playing easy first-time passes but every now and then suddenly turning, shrugging off his marker, and slicing the ball through their defence.

Salim was both our colleague and our teacher. The only thing he couldn't stand, and wouldn't tolerate, was stupidity. He didn't mind missed chances or inaccurate passes, he was always encouraging: 'Unlucky. Well played. Good boy. Try again.' But if someone over-elaborated or hoofed the ball upfield instead of playing a simple pass, Salim glowered and scowled and tore strips off us. Losing possession irked him. He showed us that you can always get out of trouble by playing simple one-twos, and move around the pitch with a series of wall passes. It's a simple game, he told us: pass and move, pass and move, that's all. The brain's the most important part of a footballer's anatomy. The key's movement off the ball: football is geometry in motion, human beings creating patterns Euclid never dreamed of.

Keep thinking, keep moving, but be patient too. In England we grow up playing at full tilt the whole time (mainly, one suspects, to keep warm in this, our winter game; if our season ran from March to December standards would soar). Slow, slow, quick quick, slow: that's how the brain can best reach peaks of imaginative expression. When the body's fully extended the brain can only reach a certain level and maintain it. You need patient, purposeful probing, then sudden bursts of creativity. 'Play like Liverpool, for fuck's sake,' Salim exhorted us. 'It's not difficult. Just use your bloody brains.' Of course in sport, as in art, simplicity is the most difficult thing of all.

Most of us were in our late twenties or early thirties, hardened football nutters from all over the world. Like Mario, a free-scoring Brazilian who mangled his arm in the pasta-making machine in the pizza place where he did the washing-up. Like Iranian Mohammed and Sala the Iraqi Kurd, who played either side of Salim in midfield. Like the Italian who insisted upon being referred to as 'The Prince'. Like Moroccan Rashid, who could miss from two yards with his right foot but score from anywhere with his left.

But the best player any of us played with was a sublimely talented, sixteen-year-old local boy.

Kenny was on Tottenham's books, and travelled to London for training once or twice a week. He played for a top-class Oxford team on Saturday and then turned out for us on a Sunday, like a kind of guest superstar. He was an attacking midfielder with the most precious commodity: vision.

The source of satisfaction for a spectator is watching a good player accomplish what can be seen – from beyond the participants' limited perspective – as the most useful option open to him. The exceptional player improves upon what the most privileged spectator can see. Kenny used to pass the ball into what appeared to be aimless space, and it would take a second or two to realize that he'd prised open their tight defence, had invited our winger to run clear. He'd both anticipated and prompted the unfolding geometry into a new phase; the moment of appreciating what he'd just done was breathtaking.

IQ tests shouldn't be carried out simply sat at a desk; they ought to include at the very least some simple ball skills. I've seen brilliant academics in University Parks utterly incapable of judging a ball bouncing towards them. Gazza may be daft as a brush, but he's also an Einstein.

When Kenny received the ball it became part of him. He accepted it lovingly, caressed it, and when he stroked the ball on towards a colleague it was a gesture of affection.

Our league was constituted so that the top two teams in each division had to play-off for the title, and we met our arch-rivals, the Nag's Head pub team. We'd thrashed them 8–1 in the league two weeks earlier, and their manager responded by sending them out in a new bright purple kit splashed with black dots. A couple of hundred friends and family came along to watch on a bright sunny day.

The truth was that having Kenny on our side was unfair: we were well-matched teams but he was on another plane altogether; he was irresistible. We were sometimes guilty of standing back and gaping at his skill; he reduced his own colleagues to spectators. He laid on an early goal for Jay, our African striker, and the game was as good as won.

When a player commits a nasty foul it provokes instant rage, but when someone's actually hurt, when you hear the crack of bone, anger doesn't even rise. Anyway, bad injuries are usually accidental. Midway through the first half Kenny had an innocuous collision with their captain, and his right thigh-bone snapped. One of the Nag's Head players' mothers was training as a physio and she had a kind of cushioned padding with which she supported Kenny's leg while waiting for the ambulance. It came eventually, driving across the council pitches, and took him to the John Radcliffe.

Willy said afterwards he wished he'd abandoned – and forfeited – the game. Our hearts weren't in it, we lost 2–1, but we didn't care. Kenny was in hospital for weeks. He didn't kick a ball again for another year and he was never the same. He played for Ipswich reserves and has gone on to a minor professional career on the Continent, but a diffidence entered his play that is the difference between mediocrity and brilliance. Our grizzled dreams were with him, and we saw them dashed. It was the saddest thing.

Willy worried all week about selecting his team. At our level, friendship complicated the process, but, although he had our affection as well as respect, Willy had that strange measure of aloofness necessary for leadership, for painful decisions. He gathered us together before games and read out the starting line-up from a wrinkled scrap of paper. And then he said: 'Play, guys. Play football.'

I don't remember Willy ever giving a team talk, or discussing tactics. He attracted the best players he could and let them get on with it. He wanted us to express ourselves and he wanted us to surprise and entertain *him*. He said there was no point in watching players do what he'd told them to. Where was the fun in that?

An Oxford paper covered our results, scorers and league tables with an additional round-up, and during our second season the local FA got in touch with Willy to request a meeting. I accompanied him and Geren, our league secretary, to a conference room in the Moat House Hotel. We sat across a table from three men in blazers worried by the success of a league outside their monopolistic control. They offered us inducements – insurance, contacts, qualified officials – to come under their umbrella. It would have meant agreeing to all their rules, which included, once becoming affiliated ourselves, being unable to play even friendlies against unaffiliated clubs; and also women being banned from playing. This wasn't merely an academic point, since a couple of American women had played for one of the tutorial college sides. But even if they hadn't, Willy wasn't keen on banning anyone.

Willy listened to the FA functionaries' arguments, and declined to join. They responded with threats, warning all players and officials that if they took any part in our league they'd be banned from the FA. Whether or not they found out by sending spies, the following season a couple of referees and a number of players (in FA teams on a Saturday, in ours on a

Sunday) were suspended. It was a spiteful action, and it turned out to be needless: Willy was stitched up in a business venture and had to start commuting to Paris to work, leaving no time to lead the league he'd started, which ground down at the end of that season. We'd had three great years together.

Football is so compelling an activity partly because, like any sport, it requires utter concentration of mind and body – in the act there is no duality and no ego, only total absorption in the moment, pure individual expression – and also because of its nature as a team game. Football combines two quite different human endeavours in the act of defence and of attack. The one – anticipating danger, racing back, getting behind the ball, marking, covering, blocking, tackling – is that of mutual support in a crisis, working together with courage and selflessness in an emergency.

The other – constructing the complex, improvised patterns of passing movements, running off the ball, offering options, dribbling, crossing, shooting – is collaboration in creative expression.

These two different activities are contained seamlessly within the same game; play oscillates constantly between them. When it's successful the result is a profound communion, an intimate fellowship with one's colleagues, with, in Ebony, our French leader and his rag-tag team of Oxford lads, odd academics, refugees, migrant workers and other gentlemen of the beautiful game.

Born in 1956 in Kent, Tim Pears now lives in Oxford. His first novel, *In the Place of Fallen Leaves* (1993), won the Hawthornden Prize and is published by Black Swan. His second novel *In a Land of Plenty* will be published by Transworld in March 1997.

Conrad Williams

aet

In delicious BBC slo-mo: Tierney's red shirt moves like arresting fluid as he slips one tackle and shrugs left in order to get the ball on to his favourite foot. A window appears, very small, but it's all he needs.

Impact.

The crowd rises like the black swell of oil in a polluted ocean. The ball, captured in the impossible detail of rotation – sponsors' names clear upon its equator – moves as if in deep space, forever to follow the trajectory its launching boot has ordained. Tierney's leg sweeps round, muscle and sweat. Spent, he can only watch, the shimmer in his shirt ceasing.

Foley springs but his fingertips can't gain purchase. His face is etched with the kind of expression found upon disbelievers.

'GOA—'

The ball collides with the underside of the crossbar. Udney scuttles back and hoofs to Kingdom Come. The ref blows for the end of extra time and that magical word dies in Tierney's throat.

'Jim's here, Paul. Come on, drink your tea.'

Cyn tore the curtains apart; a chunk of sunlight staggered through the window as if grateful to find a resting place. Images fell away from Tierney as the years piled against him.

'Goal,' he said, flatly. It never possessed the same taste these days.

In the bathroom, he scrutinized himself in the blanched honesty of the striplight. Scars mottled his legs like the bark of a silver birch. Six holes in his chest: a souvenir from an end-of-season tussle with Wigan Athletic back in '99 which clinched Liverpool's third successive title. That August had been the start of Tierney's last season in league football, although he'd been playing at his peak. Same for his team-mates. He still felt deeply for Morris, who had been poised to go to Marseille. And Cat, of course. Their keeper.

He showered and gulped his tea. Boucher was leaning against the sink in the kitchen, his arms folded.

'Jim,' Tierney acknowledged.

'Today's the day, hey, Paul?' said Boucher. Tierney didn't know whether to be impressed with Boucher's ebullience or appalled by it. Of the four scheduled days they spent in each other's company, he always came out with the same crass greeting, capping it with the kind of noiseless chuckle an asthmatic lizard might loose. The novelty of being guarded had long paled for Tierney, a top midfielder capped for England on fourteen occasions and a Liverpool stalwart since the Golden Age returned to Anfield in the mid-1990s. Now it was just another job. Four visits to and from Wembley One each week, plus the occasional radio interview or TV appearance, where he was wheeled out like a circus freak and patronized with the applause usually reserved for old ladies who'd reached the age of ninety.

Tierney had sometimes questioned Boucher's necessity. Not since the goal-line incident of 2001, when he'd successfully appealed to the referee that Liverpool's penalty be retaken because Manchester United's goalkeeper, Iain Foley, had been doing a Grobbelaar shuffle on the line to put him off, had he needed recourse to

Boucher. It was one of the reasons he was invited to do interminable lunch-time interviews for *Pebble Mill* and Radio Five Live. 'Must be doing my job well, then, hey, Paul?' he'd countered, with that scabrous enthusiasm. He guessed he kept on at Boucher because it had been so long since he felt captain of his own ship. He lashed Boucher because he wanted to feel alive.

'Doing anything special for the anniversary, Paul?' Boucher twinkled. 'Like, say, winning the bloody thing? Hsss-eh-heh-heh-ehhhhsss.'

'Yeah. That would be nice.'

'"Nice", he says.' Boucher tipped a wink at Cyn, who looked as listless as a dead pond. 'It must be demoralizing, eh? Week in, week out, twatting a piece of leather from twelve yards into a net? Paint me black and call me Mabel. I'd rather watch me mam soap her arse.'

'I didn't realize you were such a football fan,' said Tierney, bitterly. He felt the compulsion to defend his corner despite the fossil of his love for the game inside him.

'Oh, I *am* a football fan. I *am.* But *you're* not playing football, are you? *You're* playing silly buggers. Hssss-eh-ehssss.'

'It's keeping you in pie and chips, isn't it?'

'Aye. Mustn't grumble. We've been getting death threats, by the way.' He might have been asking the time.

'From whom?' Cyn's colour pushed through the dough of her face, animating her. 'The same one as before?'

'Probably. It looks like it. I wouldn't fret. It's only because of the anniversary. There'll be extra men on, come Saturday. And you could always duck out of it if you want, Paul.'

'Yeah, right.'

'What about these death threats?' Cyn asked. 'Have you got them on you?'

Boucher nodded. 'Got copies. The police have got the originals.' He opened his suitcase and pulled an envelope from one of the pockets. 'They were sent to Anfield, which might mean he doesn't know where you live. Which is good.'

'Yeah, right,' said Tierney again. 'I'm tickled fucking pink.'

He took the envelope from Cyn after she'd studied the contents, as someone will study an unexpected photograph. The paper was cheap and smelled faintly of vomit. Without resorting to cod frighteners such as clipped letters from newspapers, he'd gone for no-nonsense handwriting:

YOU'VE WRECKED OUR NATIONAL GAME,
BASTARD.
I'M GOING TO WRECK YOU.

and

HOW DO YOU SLEEP THESE DAYS? MAKE NO
MISTAKE, I'LL SEE YOU
SLEEP FOR EVER.

As always, a photograph of his old friend Cat was the last thing he saw as he left the house, standing on the telephone table by the front door. Kissing Cyn, he told her not to worry, because he wouldn't, and went to Boucher's car, forcing himself not to take nervous glances up and down the street.

They travelled through north London, the last stint of his four-day shift. Through tinted windows, Tierney snatched glimpses of boys in alleyways kicking a ball back and forth on the way to school, as he had once done with Cat. The memory stirred in him, a pure bubble trapped deep in mud. They'd followed each other on to football pitches at all levels. From infant school to county level to signing for Liverpool as a package from Runcorn FC they'd shared the glory and the pain. Cat was the unlikeliest figure of a goalkeeper since Willie 'Fatty' Foulkes. He was short and wiry. And he wore glasses, round-framed affairs which shone like tiny suns whenever the light fell on his face. He had to switch to contacts when he became a professional because players were complaining about being put off by his brilliant stare.

But he could *move*. One game, back in their first season at Anfield, they'd been playing away against Arsenal and Cat had saved an impossible shot. Gordon Banks' save from Pelé in Mexico, 1970, was the fumbling of an amateur compared to this. Wrong-footed by the mercurial striker Steve Jones (whose trademarks included a trimmed eighties beard and white boots), Cat had somehow flitted back the full length of the goal-line to tip his curling shot around the post. It had been hailed 'save of the century' and shared front-page status with John Major's prefrontal leucotomy and Jimmy Hill's suspension from *Match of the Day* for punching Des Lynam. Athletes had been invited to make the same demands of their bodies, to see if such movement was possible. None could achieve it. Cat's save was a fluke, bawled the commentators.

They'd spent an evening together, towards the end, when Cat's drinking had been noticed by the manager, who had replaced him with the new boy, Pucill. Cat looked haggard, his body no longer agitated by its inner compulsion for movement. Once, Tierney had been irritated by Cat's constant fidgeting. Now he silently pined for it.

'I'm a freak,' Cat, soused, had whispered over the

rim of his pint. 'I did something nobody's ever done before. I did something *I've* never done before and will never do again.'

'How do you know?' Tierney had asked.

'Because it wasn't a physical thing, Paul. It's the reason all those clowns from the athletics clubs couldn't do it. It was all up here.' He tapped his forehead with his glass. 'You know what I was thinking when I saved Jones' shot? When I made the "save of the century"?' The phrase was spat.

Tierney hadn't said anything. He wasn't sure he wanted to know. A magician never explains his tricks.

'I wasn't thinking of angles, or closing the bastard down. I was thinking of me and you. Up on the embankment near Seven Arches years ago. Kicking a tin can around. I was a kid again for that crucial second, mate. I've tried it since but it's hard to stop concentrating, to let something out of whack like that to get through. Just happened. Came out of nowhere like a sneeze.'

They were quiet for a while. Then Cat had said: 'I don't have the passion any more.'

The twin towers of Wembley One loomed; just behind, Wembley Two's copper lion glinted green in the quickening light. As they approached the players' entrance, bypassing the Venables statue, Boucher peered round the driver's headrest and winked at Tierney.

'Don't get out when we park, OK? Wait for my signal.'

Shepherded inside, Tierney left Boucher by the changing-room door. Most of them were there already: Coady, Pucill, Morris and the goateed Smith looked like suicidal, lost troops, complete with a twelve-yard stare.

'Where's Fricker?' asked Tierney, shrugging out of his jacket.

'Probably down the pub,' said Morris, 'where the rest of us should be. Right, Ric?'

'Isn't it just,' said Coady. 'Absolutely.' He was already in his kit, staring at his boots as if they were the shells of reticent molluscs and he was waiting for their inhabitants to emerge.

Smith touched Tierney's arm. 'Are you all right?'

'No. I've had death threats again. You'll excuse me if I don't hug you till your tits squeak when I knock mine in this evening.'

As they were filing out into the tunnel, Fricker arrived.

'You're late,' Tierney barked.

'Fuck your mother, Paul,' came the unimpressed reply.

Tierney was about to pile in when strong arms dragged him away. 'Forget it, Paul,' said Morris.

Smith ground his cigarette out and guided him towards the floodlit strip of green. 'Two things about Fricker,' he said. 'A: he's an arsehole. B: he's pissed off because he's the substitute. Find it in your heart to feel some pity for a man who has had to sit on the bench during the penalty shoot-out for the past five years.'

'You fuck your mother too, Smith,' called Fricker.

Even now, emerging from the tunnel into the grand old bowl of Wembley ('Wembley Tedium' as the newspapers had christened it), Tierney tensed himself for the roar. When it didn't come – just the tepid clap of fifty or sixty 'Pen-Pals' – that scintilla thrill winked out so fast that he couldn't even be certain it had been there at all.

The Manchester United team trotted out a few minutes later to similar underwhelming applause. Someone tried a chant: 'Bry-an Rob-son's Red And White Ar-my,' but nobody took it up. A lone Liverpool pensioner felt the need to cancel it out nevertheless.

His voice drifted down from the stand, enfeebled with age and a reedy Scouse accent: 'Fook off, yer Manc twats. Yer fooking shite, the lot of yez!'

Tierney waved at the fans while trying to spot a potential assassin among them, but they were too far away. Fricker was on the bench in his tracksuit. When he caught Tierney looking at him, he gave him the Vs, pulled out a magazine and put his feet up.

'Come on, Paul,' shouted Coady. 'Are you going first?'

'No, Ric. You go. Then Mike, Marky and Puey. I'll go last.'

The players hung around the centre circle while goalkeeper, striker and a corpulent referee prepared for the first pen of the night. Alan Udney slapped Tierney on the back and swung his blotchy face into view. He looked a lot heavier than the scampering wraith that had kicked that final effort off the line all those years ago.

'All right there, Udders?' said Tierney, groping for a smile.

'Nowhere I'd rather be,' he returned. The referee blew his whistle. Coady lumbered up and slotted the ball past Foley, who hardly moved.

'Ooh,' Tierney joshed Udney's arm. 'Now the pressure's on.'

Udney yawned and trotted away. He placed his penalty to Pucill's right. The net billowed. Pucill looked at his watch. Someone in the 'crowd' went home.

From behind Tierney came the improbable harmonies of a real gathering as a real goal was scored. A thick, silvery glow hung around the mouth of Wembley Two, which, along with the roar, thinned to nothing as the night teased it skyward. A fanfare of synthesized trumpets and a hologram projected into space:

SUPER LEAGUE CUP FINAL
GOOOOAAAAAL!!!!!!
EVERPOOL ALLSTARS FC 1
LONDON TOWN TEAMSTERS 0
TONIGHT'S SPONSORS: 'DOVE' BY DAMERAU
LTD . . .
. . . THE FOOTBALLERS' ECSTASY

The prickle at Tierney's neck receded and these drab confines folded around him like an Oxfam greatcoat. He wondered briefly if he was unconsciously sending the death threats to himself, to pepper the monotony. Smith, Morris and Pucill – penalty kings all – drove their kicks home and, as usual, stepping up to the spot he felt the old burn in his stomach, but either the layers of hide which had accumulated on his body or the lack of external stimuli had cancelled its significance. He delved for the recognition of that magic but it wouldn't come. Not that it would help his cause. If anything, rekindling the glory of his life – the beautiful game – would only send him deeper into a funk. Better to carry the dead baby inside him. Better to—

Without thinking, he'd buried the ball in the top left-hand corner. It wasn't hard these days, not since the FA had bowed to the cash registers of the burgeoning American influence on the game and increased the size of the goal. Yes, it had done much for the game, really cheered up the masses who craved goals. But nobody had thought of the consequences for the penalty competition. *Here we are*, Tierney thought, utterly without bitterness – years of the same notion had rendered that emotion pointless – *here we are, dinosaurs on show, the old footballers, the clowns.* Was the lust for competition really so great that they had to battle this out till someone took a 'Chris Waddle' and forfeited the old FA Cup? Did they really give a shit?

'Yes, of course, you arse. Of course we give a shit!' It was Morris, answering a question Tierney hadn't meant to ask out loud. 'I support my kids on this, you know. Five minutes on *Penalty Corner* with Tony Gubba keeps me in custard for a week.'

'Yeah,' sighed Tierney. 'I'm sorry.' He ran down the pitch, as he always did at the end of the session, to touch the black ribbon pinned to the bar over the opposite goalmouth. He remembered a grey, dripping dawn, when he'd come here to meet Cat, who'd called him in the night asking if they could talk. He knew what was wrong as soon as he entered the stadium and saw the limp, dark figure depending from the woodwork. Cat didn't look terribly unwell, considering. He appeared bored, his eyes gazing at a portion of pitch in the disaffected way children deflect their attention if they are being chastised. Before calling the police, he'd relieved Cat of his spectacles. They were at home in his top drawer with their odd, purple plastic rims: his only concession to gimmick.

After his shower (not that he needed one, having barely worked up a sweat), Tierney dodged Boucher and slipped outside via a service door. It was when he was trotting along the approach to the stadium that he realized what he'd done, and then only because of the riot of his heart. *OK*, he told himself. *It'll be OK.* He reinforced that by imagining how insane he was likely to get if he didn't flee and get a little wind in his hair occasionally.

He walked the dismal streets till he found the station – it exuded a warm belch of burned oil, which he found perversely enjoyable. How long since he'd Tubed it any-where? Christ. All he'd known in the last five years were leather seats, tinted glass and the back of Boucher's badly shorn head. He travelled to Baker Street to inter-cept his connection. The platform was sparsely populated. A woman, reading the latest issue of *Mizz*, a gent carrying a tightly furled brolly and a dangerously sharp *FT*, a pair of kids snogging with a desperate circular motion, as if their mouths were governed by gyroscopes. Further along, a pair of tracksuited legs thrust out from a bench tucked into an alcove, the rest of the body was severed by its leading edge. Something about its complete lack of movement troubled Tierney. As the train barrelled into the station, punching hot air before it and a tide of grit into his face, he wondered if the person was asleep, or worse. Tierney couldn't allow the fever of his liberation simply to die down; the platform became littered with people leaving the train. Some of them cast glances at whoever it was that was hidden from him. A girl laughed. He hoped that by the time the passengers filtered out, the legs would be gone, revealing his panic to be folly. But they remained.

From behind the wall's extent, Eric Cantona's head leaned. For one bizarre second, Tierney thought it was Bert from *Sesame Street* but then he saw that it wasn't Eric, it was someone in a rubber mask, and he laughed out loud; a nervous bark. When Eric stood up and came for him, Tierney knew better than to hang around to discern his purpose. Finding a swiftness that had long been unasked of his body, he sidestepped between the closing doors. Whether Eric had been intending to follow suit or merely wanted to give him a fright was academic: his empty eyes tracked Tierney from the platform as the train gathered pace. He would have kissed Boucher's head if it were near him now.

He rode the lift alone at Tufnell Park and walked up Dartmouth Park Hill, turning left into Churchill Road where shouts and the unmistakable sound of a cheap, over-inflated plastic ball skidding on tarmac halted him. They had set up goals on the school car park – four clumps of duffel coats and jerseys. Six-a-side. Punt and chase.

'Pass the ball, Cudge!'

'Leave it out, he couldn't pass a fucking stool!'

When someone contrived a goal from all that messy endeavour, Tierney was startled into applause by the force of their celebration. He watched till the ball ended up on the school roof and an argument broke out about who should retrieve it.

Cul was in the window, hands in his pockets. When he saw Tierney he waved – or rather, flapped his hands with shock – and ducked out of view, reappearing as a shapeless white mass through the frosted glass of the front door.

'Where the fuck's your fucking wotsit … your chappy?' he babbled, like hot chip fat.

'Calm down,' soothed Tierney, easing past his brother. 'If you mean Boucher, I ducked him. Fed up to my tits of being in each other's pants all day. I've had a cracking time on my own, if you must know. Kettle on?' He didn't mention what had happened on the platform.

'Cyn rang me about an hour ago. Blow me if she's not feared to Christing buggery, lad. Why couldn't you give her a call?'

'I didn't want anyone, Cul, all right? I just wanted a bit of space. A bit of the old me. I've been cooped up like one of Dad's chickens for too long.'

Cul left him for a while and the warmth and the peacefulness of the house crept into him. When his brother returned, pressing a mug of tea into his hand, he was ready to fall asleep.

'Why did you come here? I haven't seen you for fucking donkeys.'

'You've still got that box I gave you? Well, I want a look, don't I?'

'It's in the loft. Honestly, I don't know why you don't just chuck the lot of it. I mean, it's only a pile of rotten old leather and shite. Good for bugger all but the flame if you ask me. Ah but, Paul, you're a daft bastard, you are.'

'Yeah, well, thanks. And I'm not asking you. I'm just— I haven't got a grip of me any more. Can you at least understand that?' Tierney put his mug down and made to stand up. Cul gestured with his head: go on then.

Upstairs, he unfolded the stepladders beneath the loft entrance and slid the cover away. He felt around for the torch and switched it on before lifting his body into the balmy pyramid. A pale cone of light from the torch licked the rusting frame of a camp bed and a single novel bloated with damp. He drew the wooden box towards him – his father's initials ingrained on the lid – and flipped it open.

Inside was a plastic wallet stuffed with programmes he'd collected as a boy, along with football cards and a pair of shinpads he'd used all through his childhood. Here was an album of photographs Dad had taken of him during his Penlake Under-13 days. But it was the pair of desiccated boots he lifted from the box. If he closed his eyes while he breathed them in, he could just about smell the phantom of soft fields. A few tufts of grass were bonded against the rusting studs with mud and time. For a short while, they seemed alien compared to the moulded rubber blades everyone wore today. But then they called to something inside him that he'd guessed was dead and he rubbed his hands over their insteps, remembering the goals he'd scored, the legs he'd clattered into, the acres he'd covered.

It was almost dark when he came back into the living room.

'What it is, Cul,' he said, 'is that I don't get dirty any

more. It's been five years since I got kicked into the air, or muddied my knees, or headed the ball. All that we are now is a freak show, the reason they switched from penalty shoot-outs to bringing a man off every ten minutes till someone scores.' He slumped on to the sofa and ground the heels of his hands against his eyes.

Into the silence, Cul said: 'European Cup winning side, 1977.'

'Oh God,' said Tierney. 'Oh God, yes. Borussia Mönchengladbach. Three bloody one. Clemence. Neal. Jones. Smith. Kennedy. Hughes. Keegan. Case. Heighway. Callaghan. McDermott. What a beautiful bunch. What a beautiful evening.'

Towards midnight, he let himself in through the back door. He could hear the motion sensors chirruping, and a few seconds later Boucher appeared carrying a baseball bat.

'Sophisticated weapon you've got there,' Tierney yawned.

'You're bloody lucky I didn't brain you with it. Where've you been, you idiot? Why did—'

They were interrupted by Cyn, who said not a word, simply took Tierney's hand and led him upstairs.

There was, in Boucher's words as they approached the twin towers the next morning, 'a bit of a kerfuffle'. BBC and Sky vans almost outnumbered the police contingent. There were more fans around than usual. When Tierney stepped out to inspect the pitch a Liverpool v Manchester United old boys was in full swing. Somebody fed: 'What's the time?' and the ancient punchline, 'Ten past Stepney', was returned by a dozen voices.

On his way to the dressing room Tierney was cornered by Ray Stubbs. 'Paul. Five years on. How does it feel?'

'Are you still doing this shite?' he asked, closing the door.

There was some kind of pep-talk from the gaffer, Hansen, who had sacrificed a training session with the first team for today's anniversary. Tierney hardly heard him, apart from the odd mention of 'percentages'.

Last night, with Cul, he'd understood again what it was about football that lit him up. It wasn't this panto-mime of penalties. It wasn't the shitloads of money bandied about in transfer deals. It was the simple joy of kicking a ball around a playground. Nobody looked as if they enjoyed the game these days. Cat was right. He couldn't remember a time when he'd been happier, playing three-and-in by the garages back home.

In the tunnel, the players had the same old dimin-ished look about them and a suggestion of bemusement at this media involvement. A celebrity spot-kick was in play on the pitch, to the accompaniment of a Scanner remix of Phil Collins singing 'I Missed Again'.

'Do I not like that,' muttered Smith, devouring a cigarette.

'Where's Pucill? Did anyone see him come in?'

Morris shook his head. Coady shrugged.

'Arses. Fricker. Strip off. And smile for a fucking change, will you? Your mother might be watching this.'

The two teams trotted, not without embarrassment, on to the turf. A slightly more vociferous crowd greeted them.

'Uni-ted!'

'Wank!'

'Uni-ted!'

'Wank!'

When they reached the centre circle, there was still no sign of Pucill.

'Hold on,' said Smith, pulling a mobile out of his shorts. 'Does anyone know Puey's number?'

It transpired Pucill was caught up in traffic on the North Circular. 'No sweat,' said Coady. 'You could stick a cardboard cut-out of Dani Behr in goal and it'd make shite all difference.'

'I'll go in goal,' said Tierney. 'And I'll take first pen. Fricker next, then Mike and Marky. Then Ric. And then we can all piss off home.'

From here, he could see the comma of ribbon on the opposite goal. He was still looking at it when the net ballooned behind him and a cheer went up from the Manchester United supporters. His colleagues gave him an ironic clap. 'You snake-hipped demon, you,' said Fricker, flatly.

And so it went on. Udney pinched him on the arm when he was returning to the goal-line for the last time that evening. 'You do know,' he said, 'that if you hadn't hit the bar that night, five fucking years ago, we wouldn't be here. You do know that. This is all your fault.'

'Yeah. And I'm sure that, with hindsight, your mother would have used a condom.'

Once the referee had separated them, Tierney found his mind retracing the steps of his and Cul's conversation. The achingly evocative sound of studs clacking on concrete. Wintergreen in the changing rooms. Saving shots from Dad (who'd played professional football with Witton Albion back in the fifties) in their garden in Warrington. The thrill of scoring a goal in front of him and—

What was he doing lying in the mud with a ball clasped against his chest?

The world outside him had frozen, trapped like an image in a photograph. Everyone wore open mouths.

So much time had passed that he couldn't get excited. The crowd clapped politely. The players shook hands and were about to walk off when the referee called them back. They stood around looking at the grass while officials worked out where the Cup had been stored and who had some red ribbon to hang from it. Tierney accepted his medal and lifted the trophy to a crowd that was already filtering out of the exits.

'Barry Davies wants to write a book,' said Smith, as they dressed.

Fricker sneered. '*I'll* tell you what Barry Davies wants—'

'I want something to eat,' interrupted Coady. 'I'm so hungry, I could eat a baby through a wicker chair.'

'Shall we go to the pub?' said Smith. 'I really think we should go to the pub.'

Tierney left them to it. Such a weight had lifted, but it was replaced by a profound tiredness, as if the years he'd been staving off during the game had finally been allowed to make their home in him. A shadow at the end of the tunnel leading to the road straightened as he approached.

'Boucher, you old git,' Tierney shouted. 'Today was the day. *Hsss-eh-heh-heh-ehhhhsss.*'

When he was close enough to realize it wasn't Boucher, he was too close. 'Nowhere I'd rather be,' came the muffled voice and Tierney, in the moment before it happened, smelled rubber. He never imagined that his reward for saving a penalty would be to pay one.

Having published his first story at the age of eighteen, Conrad Williams went on to sell a string of increasingly ambitious tales to a range of magazines and anthologies, from *Dementia 13* to *Panurge* and *Darklands 2* to *Northern Stories 4*. Seven Arches, which gets a brief mention in 'aet', is a typically unlovely piece of Warrington railway architecture which has acquired mythic status in Williams' stories and indeed in his forthcoming novel, *Head Injuries*.

Nicholas Lezard

The Beautiful Game

The year's last swallows dipped and weaved in the twi-light; pipistrelles fluttered beneath the arches, and the college fountain plashed and tinkled as musically as it had done every day for the last four centuries. The crisp, smoky smell of autumn was in the air. Softly the ancient clock chimed the quarter-hour. As he drank in the scene from the Senior Common Room windows, Gervase Dewell, JVC Professor of Passing Technique, shrugged his ageing but still bearish shoulders beneath his gown, and thought, happily, as he always did around now: It will be dinner soon. Time, perhaps, for a little something?

As if his thoughts had taken on material form, he heard a clink and, barely audible beneath it, a velvet footfall as it neared him through the thick pile carpet: Simmons with the drinks. Dewell turned round and bestowed a happily superior smile upon the servant. Uncanny, and how pleasing, Simmons's ability to just turn up like that.

—A drink before dinner, Professor? asked Simmons.

—Ah, splendid, Simmons, splendid, said Dewell, taking a frosty Labatt's Ice from the silver tray. He admired the condensation coursing gently down the gaudy label and turned back again to the view.

—A beautiful evening, sir, if you will permit the observation, said Simmons.

—Absolutely, Simmons, absolutely. The start of another fine season, I'll be bound.

Simmons briefly closed his eyes and tilted his head at just the right degree to indicate acknowledgement and deference, and Dewell made a similar gesture which said, instead: You may go now. There was something about his ability to butle which reminded Dewell of something – something not even half-remembered, something vague yet troubling at the edges of his consciousness. But what? Dewell watched his retreating form with a kind of sadness. Poor Simmons, he thought: an attenuated, lanky frame, all spindly legs and long, wraith-like arms. He would never make a good footballer; the first tackle would crush him like a leaf. Tall, yes, but no good in the air: the neck too long, the cranium, blue and delicate as china, too frail to head the ball. If he'd come from a rich family he could have crammed and bought himself a place as a boy, but would have struggled to get a third; a waste of his time and of ours. But a damn fine college servant. Good to see these local boys being put to some kind of use. (And as he contemplated the reality of that locus, the world beyond the college walls, with its skewed priorities, its surly inhabitants, radiating defiance, a secret agenda, resentment, he shivered.) Dewell watched the boys in their gowns begin to drift through the quad towards the dining hall. Look at them all. Stocky, deft performers to a lad. So much potential. So much talent waiting to be teased out of their fluid sinews, their solid bones.

The muted gong sounded through the corridors of the Master's Lodge: dinner was served. Dewell looked at the menu: tomato soup, chips, peas, lobster and a fried slice, followed by the chef's renowned *Roues de Charrette* served with a delicate *crème au lait* and chocolate ice-cream. The college's curriculum might have changed over the centuries, but its kitchens were still the best. He finished the last drops of chilled lager from the bottle and thought of the pleasant hour or so ahead of him: the first Formal Hall of the academic year; the boys, hushed and awed as the Master, bowed yet venerable with all the accumulated seasons of his service to club and country (forty-eight caps! and fifteen of those as captain!), takes his place at the head of the table, his Adidas gown weaving a subtle pattern in the air behind him, the hushed yet penetrating grace ('Que sera, sera'); the clink of cutlery and china as food is shovelled down the hungry mouths; the scrape of chairs as heads bow for the valedictory ('They think it's all over,' says the Master, and two hundred throats murmur in response, 'It is now'), and all followed by liqueurs and Silk Cuts in the Master's drawing-room. Dewell's stomach growled.

—And what is your opinion, asked the Master, in his piping, earnest voice, of the new lot?

Dewell brushed some cigarette ash from his gown.

—What can I say, Master? he chortled. Another golden year. I flatter myself to think – hmmf hmmf – that the admissions procedures are as far-sighted as ever.

For in the last five years alone – ever since Dewell had been given the honorary post of Admissions Tutor, with special responsibility for talent-spotting, the college had supplied the following: thirteen caps at international level, forty-nine Premier League caps, of whom eleven were now captains, dozens of first-, second- and third-division places; a healthy clutch of promising coaches, linesmen and referees. Even those who had squandered their time, which, after all, every student had a right to do, as long as the sponsorship money still kept coming in (and their failures, however much they grieved him and his colleagues, only served to bring the other successes into sharper, more brilliant relief), had managed to get jobs in sports journalism or match-funding. The college's reputation stood so high that even someone with two left feet would make a living from the touchlines somehow.

The Master sucked contemplatively on his Southern Comfort.

—And whom do you rate best among the new boys?

Dewell, accepting a schooner of Tia Maria from the humbly inclined figure of Simmons, loved this question above all others. There was nothing more exciting than the spotting of some prodigious new talent, raw, inchoate, but alive with energy; every year contained at least one such, but every so often the interview process threw up someone with such dazzling ball-control skills, such imaginative intelligence in the air and on the ground, that one perhaps saw another Pelé, another Cantona, in the making, and only the ruthless procedure of tuition and training would determine whether this was a freak flash of inspiration, an uncommonly good day, or whether, on the day, and at the end of ninety minutes, it would all come good in the end.

As it happened, there was one such whom Dewell had interviewed personally, with mounting, quivering excitement, and what made this discovery so thrilling, almost gaudily serendipitic, was the amusing coincidence of his name.

—Well, Master, there is one lad I'm keeping my eye on, said Dewell, mischievously twirling the ruby liquid in his glass. By a funny coincidence, he's called Gascoigne.

The Master's eyebrows shot up in amusement.

—Is he—

—No, no relation, Master. Or at least certainly not close. Still, you never know. I do hope I am not letting this fortuitous circumstance cloud my judgement. After all, we remember what happened to Hopkins.

Hopkins, Dewell's predecessor as Admissions Tutor, had made the unfortunate mistake of rashly admitting a boy into the college called Liam Brady; as it turned out, the boy had had to leave after five terms (asthma, china shins, almost total lack of proprioception, and, on the big days themselves, a guaranteed tendency to choke), and Hopkins had wisely been moved back into his special area of expertise, throw-ins.

—What's good about him?

—Difficult to say at this stage, as you well know, Master. Yet he was able to demonstrate the most brilliant control. The ball seemed glued to his feet. Doctor Amarosa couldn't get the ball off him at interview. Had to bring him down in the end.

The Master whistled softly.

—Amarosa, eh?

The fiery Italian was not normally used for interviews. A brilliant tactician – brilliant – yet with a ruthless and savage temperament which had caused him to be sent off once too often, and if he had had to be curbed, not so much for his own good as for the good of his pupils (there were a few graduates still on crutches as a result of his 'enthusiasm', fulsomely aegrotated and handsomely, if silently and through well-worn but unofficial channels, generously recompensed), he was still one of the jewels in the college's teaching crown.

The Master picked at a stray thread where his ancient sponsor's logo had been, lovingly transferred from his last, fallen-to-bits gown ('Either that gown goes,' said his redoubtable wife, 'or I go'; he had thought about it).

—Well I do hope, Dewell, that this young Gascoigne does not bear any of the – ah – unfortunate character traits of his *illustrious* namesake.

—I do hope so, too. But he does seem, on initial acquaintance at least, to be a reasonably well-adjusted young man. One would not like to let Mr Hackenfasser loose on any more students than is absolutely necessary.

—Yes, Hackenfasser, said the Master uncomfortably,

and they both shuddered, as if a chill had entered the room.

—Another Southern Comfort, Master? asked Simmons, who had once again turned up with his silver tray to save what was left of the evening.

As Master and don talked, not two hundred feet away, Gascoigne himself was in his new rooms unpacking his trunk, hanging up his tracksuits, reverentially folding his match shirts (how proud he was that day when, with his parents, he had been fitted out in his first college kit), uncoiling his sweatsocks, unwrapping the newspaper from his plate, his knife and fork, his mug. He felt monkish, absorbed; the bare walls, the uncluttered room, lending an air of intense and scholarly application, and holding, therefore, the promise of sponsors' riches all the more justifiably and tantalizingly in prospect; he was nervous, but proud. Like so many of his fellow freshers, he had never stayed away from home before for more than one night, unless it had been for European matches, and then only in the company of brothers and schoolfriends. He had cautiously taken the first few steps towards friendship with one or two of the boys; the first cuts and thrusts of intellectual debate had started when a rather confident and severe-looking young man to his left had asked, in a voice of jocular contempt, whether Ruud Gullit's contribution to the game had really been anything more than an audacious hairdo. Such iconoclasm! The others had gasped, and then angrily counter-argued, citing his dazzling midfield ability, his rocket-like shots, and Gascoigne had argued with them; but he had been secretly thrilled by this young man's nerve.

In the lower shelf of his trunk lay his rolled-up posters, his father's tearful parting gift, a cherished poster of the Arsenal Double-winning team of 1991–2, his picture of his honest, homely girlfriend, Debbi ('I'll wait for you, Paul'), in its silver frame. And underneath them, something else; something private, something he had never, somehow, been able to relinquish, however hard he'd tried, been encouraged; something – well, a few things, technically speaking, but of one family – that he knew he would be unable to speak of with anyone. No one at all. Until he knew whom he could trust.

Dewell's preferred lecturing style was to pace slowly up and down the length of the hall, head either facing the ceiling or his shoes but never anywhere else, hands gripping the lapels of his gown in a thumbs-up position, and delivering his speech (now so familiar to him that he could, and indeed once did, in the privacy of his bathroom, recite it backwards) in a weary monotone. He had seen it done like that in a video decades before. He relieved the tedium by injecting swoops of emphasis and register entirely at random.

—*When* Sepp Blatter, who of course should need no introduction from me, but *was* of course Chief Ex*e*cutive of FIFA in the nineties, said that the English game was lagging thirty years behind the rest of Europe, he knew *what* he was talking about. And we can, *too*, bear in mind the words of Matthias Ohms, the guru of Eintracht Frankfurt, when he said how the *Ge*rman game freed itself from the tyranny of the kick-and-rush game . . .

It was all simple background stuff, it should have already been crammed into their heads by their mid-teens, but it never hurt to go over old ground.

—. . . in Argentina's game against Greece in the 1990 World Cup, Maradona's goal was the result of an extended row of *wall* passes; indeed, Can*igg*ia himself hit the bar after a wall pass . . .

He stopped. The lecturer's sixth sense told him

something was amiss. He glanced slyly to his right. There was Gascoigne, right by him, but unlike the others, who were taking down notes with ham-fisted earnestness, he was looking at something in his lap, beneath the table. It looked like a book. Dewell picked up again, after a discernible beat. Gascoigne had not noticed him.

When the lecture was over and the students gratefully packed up their pens and papers and went off to do some warm-up exercises, Dewell gently stopped Gascoigne.

—A quick word? he said. Gascoigne nodded.

—Now, dear boy, was it my imagination, or were you slightly distracted during the course of my little speech?

Gascoigne flushed horribly.

—Let me see, said Dewell, holding out his hand. Gascoigne fished nervously in his kit-bag and pulled out a battered paperback.

—Hmm. *The Idiot.* By Dost ... Dosto ... hmm. Whatever.

He handed it back.

—Gascoigne, this is not a school; it is a university. We do not punish or humiliate. And I have no objection to our undergraduates having any kind of extracurricular interests, as long as they are legal. And reading – I go against the grain of my colleagues' inclinations – is not a hobby which I would be minded to campaign against. But it is somewhat *mal vu*, is it not, to bring one's hobby – especially one as proletarian and useless as this – into the lecture hall of a venerable university. Hmm?

Gascoigne, who looked on the point of tears, nodded. Dewell rested an avuncular hand on his shoulder.

—We'll forget about this. You're a promising player. Perhaps the most promising of this year's intake. I understand how this places you under pressure. But you must face that pressure, use it to your own advantage. Remember what the immortal Vinnie Jones said:

'That which does not destroy me makes me harder.'

Gascoigne nodded again.

—This book, said Dewell. Is there any football in it?

—I haven't come across any yet, said Gascoigne.

—Well then, said Dewell, with a smile. Gascoigne, too, smiled.—If it's books you want, there are plenty out there, you know. You could try Jenns Bangsbo's history of Athletic Bilbao; or *The Premier League: First Among Equals?* by . . . by . . .

—Klinsmann, sir.

—Exactly. Or Alberto Parreira's memoirs of coaching Brazil. It's all out there, this rich history; there is always something new to learn in the beautiful game. You see?

—I see.

—Good. Now get into your kit, Gascoigne, said Dewell, patting him. He watched Gascoigne rush off to join his peers, and shook his head.

That evening found Dewell still preoccupied with what had happened. As Simmons approached with the tray, Dewell found himself in the extraordinary position of having to ask him a question whose answer he genuinely wanted to hear.

—Simmons?

—Sir?

—You don't play football yourself, do you? You know, on your days off or anything?

—No, sir.

—No five-a-side?

—No, sir.

—Seven-a-side?

—No, sir.

—No other sports?

—No, sir.

—You know, rugby, cricket, hockey, snooker, darts, fishing, running, javelin-throwing, that kind of thing?

—I regret to say, sir, that I have not been blessed
with the capacity for prowess in any of those activities.
It is a source of some frustration, I hasten to add.

—No, no, don't worry about it, it's not what you're
here for. But what I want to say is that, um, well, I think
I heard someone once say that, um, that for recreation
you, er, you, that is to say . . .

—I read books, sir.

—Exactly. That's the thing. But what I want to know
is if, in your opinion, an attachment to reading might
. . . how can I put this . . . *interfere* with the development
of a talented footballer?

—I couldn't possibly say, sir. A Labatt's?

—Yes, thank you, Simmons. That will be all.

Dewell pulled at his beer miserably. It didn't seem
to taste of anything.

Gascoigne was in the infirmary, having some physio
after a spectacularly late tackle by Doctor Amarosa.
Amarosa visited him, as he often did those he had
tackled, to show there were no hard feelings.

—You OK, Gazza?

Gascoigne smiled at the familiarity. Amarosa pronounced it in the Italian style, though.

—Yes, Doctor Amarosa. Should be up and running
in a day or two. It's only a scratch.

—Hey, maybe I tackle you better next time, eh? Put
you out for a week?

They laughed. Then Amarosa noticed the book on
Gascoigne's lap.

—You mind?

He picked it up.

—*Inferno*. By Dante Alighieri. Why you read?

—Er . . . well, it's jolly good.

Amarosa waggled the volume contemptuously in
Gascoigne's face.

—You leave offa this shit, OK? It fuck up your game for good. In Italy, only *stronzi*, only the *teste di cazzo* read this, you know what I mean?

He tossed the book back to a suddenly despondent Gascoigne. He tapped his head.

—You only got room for one thing in there, and that thing is football. The beautiful game. OK?

—Yes, Doctor Amarosa.

—Say after me: 'The beautiful game.'

—'The beautiful game,' repeated Gascoigne.

—Good, good. Now you get well. And – he punched Gascoigne on the arm – you be good now, you hear?

Amarosa, of course, had to have a quiet word – well, as quiet as he could be – with Dewell, who groaned.

—Dear God, it's worse than I thought, he said, and called for the College Chaplain.

The Chaplain was a timid, ginger-haired man without much practical footballing experience beyond his post as Spiritual Adviser to Wolverhampton Wanderers. His function, as far as he could tell, was to direct the students' prayers for victory and success in what he called 'a useful and relevant direction', although how God could answer the competing prayers of opposing teams without some disappointment was something he did not care to think about too much. But, as Dewell had said, if Gascoigne was in the grip of a spiritual crisis, then it was the Chaplain's responsibility to pull him out of it. After that there was only Hackenfasser, with his thick spectacles, his psychoanalytic gobbledegook, and a lamentable track record among his charges of depression, suicide, and voluntary rustication.

The Chaplain tapped on Gascoigne's door. At least the oak was unsported. A good sign.

—Come, said Gascoigne, who looked up from his bed with surprise.

—I'm the College Chaplain. But please call me Brian.

—Hello, Brian. Do have a seat.

Brian sat down in the only chair in the room and looked about him.

—Gosh, you've got a lot of books, he said, looking at a shelf with perhaps a dozen battered titles on it.

—Just a hobby, said Gascoigne.

—I know, I know, said Brian. I like to read myself, you know? There's something about it, isn't there?

—Yes, said Gascoigne uncertainly.

The Chaplain rooted around beneath his gown. For a horrible moment Gascoigne thought he was going to do something indecent. He'd heard about the clergy. He'd *read* about the clergy.

—In fact, said Brian, I've got something for you you might like.

He finally pulled a book from his jacket pocket.

—It's one of my favourites.

Gascoigne looked at it apologetically.

—Actually, I've read it.

The Chaplain looked disappointed. And no wonder: this was his only plan, and it had backfired.

—I think you'll find that just about everyone here has read *Fever Pitch*.

—Oh, have they?

—Well, it is a set text. It's the only set text, I think.

—Oh, well. Brian looked about him, at the unlovely room.

—You've got a spanking set here, he said hopelessly.

—Yes, they're very snug, said Gascoigne.

—What's that you're reading?

—Michel de Montaigne. A philosopher.

111

—Oh good. Well, the philosophy of the game is important. The spiritual side, you know.

—Indeed. (Gascoigne was alarmed at how easy it was to be rude to this man.)

Brian stood up and flapped his arms a couple of times against his sides.

—Well, must dash. Give us a call when something's on your mind.

—Yes, bye, said Gascoigne; pleased that the irritating man had gone, and above all pleased that he had not been asked to recite the last sentence of Montaigne's that he had read: 'Never trust a man whose mind is full of sport; for that means there will never be room for aught else of import.'

Only two terms in, and Gascoigne was in a mess like this! His term project, *Stand Up and Be Counted: All-seater Stadia, the Taylor Report, and the Decline of Hooliganism*, was dreadfully stalled; and his game had, to everyone's observation, gone dramatically off the boil. The news that Gascoigne had had a short story *and* a poem published in some oiky little townie rag was, it turned out, the last straw.

—I think a break for you, until you sort yourself out, said Dewell.

—You're throwing me out, aren't you?

—No, we're not. We're just giving you a little time to think about your priorities, that's all. Do you want to take this place seriously or don't you? We'll have you back whenever you want to come back. Maybe a spell in the real world will sort you out. People within these walls can become . . . *cut off.*

He sighed deeply: so deeply that it was nearly a sob. And Gascoigne, too, nearly sobbed, heavy with the burden of his betrayal. He had not meant it to be like this. He had not meant it to be like this at all; and as he packed his trunk later in the evening, wondering what on earth he was going to tell his family, the ever-faithful Debbi, he thought of the world beyond the college gates, a world where the wind blew fiercer, where snarling aesthetes padded through their murky *unterwelt* of literature and art; unknowable, terrifying, and dark. Debbi would not understand. *He* could hardly understand it himself.

There was a soft tap at his door. Gascoigne opened it and was puzzled to see the willowy figure of Simmons standing respectfully in the hall.

—You're that chap who serves at High Table, aren't you?

—That's right, sir, said Simmons, giving his name.

—Come in, said Gascoigne.

—I won't, sir; but I have heard of your . . . difficulty. If I may take the liberty of doing so, I would like to present you with a small token which might lighten your mood and make the vicissitudes of the outside world easier to bear.

And he handed Gascoigne a book.

—Why . . . why . . . I'm sorry, but I've heard of this man, but never got round to reading him.

—I have found it, on a personal level, highly amusing, and occasionally even instructive.

—I shall treasure it, Simmons. This is too kind.

—We readers have to stick together, said Simmons. Not a word, if you please, to the authorities.

—My lips are sealed, said Gascoigne, and as he looked up from the book he found that the butler had disappeared without the trace of a footfall, as if he were no more than a dream. And, as he hardly had any more packing to do, he lay down on the bed and began to read this book, with its absurd title, pausing only to wonder: did one pronounce it 'woadhouse' or 'woodhouse'?

Nicholas Lezard

Nicholas Lezard has been reviewing paperbacks for the *Guardian* since time began; he also writes for *GQ*, the *Sunday Times* and the *TLS* and he was literary editor of the *Modern Review* under Toby Young's editorship. 'The Beautiful Game' is his first published short story. He lives in west London, close to Loftus Road, no more than a couple of miles from where he was born in 1963, although he has moved around a bit in between.

Glyn Maxwell

Injured Men are Talking

It's Burns and Berry on tonight, which is our favourite
pairing. Burns is so good, so very experienced, he tells
it so well you can almost see it. They say he makes
eyesight a luxury. We want to tell all the people who
are blind, we want to tell them *don't worry, don't fret*
because it's Burns on tonight, and when he tells you
what's happening down there we guarantee you, we do,
you will see it in its flesh, its glory. England in white,
Isle St-George in red, the pitch plush green, the referee
in all his silver. That's all it needs, according to Burns.
Dabs of colour.

He said that at a talk we attended. He said that in
the first days of radio commentary the pitch was divided
into eight rectangles, for the benefit of the blind
listeners, those blinded for any reason, though this is
so long ago that war was obviously often one. You could
hear them say *the ball is coming out of 4 into 7, where
Silversmith* (for instance) *controls it well and passes it back,
deep into 3.* This was a code that meant something to
that generation. The first radio play ever broadcast by
the BBC was set in a mineshaft, because, of course, no
one could see anything. There had been an accident,
and injured men were talking. We've never heard this
play, but we were told this was the case. After that first
pure play, things started to slip, at least with radio.
A certain cleverness takes hold, we've noticed. Things
slipped so badly you have the situation you have today:

We're all on a ship. The action takes place in a dining room. The ghostly Irish soldier-boys are coming over the hill. When any fool could tell you we are still all in a mine in which there has been an accident, and injured men are talking.

Dabs of colour, said Burns at the talk, privately this was, to us, at the signing session. Amazing to think that we are all still here, still around, us and Burns, though far from meeting to chat amiably among other keen fans of Burns in a bookshop on a freezing Monday night, we are far apart, Burns in his lofty commentary position, high up in north-west London in the clean June sunshine after the rainshower, us here at home on our patio, drying our hair with white towels after the very same rain. Some of us, me included, are breathing deeply to relax ourselves as we sort out the cold drinks order. We will have to order enough to get us through the full ninety minutes. We are not expecting extra time.

We're all agreed we're glad it's Berry, Berry on Expert Comment. When Burns works with, for instance, Kirkup, you get nothing but aimless chatter, mere cramming of airtime for no good reason. *Talk us through the goal, Kirkup.* And he plunges like a stupid boy into a pool, saying *I'm happy to do that, quite happy, Burns. You've got a good ball played in by the big lad, a good ball for a big lad* – as if Burns hadn't pointed out that anomaly as early as the fifth minute – *he's played it in short, the new lad's turned on it, checked, and he's proving worth every penny of that twelve million, Burns.* Which infuriates us, because what all the blind listeners want to know is where the ball went, and with what power, and what the goalscorer did next by way of celebration, and what the goalkeeper's face was like, and who was blamed, and the whole picture of a moment that meant something to everyone; instead you get Kirkup telling you the new lad cost twelve million, which is information available from any newspaper that covered his transfer. Fortunately for everyone, Burns has already described the goal with his customary brilliance and verve at the moment of its execution, and those of us smart enough to have considered recording the commentary for another day are smiling all over our faces.

The thing with Berry on Expert Comment is the silence. This may sound strange, but, given the exact same circumstances, this is what Berry would do: to go back to our 'for instance', the goal is scored. Burns leans across to Berry and says to *talk us through the goal, Berry.* You won't get any of this *I'm quite happy to do that, Burns* – there's not a persuasion issue. Berry knows that his personal happiness doesn't matter. There are words to be said. But always what you first get with Berry is the silence. As if he hasn't heard Burns's request! As if he's walked away to get the half-time refreshments for both men. But oh no he's there all right, and in the silence you begin to experience the triumph of the goalscorer, and the pain and resignation of the goalkeeper, and the bitterness of the defenders, and the businesslike notation of the referee. And then maybe all Berry will say is *the ball is still spinning, Burns, the ball is still spinning.* Burns knows enough to let that comment hang in the air. Whereas if Kirkup had anything to do with it, it would be *it certainly is, Burns, that white and black ball, spinning away there on the turf at a packed Goodison tonight, but slowly it's slowing down* ... You can see the difference. *The ball is still spinning, Burns.* We are particularly pleased that Burns and Berry have been chosen for this match.

We were talking before we arrived here, about what a mismatch it is, England versus Isle St-George. Of course, the newspapers have had one of their field days with the saintly symbolism, the dragon and the damsel, and children have had a lesson in geography, peering low into maps to find that tiny island off Jamaica, itself only an island. One child said *there's not even room for a pitch on that.* Another observed *we could boot the whole country into the net at Wembley, it's round enough!* A third child said curtly *that's only what we're going to do.*

It is, and when we've done it, we will be one of the last sixteen teams in our own World Cup finals. We're hosting them, we're staging them, they're ours. And we don't even need to win tonight, we only want a point. It's the last game of our group stage, so we know that even if we only *draw* – and so far Isle St-George have conceded sixteen goals in two matches, so a draw has not entered anyone's calculations – we would still qualify as one of the best third-placed teams. We don't see any difficulties. The chance and mathematics have dealt us a great hand, and our nil–nil draws with Russia and Spain will carry us through. Burns has described the table to us in fine detail. *Russia will be ruing their chances in the match against ISG* (Isle St-George). *They took their feet off the pedals, and allowed the plucky lobsterfolk to hold out for the last ten minutes for a creditable result.* What he means is (and he knows we know this) Russia – think of it, the might of it! – could only beat ISG eight–one, whereas the strong Spanish side defeated them eight–nil, which is a crucial goal difference of one goal. Berry said quietly *there is a monument in Dear Mary Square,* and Burns explained through peals of laughter *there are bronze statues of eleven men running, the eleven who scored a goal against mighty Russia! And Alphonse Dawes* Berry added *has a garland on his head* ... Alphonse Dawes scored the goal, after a comical mix-up among the Russians. One of the blond-bearded defenders clapped Alphonse on the back as he ran past, leaping in the air. *Giving thanks to his ancestors,* is what Burns said he was doing. *They still lost,* said Berry, *they were slaughtered.*

Injured Men are Talking

This is the table as we understand it. We've written it out with four felt pens and placed it on our own table in front of us. It reads as follows:

team	games	won	drew	lost	goals	points
Spain	2	1	1	0	8–0	4
Russia	2	1	1	0	8–1	4
ENGLAND	2	0	2	0	0–0	2
I. St-George	2	0	0	2	1–16	0

The ball is in our court, is how Burns characterized this moment in the championship. Spain and Russia, meanwhile, are playing each other at Villa Park in Birmingham. If they draw, and we score more than eight against the *lobsterfolk* (as Berry calls them) we shall win the group, in which case we will face a weaker team in the next round, probably Hungary but possibly Belgium.

The tension is increasing among us. Burns is asking the club managers for their predictions. So far they have hazarded ten, twelve, and a rather pessimistic seven, which could leave us looking foolish in third place. He says that old chestnut, *there are no easy games left in football,* but that makes them laugh and all say *well, maybe just this one.* Around our own table we have bet nine, nine, ten and twelve – but the one who said twelve thinks we may let one in. They would need a new statue in Dear Mary Square. I am sticking to eleven. Eleven men, eleven goals, top slot, Hungary. This is exactly what Berry believes, after his customary pause for thought, but now he hands back to Burns with the words *let us open the gates . . .*

1 Kambeau; 2 Marius, 15 Frederix, 5 Ruby, 11 Billy-Clair, 3 Pierre Taureau; 4 Juru, 17 Clydie Taureau, 20 Costaigne, 8 Dawes; 9 Bonne-Jean. Substitutes: 6 Strassner, 12 Daladier, 22 Goto.

Why is it, Burns asks as we hear the national anthems and picture the teams lined up in their white (England) and their red (Isle St-George) *that the longer a country's national anthem, the more, with all respect, challenged they seem to be on the field?* Berry doesn't answer, but we feel he has appreciated the observation. After all, it's the type of observation *he* makes. As the cheering of the crowd signals the breaking of the two teams from their ranks – and the Wembley crowd do give a huge cheer for the little islanders on this big day of their lives – now Burns relates to us again the peculiar circumstances of Isle St-George's qualification for the World Cup finals, the tale of a small island (pop. 72,456) catapulted into the global limelight by chance and the pernicious attitudes of poor nations.

If they want to bemoan their lot, there are better places to do that. Berry agrees *what should be a celebration of difference has been turned into an orgy of envy.* Burns says *an orgy of envy, and the, let me say, ignorant stubbornness of the boycotting African and Caribbean countries has, ironically, opened the door for one brave little island State. Brave enough to say 'We are not envious, we do not envy you your riches, we will gladly play a game with you!' And this, this glorious summer night at Wembley, is the just and splendid reward for that courage. They may have earned the hatred of all small nations, and I mean small-minded as well as small in hectares, they may be threatened and insulted by the unenlightened, but the people of Isle St-George now have worldwide international respect, for their pluck, their good humour and above all their colourful – if at times bizarre! – contribution to this festival of football.*

Meanwhile the game is underway, two minutes are gone, and in the studio as well as here, they are joking about two whole minutes without England's first goal: *Crisis time, we're playing for the draw! Let me, if you're just coming in from work, remind you, if you needed reminding,*

England are in the age-old white shirts, blue shorts; St-George in a very smart all-red outfit, with gold trimmings. Really quite natty, but of course they're not going to forget this night. Nil–nil the score, three minutes gone and the islanders actually have possession: Manny Juru has the ball, big moment for him there. Berry remarks *they'll buy him a new hacienda, Burns.* Burns jokes back, quick as a flash *a roller if he passes to his own team!* But Berry just says *he's given away possession now, so it's goodnight to that and thank you.*

Five minutes into the game, by which time we've hit the post and taken three corners, one of the Isle St-Georgians is injured in a clash of heads. Burns takes this opportunity, as he did both in the Spain–ISG game and the Russia–ISG game, to talk about the professions of the eleven islanders. Our favourite is the epic poet, who goes by the name of Mr Boy Turtleman, but he's not playing because he went missing in Knightsbridge on a sightseeing ride. So we're down to the seven lobster fishermen, the two guitar-playing Taureau brothers, who had to fly over from Miami where they work as session musicians in jazz bands, the island's chief judge (Walter Billy-Clair) and the zookeeper Emmanuel Juru.

They can have a choir, can't they, the seven of them, they can sing one of Mr Boy's poems. The Taureau brothers will play their guitars, the judge will keep order on the beach, and – who does that leave, Berry? That leaves the zookeeper, Burns. He's for crowd control.

Because we have not scored in the first ten minutes, we are now required to score more than one-per-ten-minutes. Burns points out how in games like this the goals often arrive in a flood towards the end, when the inferior team is tired, and they begin to make elementary errors. *Still*, he says, *it's a disappointing start by our standards.* We have got all our drinks topped up already and someone says only eighty minutes to go. We look briefly at the clock to see how very far the hands have still to travel.

All credit to the lobsterfolk, Berry says. *Indeed all credit,* Burns agrees, *and more. What a glorious night for them. They'll remember this for the rest of their lives, they'll call their grandchildren in from the beach to hear this one. Don't you think, Berry?* Berry thinks and says: *They'll turn it into one of their spiritual songs. The glorious ten minutes.*

Eighteen minutes have gone when we are awarded our first penalty. We had to break them somehow. *Their tackling is so clumsy, it was an accident waiting to happen.* They should send off that Pierre Taureau, he's a bit of a thug. *I think that would be a shame on such a big night for him. And I really don't think there's malice involved. That, sorry to say, is a disease of the more sophisticated footballing powers. No I think he went in hoping for the best, and just mistimed it.* This will punish him. He'll have learned something tonight, that lad. Here we go, bury it. *Here we go.*

We friends sit up together in my house and hear the whistle blow and the shot taken, then a brief rustling quiet from the radio to the hedges. We feel in that quiet a shudder of something, as if we knew there was no hope, no sense in trying. We take sips from our drinks and find it in ourselves to enjoy the embarrassment and pity of the moment. A car goes by on the street and we all feel the same: who could that be? What ride is so important? A baby must have chosen this moment to come out into the world! Then we return our full attention to our disappointment.

Berry? Berry? . . . I should have taken that, Burns. Well yes Berry, time to roll our sleeves up, I think. You know, Burns, I don't like the way goalkeepers go berserk – they're all hugging him on the ground, and I hate to say it, but FIFA have issued guidelines about I'm talking about health guidelines in view of recent anyway, Burns, after all he didn't save it, the lob-sterman, he didn't punch it out with any big red lobster claw, you know, Burns, he didn't do that it was a missed *penalty, that's all, it hit the bar which after all is no shame in fact it's very unlucky, I'm sorry, Burns, it is. They ought to get on with the game. There's no time for this childishness. I mean look.*

I'd drawn that player to score first in the sweep. I have a more personal anger than that of the commentary team. One of us has gone outside to collect his thoughts, he said, which is unheard of. He'll miss a goal, he always does. One of our players has collected the ball on the halfway line, Burns is informing us, but his clever run through the simple and wildly lunging defenders comes to a sudden stop.

Look, he's done it again. I mean really. He's got to go now, Berry, he's done it before. It's not Pierre Taureau, Burns, it's Clydie Taureau who hacked our man down. Those brothers look rather similar facially. I still think he should go, Berry. They think that, we think that, I mean fair's fair and it's good to see them in the tournament but that man's an animal, frankly. Surely off he goes under the rules. No . . . you see, benefit of the doubt, every time. It's not just in football, you know, I'm sorry, it's not. *Again, I think it was just over-eagerness, Berry. Do you not think, Berry? He was over-eager.*

We waste the free-kick. We put a corner straight into touch. Half an hour has been played and the commentary is simply a terse roll call of English names as they pass the ball among themselves to not much effect. Berry seems to have left the position, to collect his thoughts perhaps. But then we hear his deep harsh breath.

No, Burns, it's not, I'm sorry, 'just over-eagerness'. He should have gone. He should be in the changing room by now, him and his brother and that other lobster one with the claws.

There it is. A foul is a foul. That was a criminal act by decent standards. 'Over-eagerness.' 'Over-eagerness.'

They had interviewed the ISG captain before the game began. Oddly enough, it's not the island's chief judge who captains the side, but one of the lobstermen, Nelson Costaigne. He was smiling broadly, Burns felt it necessary to inform us. Was he proud to be leading his players out on the famous Wembley turf? He was, he was very proud to be captain of his nation's team. Did he not think his players would find it difficult out there tonight? Yes, he did, very tough, very tough. Which of the English players did he most fear? It wasn't so much the players, he said, and Burns said you could see the wide white grin vanishing slowly. And would he be swapping shirts with his heroes afterwards?

I don't like the way he answered that, say the club managers at half-time, as they sit gloomily in their small cabin, smoothing their red-and-blue ties. *He said he wanted to keep his own shirt as a souvenir,* says Foster. *Well perhaps he doesn't understand the way it works,* suggests Sinclair, *the shirt-swapping idea.* Young Mason says: *It's an old thing, you know, to be honest with you. We don't do that any more, you know, drenching each other with some player's sweat, some player you don't really know in terms of personal habits, you see what I'm saying? How many lobstermen have you swapped shirts with lately!* Someone says *point taken.* Foster makes a sound to indicate shuddering: *Perhaps yes it's just one of those other great traditions we have to say so long to these days.* Young Mason says quietly *if we want our game to develop, you know. My experience in the game tells me* but the others roar with laughter *his experience in the game! Barely out of short trousers and he's running football!* The laughter stops abruptly. Burns and Berry are back in the room after their half-time break. Young Mason is the last to stop speaking, still insisting he wants our game to be developed then his voice dies off.

Our game is developed. It's not our game that's not developed. It's only that it's being destroyed. I think we should talk about immediate substitutions.

We reach the bottom of the garden without speaking. We take deep breaths. It's not a bad day weatherwise. Over the fence are sitting many of our wives and girl-friends. They have their own radio, but we have split into two parties for the duration of the broadcast. They are smiling shyly at us over their wine-glasses, as if we had not met them yet, as if we were all young and they had just stopped talking to concentrate on this moment when they might meet us, might like us. But we are unable to affect the silence, and retreat back up the lawn, listening to the gentle resumption of their private talking, until it is drowned in the noise of the Wembley crowd, and the commentary team high above them.

Who are they, Berry, who are they? What we appear to have is a large section of the crowd cheering the West Indian side as they reappear for the second half. I can only think that's ironic in tone, perhaps because of their filthy play. It's certainly not sporting to be cheering that brand of dirtiness, irrespective of the scoreline. That's in a way a black day for football, that cheering of them.

Spain were beating Isle St-George six–nil at this point in their game; Russia were winning three–nil. Why is it always us who can't do it? Why is it always us? We will have to settle for four or five. We are back in our chairs, with new drinks, chocolates, a relaxed attitude. We spread ourselves out. We note that no English substi-tutions have been made, but the lobsterfolk have brought on a little defender called David Goto, number twenty-two in their squad. We are expecting Burns and Berry to comment on his ludicrous name, but instead Burns says *Goto plays for Kingston, Jamaica, and scored three goals last season, including the winning penalty in the*

Glyn Maxwell

Jamaican Cup Final. Berry says *Well he's not playing beach football now,* and Burns goes *indeed* in a flat voice.

We have been altering our table during the half-time break, because Russia are now leading Spain one–nil. We all agree that their game seems very far away, in a real world that is a world we miss, where the teams are more like we are, they know what they're doing, they're serious and if they foul, they foul for a reason. We feel abandoned by Spain and Russia, leaving us to plug away at this impossible bunch of grinning part-timers. If the games were to end like this, one of us says, the one who *would* say that, and we all shriek with laughter, then the table would end like this:

team	games	won	drew	lost	goals	points
Russia	3	2	1	0	9–1	7
Spain	3	1	1	1	8–1	4
ENGLAND	3	0	3	0	0–0	3
I. St-George	3	0	1	2	1–16	1

We'd still qualify, one of us says as we ponder the changes, that's what matters. By two clear points, says another. Yes, says a third, but we'd get Germany. That's the only thing.

It's sad to see a side play so defensively, Berry, that's what my concern is. We're now in the what is it fifty-third minute and these people are simply packing the penalty area they are without ambition. *It's really not exactly much of a spectacle and you know it's surprising, Berry, because after all we're supposed to believe that the people in these nations are lively, happy-go-lucky people, do you follow? with their dancing and their you know colourful traditions their harmless ways handed down and that. They play as if they don't have a care in the world. Don't they, Berry?*

Do you know what I think it is?

Oh. We're now joined in the commentary position by Kirkup,

Injured Men are Talking

for Expert Comment as we enter the last half hour of this extraordinary and from a footballing viewpoint quite disgraceful so far game. Kirkup, do you think the world wants to see this team of, well, lobster-fishermen putting what I call a clamp on the game like this especially here in the Mecca of football? I would think this might be an embarrassment to them. I think if they were responsible for the host nation, the country that gave football to the world, having this kind of difficulty, don't you think it might embarrass them in terms of well history. I'm thinking particularly sixty-six in indeed this very hallowed this don't you think, Kirkup? There's a certain kind of I don't know, a certain spite about it in some ways, maybe a sense of even who knows glee perhaps glee is not too strong even.

No mention at all of whether Berry's gone, but he hasn't spoken since he made the observation about the Jamaican Cup Final. Kirkup, of all people. That's going to be no help at all. Berry was willing us on. Christ.

Burns, I think it's gods. I do I think it's gods if you ask me. Another free-kick, a good position. Three lined up to take it, only one of them can. See, that's pure Kirkup. *Up comes – no, it's wide. Well wide, Burns, wincingly wide. He might as well have kicked that ball clean out of the ground. Like I say, Burns, it's the gods you get there. Well I don't think so, Kirkup. I think it was just well wide. Actually, Burns, I didn't think it was even a free-kick but can I say that?*

Can we turn it down when Kirkup is speaking? We need Berry, Berry knows what's happening. If we're going to feel anger we want to feel it through Berry. We waste another corner. We hit the post. We score and it's given offside. Burns cries out in fury.

That was simply not offside. I'm sorry, it simply wasn't, you have to take a hard look at the standard of some of these officials, we have as I say a Greek linesman and one from of all places Singapore, under the eye of a referee from Korea and I'm sorry, I'm sorry, but some of the perhaps younger footballing nations are perhaps not maybe ready quite to take on these

responsibilities, Kirkup, at least at this level. There's the neu-
trality question to be looked at, I think in terms of perhaps the
less European nations. There's an underdog thing is what
there is here.

Burns, I'm in agreement with you. Some of the more, you'd
have to say, emotional nations have been asked to take up
positions where they couldn't really understand the subtleties,
the give and take of modern football. It was handball, though,
Burns, not offside.

Well, I didn't think so. Well it was. No it wasn't. Yes it was.
Not if it didn't touch his hand. If the referee gives handball, it's
handball. Let's drop it. It's true. I said drop it. It was his
elbow. Drop it, can't you.

This is the goal, I say, a private game, where I pretend
this is not now, not live but a recording I heard and
nobody else did. This is the goal coming up, I say, but
they all know that game, they all know this is live, real,
now. Burns described the sunset earlier and it was just
like ours was.

Clear use of the arm, Burns. Look shut it.

He does, and for a while they all do, so that we are
unsure whether we have lost the signal. We gather
nearer the set to hear the crowd, but they are quiet
too. We will not look at each other. Our clock says
eleven minutes to go. One of our midfielders thumps
in a long-range shot so hard we hear it from here. We
know before we hear the news. We are already rising.

YES! cries Burns *CHRIST YES!*

And we are knocked back, tumbling away in a friendly
fight as we bang heads and knock drinks over, and some
of us are punching the air in the garden by now and
others are kneeling and making the cross sign like
Brazilians used to and the wanker sign like we do sometimes, but did you know that one of my friends has
come tonight in a Death costume and he comes to the
edge of the patio to say *no, that didn't happen, it was a*

mistake, it was an illusion. Kirkup saw the ball hit the side netting. It was only an optical error. We sprawl in the remains of the moment, we remember physical laws, we feel that hopelessness, that delicious horror. *We have another corner though.* This time we don't sit, we stand, supporting each other. Kirkup has left the commentary position. They won't use him again ever. Berry is back.

Look, Burns, look. Move your eyes from the pitch and look . . . Mad ludicrous dances away to our left. They are swinging their arms, and beating their drums. They are waving sheets with children's pictures on them and they mean it to be a national flag. They're not even them, *Burns – it's Englishmen doing it, doing it* with *them as if what, we had to impress them in some way do we? Are they some suddenly bloody great power, Burns, we have to be* in *with do we?*

The corner is cleared. *Pierre Taureau boots it clear, no style, no vision, just a kick into the sky. He's bleeding from a head wound, his socks are rolled down—*

And that's against cunting FIFA rules for a start—

And the ball lands improbably on the edge of would you believe it, the English penalty area.

'Head wound?' 'Head wound?' If he'd made tackles like that on my street he'd have more than a bleeding head wound, Burns, he's a thug, he's a fucking drug-dealing bastard gangster—

One of them, don't know which, has ventured into English territory, must surely be way offside—

Or lost, thinks he's back in the fucking Sahara, Burns—

And That, Feeble, Pathetic, Shot towards goal will probably net him a fortune—

Another shitting statue—

Rolling pointlessly towards one very bored goalkeeper, who simply, contemptuously, reaches down and rolling pointlessly towards one very bored goalkeeper, who simply, contemptuously, reaches down and reaches pointlessly who simply reaches rolling reaches simply rolling simply.

Glyn Maxwell

We are walking down Ashlock Street, all of us. We didn't tell the women. They'll know where we're going. One of us said there were four minutes still to play but we've been walking for seven and we have heard no cheers from our neighbours. What we have heard is gunfire from far off to the south, the centre of town, with whistles and screams, and one of us said 'storm coming' because he said he saw a flash of light, but as we listened we heard drums from the Harris Estate, then saw more fireworks from there. A single rocket detonating in the warm sky, raining green, yellow, red, white. We are out, we are out but we are friends. So we are walking out of the world before we are asked to.

We are out, we are out, we are out. We are heading down Ashlock Street towards the canalside, opening the last of our chocolate. We are out for ever. We are dropping down to the place where we have no more fixtures, to the empty fields and shut stands. We will not need to meet again in any of our houses. There is going to be a monument in Dear Mary Square, but we have lost and are out now for ever.

They are waiting for us, though, the people we wanted to be waiting for us, they are taking the back off their great radio and casting it on to the filthy water, then rummaging out the wires and boards and flinging them in after, then all the broken front and collapsed sides floating off in the dirt. There's Foster, Mason, Garrett, Poole, and Hedges. There's Burns, covering his eyes, but shaking his cigarettes out to the air as we approach, meaning we can have them, go on take them, then up the towpath now comes Berry in his raincoat, and we know we won't speak until he does.

Glyn Maxwell's first novel, *Blue Burneau*, was published by Chatto & Windus in 1994, by which time he was already one of the most prolific and acclaimed young poets in the country. Among the prizes he has won for his work are the Somerset Maugham Travel Prize and an Eric Gregory Award. He lives in Hertfordshire and during the football season plays for a five-a-side team on Sunday mornings.

Steve Grant

Casuals

When I go home to visit my parents these days, both of them still perky into their eighties with a social calendar more advanced than my own, it doesn't take my dad long to get started about the modern game. I'm old enough now to realize that we've had almost the same conversation for close on thirty-five years. That, and this seems genuinely astounding, the mediocrities and one-season wonders of today used to have names like Bobby Charlton, George Cohen, Roger Hunt and Alan Ball. Though never Jimmy Greaves. Now, after the preliminaries – Dad telling me about neighbours I've never met and relations I've never seen since 'Love Me Do' entered the charts; their precise and to-the-day recitation of my last visit; their enquiries as to the length/comfort/cost of the journey forty or so miles up the railway line from King's Cross; their inventory of television programmes watched, bingo calls heard, outings enjoyed, concerts endured, pool games won or lost (Dad) and garden gnomes painted (Mum) – the subject of football will come up.

My mum, who hates the noise of the clan screaming (her description and where did her genes go all of a sudden), heads for the kitchen and starts furiously peeling spuds. My dad's first move, his long ball down the middle, will be something like 'I can't watch it any more', to which I won't say anything. Then he'll do a quick interpassing movement, Johnstone to Matthews

style, 'It's rubbish, it's boring, they aren't worth three-
pence, never mind three million, Sky has ruined it,
England have never been worse, you should have seen
Alex James, you should have seen Lawton, you should
have seen Matthews.' I have seen Matthews, Dad, I'll
offer at this point. It's true. Early sixties. Playing for
Stoke against Chelsea, aged about seventy-four, making
one of his regular 'last appearances in the capital'. But
then Dad had a point about Matthews: now, they go on
about Peter Shilton and John Aldridge, but Matthews
was playing First Division football into his fifties. And
he was a *winger*, for Charlie George's sake!

Next to the pictures of the kids, mine, not his (they
only had the one) and the strange copper sculpture
entitled *Between Solstice and Equinox* which they bought
on holiday in Scarborough, there's a red and blue
Crystal Palace rosette hanging on the wall. It comes
from the year that Palace actually made the FA Cup
Final and came so close to winning it before that inevitable bastard Mark Hughes came along to force the old
pretty-near-last-gasp equalizer.

All my adult life I have been browned off to the
Wagon Wheels with all those broadsheet confessionals,
all those cloth-cap-and-muffler reminiscences and nos-
talgia kick-abouts usually by Liverpool playwrights trying to flog a new series, or degenerate comedians,
almost invariably Tottenham supporters, who will tell
you that they first went to football on their father's
shoulders, through long cobbled streets reeking of hot
pies and memorabilia, with their newly painted rattles
clattering above the din of cheery vendors and regulars
and die-hards just back from their shift on the docks/
in the pit/yards/mill/jellied-eel stall, etc.

My parents' marriage has lasted more years than
mine managed months; casual friends, or occasional
companions who come up to give my dear mother the

illusion that I have a stable sex life, note their obvious love for each other, their domestic fusion into a two-headed dispenser of sausage rolls, teas and insouciant *bonhomie*. And yet in football terms, we are a sorely dysfunctional family. We started out in Kennington (Millwall, Chelsea poss.), moved to Luton (are they still up for sale?) a year after they too failed to win the FA Cup Final. At eighteen I left home never to return for any length of time. Dad supports Crystal Palace, I support Arsenal – and have done since November 1, 1958, when I saw them beat a pretty ropey Newcastle side, already on the slide, 3–2. I spent all of my youth trying to impress Dad, who spent six days a week at work, cycling home just before I had to go to bed, and all my adolescence after we moved to Luton in 1961 dreaming of the day when he would admit that 'Twist and Shout' was a good record, that Mick Jagger could hold a note and wasn't a 'bumbandit', and that Elvis Presley's versions of wartime Italian ballads, brought back from the front by the old man on a selection of 78s, weren't an act of international treason. While other boys stood at the back of the Dunstable California ballroom trying to work the coat queues if they couldn't score on the floor, I'd be discussing musical theory and its relation to the works of Brian Poole and the Tremeloes, or more often than not mulling over the comparative greatness of Garrincha, Didi, Vavà and Pelé, with another specimen of what educationalists used to term 'rejected by the group'.

Anyway, my footballing allegiance was fixed for ever on that foggy, seemingly uneventful Highbury Saturday in early November, when five goals was nothing special and neither were the teams on the pitch. In fact I should have been a Chelsea supporter by right because: 1) we lived in an area of London where allegiance to a club like Crystal Palace was tantamount to a lynching offence; and 2) they had a nifty young side led by the still-teenage Greaves, who had scored five goals against the then Champions Wolves before he was twenty.

Football had bubbled in me over the years: the first football I'd seen had been on our first TV: an Amateur Cup Final involving Bishop Auckland, which I remember if only because I'd rejected pleas from some street mates to go out with them, exploring the still numerous bomb-sites of the area. I'd seen Manchester City beat Birmingham in the Cup Final of '56, been more intrigued and outraged the following year when a preposterous foul on their goalkeeper prevented the Busby Babes of Manchester's other team from winning the Double. Then there had been school games, a busted ankle chasing a fifty-fifty ball in the opposite penalty area, a duffing-up when a wayward cross had shot past the goalie courtesy of my right buttock, a mob of gleeful team-mates when I did my statutory One Thing Right.

I was three weeks past my eleventh birthday: the school was playing an inter-form knockout match on a muddy expanse that seemed the size of the Great Salt Desert of Ramakutz; a ball that weighed more than the average outside-left, boots that coalminers would have discarded with relief, studs that bit into you like the rocks on which our Western heroes ran in fables, their feet bare, trying to keep a yard, a foot, ahead of the Cheyenne arrow. From a corner on the right, yours truly spun with his back to the goal, near post, edge of the box, the ball seemed to fly under the stanchion before even the full-back on the line saw it – oh my Charlie George, they even had full-backs on the goal-line for corners, not bad for Kennington Park in February and games where 'tactics' would have been a brand of peppermints. And they mobbed me, they jumped on my bones, the same kids that had duffed me up only a month earlier for the infamous 'arse-own-goal' incident.

They loved me. I loved me. And in 1971 when Charlie George of sacred memory hit that Double-winner past the Liverpool keeper and sank to the Wembley turf, arms raised in weary triumph, I felt . . . yes, Charlie, I thought I too have known the touch of sporting greatness.

Anyway, I am lucky enough to remember the precise date of my one true moment of soccer glory, although I'd give anything for it to be different. We lived in a flat on the third floor of a Victorian row of houses halfway between the Walworth Road and Kennington Tube station. I went back there a few years ago and it's now a park. That night, February 6, 1958, I'd been doubly knackered climbing those stairs, past the cantankerous 'old girl' on the ground floor and the Irish family on the first. There was my dad at the top of the stairs, Mum in her pinny. All I wanted to do was tell them about the goal. I think I'd had a cold coming on as well, which had started to encroach on the feeling of well being and triumph. Then, they kept saying, both of them kept saying, 'Son, they've crashed.' It was Manchester United, it was Munich.

They let me stay up late, all of us huddled round our small recalcitrant black-and-white TV, and I may be hallucinating or reinventing here, but I'm sure they broadcast all night, or very late, relaying news of the dead and injured: Matt Busby in a critical condition, Charlton and Foulkes almost unscathed, the colossus of Old Trafford Duncan Edwards, a prodigy not yet out of his teens, lay mortally wounded on a Munich airfield and was to perish a fortnight later. That night, for the first time as far as I remember, Dad and I talked about football and talked about it without reservation. He wasn't a banterer any more, but the Palace fan who stood on lethal terraces made of earth and watched in his own boyhood a winger called 'Harry', his own Christian name, who could score direct from a corner almost at will. Well, he wouldn't have needed me, I quipped, having managed to slip the now absurdly irrelevant goal I'd scored into our conversation as we sat crouched round the small coal-fired grate, and heard those still-memorably posh BBC voices relay the regular bulletins. It was then that Dad told me of the goalkeeper who'd hanged himself from a goalpost at Selhurst Park after his wife had run off with another player. Then he talked about the great players he saw and even talked with during his service days: Raich Carter, Tommy Lawton, Wilf Mannion, a Scotsman called Jimmy McCrory who was in his Royal Signals unit. He spoke of the day they made him act as a rugby linesman and the crossbar fell on his head and laid him out: 'My cap saved me, son,' he laughed. Then he stopped laughing. Tommy Taylor, England's centre-forward, a name even I knew well, had been pronounced dead.

Worldwide, Manchester United supporters were born out of that terrible day: years later I actually met Bill Foulkes, a lovely man who'd survived to win the European Cup alongside Charlton and had even scored an improbable semi-final goal against Real Madrid. Foulkes said that all he remembered about the ambulance ride was that he had only one shoe and sock on, and like all of us who dread being picked up by the emergency services in sub-standard skivvies, Foulkes was disconcerted by his 'improper' dress. I didn't tell him that it brought my father and me together, that and a schoolboy goal far more improbable and far classier than the one he scored that night in Madrid. I didn't even tell him that I nearly failed one of my finals papers in 1968 so that I could listen to United's victory over Benfica on a poxy tranny in a bedsit in Hull. And that it was worth every penny, every point, every mark.

Anyway, it's funny how things turn out. I'd always hankered after the big time, as I'd said before: one

Christmas we'd been to Millwall, and when relations from Yorkshire came down for their annual week in the accursed Smoke we had even made it as far as the terraces of Stamford Bridge. It was shortly after the Munich air disaster that Dad said, one Friday evening: 'Son, tomorrow we're going to see the Casuals.'

'The Casuals? What division are they in, then?' I asked.

'The Isthmian League.'

'Where do they play, Dad?'

'The Oval.'

'But that's a cricket ground.'

The Oval is Jack Hobbs, the Oval is Peter May and Jim Laker, the Oval is late Victorian over-optimism about the numbers of people who wanted to watch county cricket on a regular basis. Cricket was always Dad's first love anyway: he played for the works team during the summer and I remember long trips to Morden, postmatch dances with Mum and Dad looking smooth and irresistible on the dance floor, crisps and lemonade and the smell of mown grass, a smile from Dad's boss who looked like an RAF war hero, even the day of the charity match when I got Brian Johnston's autograph and Dad made more jokes about getting out for nought because his hair had got in his eyes – he'd gone almost bald while still in his twenties.

I'd been to the Oval a few times in the summer holidays: I'd seen Peter May score a double hundred for Surrey against the West Indies, I'd seen Laker and Lock bowl, and had always ended up pleasantly stirred, if little wiser about the finer points, shirtless and painfully sunburnt, eventually writhing like a torture victim under Mum's cotton-wool and calamine-lotion all-cure.

Those first journeys to the Casuals were fired with the gospel of Amateurism: the Casuals were gentlemen who played for the love of the game; they were university graduates, internationals, who had reached the

semi-finals of the FA Amateur Cup when the competition had a massive following and was regularly tele-
vised. We'd already seen a 1–1 draw between England
and Belgium, a friendly played before a packed crowd
of 30,000 at Selhurst Park, with a promising young
seventeen-year-old called T. Venables making a nifty
showing in midfield.

But the Casuals? 'Dad, they are toffs,' I replied as
we marched down Braganza Street towards Kennington
Park Road.

'They're a great outfit, son,' he assured me. 'They
play for the love of the game, and they're our local
team. Give it a go.'

It's rather droll in these days of iris-busting away strips
and bubble-gum coloured tracksuits, of coral blue, tan-
gerine, burnt ochre, organdie and teak, and that absurd
Celtic kit that looks like an uprooted back garden, to
remember the colours of Corinthian Casuals, which
were nothing less than chocolate and pink. This was
1958, when some clubs were still sticking out against
numbered shirts, and ten years before homosexual acts
between consenting adults in private were decrimi-
nalized. What did you shout: Come on the Chocolates?
Away the Pinks? It sounded like support for a box of
Black Magic or a flower arrangement.

But I grew to love the Casuals. And I grew to love
that brief period in my childhood when we ceased to
be a dysfunctional footballing unit, when we mulled
over the single sheet of A3 that comprised the programme, discussed the form of the portly but perfectly
balanced Doug Insole, one of the last men to excel in
both national games without having to choose, like
Hurst or Lineker, and always plumping for the one
where the wages burst the packet. Or the tricky Doug
Saunders. Or the Garth-like wing-half John Willett who
was our answer to Ron Flowers of Wolves and England,

or several lethal centre-forwards whose names now escape me, plodders and prancers across that cordoned-off area of the Oval, the mighty stadium truncated by order of the purists who resented the winter encroachment of men in long pants and thick boots on to the sacred turf where Compton struck the four which gave us back the Ashes, where Hobbs and Sandham made hay, and Laker and Lock tormented the visiting batsmen.

One thing that soon became apparent was Casuals' lack of home support: there was Dad and me, a strange but fascinating elderly woman in her own hand-knitted chocolate-and-pink scarf, a few old boys in the wooden seats at the Scoreboard end, and no doubt a smattering of Oxbridge graduates trawling around the Pavilion, which was as remote in those days as the inner sanctum of the Forbidden City. Whenever they played at home it was against teams with considerable and enthusiastic followings, teams on the map of London: Tooting and Mitcham, who wore the same colours as Sheffield Wednesday and whose supporters regularly and inexplicably screamed 'Come on, Redhill!' when anyone booted a ball into the stands; Ilford, Dulwich Hamlet, Kingstonians, the feared Wycombe Wanderers who made it to the big time; all of them bringing what seemed like hordes of perky, raucous, intimidating regulars, swaggerers and lollopers resembling at times the kind of hop-picking tribes of my own father's family whose annual holiday was a week of poorly paid shifts in the aromatic fields of beer country.

But as my father would tell me, the Casuals weren't about all that, friendly and unthreatening though it was in those far-off, pre-ICC-and-Stanley-Knife Maverick-tie days: the Casuals were named after St Paul's Letter to the Corinthians, the Biblical text for playing according to the spirit of the game. The Casuals never argued with a referee's decision; they never embraced or even shook hands after a goal (a similar method of conduct preached by the then Wolves manager Stan Cullis whose players celebrated their 1960 Cup Final win over Blackburn Rovers with little more than an exchange of eyebrows). Any other way would have been outside the Corinthian spirit: were there French kisses on the field of Balaclava? Did Horatius need a cuddle at the bridge? The Casuals were once drawn from the cream of Victorian society, just as in the seventh century my own clan had been ruling the roost in Inverness. There was Cunliffe Gosling and W. J. Oakey, whose family had been distinguished high-street bankers for three centuries, a fact of which the opposition supporters, especially those from the burgeoning, uncouth North, might have cared to remind them. The Casuals may have had their very best times at around the time that I discovered them with Dad, and got a whiff of what later became known as the Hornby effect, that perverse love of strange, grey places, of duty and waiting and longing for the inspirational moment, the light and warmth of experience's great hall before you plunge out into that darkness again, feathers clenched against the blast.

On occasions like the FA Amateur Cup we were suddenly made aware of our status as London Townies: when the Casuals beat a team called Salts by ten to nil, I kid thee not, a sour Magwitch lookalike snarled from behind his muffler: 'Come on, Salts, don't give a rat's shite for their internationals!' But normally to follow the Chocolate and Pinks was a strange, alienating experience far worse than, say, supporting the Spurs or the Wednesday, who could at least prefix their daft nicknames with some place that throbbed with history: not some bunch of Burlington Berties dressed in togas, shambling around a converted cricket stadium against a collection of draymen, dockers, drivers and artisans, saying, 'Have a goal, old chap, we're dead Casual, don't ya know?' Which is what it sounded like to my mates who were busy debating the ethics of following clubs from Manchester or the Midlands, the advantages of Millwall over Chelsea.

Eventually, like Oliver Twist with his belongings in a large hankie, I demanded to go to my first proper Saturday afternoon match. It had to be Chelsea, but Dad looked at his pools coupon and informed me that they were away to Bolton and that if I really wanted to travel on my own to a very large, very crowded stadium then Arsenal were at least a short step from the Tube station and a change away at Leicester Square. I went. Funnily enough, I once told people, because I genuinely remembered it so, that the first time I went to Highbury was for the famous 5–4 showdown against Manchester United, the last fixture the Busby Babes played on home soil before that air crash, and still judged by many who saw it to be the finest league game ever played.

Within a few years I'd become a staunch Gunners fan, with all the players' images on those little plastic badges everyone bought for a tanner, a rattle, a bobble-hat and a carefully aged red and white scarf. I'd arrive three hours before kick-off, travel for the evening games, and once threw a fit, Charlie George knows why, because we'd only beaten Bolton 6–1. Despite a promising showing in that 1958–59 season, it was over ten years before I saw them win any trophy more prestigious than the London Cup. Winning that took Arsenal, my dad and me back to Selhurst Park, and Arsenal, as Dad never stopped reminding me in between snides about 'Dicky Richards and the Shadows', were dead lucky.

Dad never bothered about my defection away from the Corinthian code: much later I understood that he couldn't follow me up the Northern Line to Highbury, not because of any Corinthian spirit but because he just couldn't afford the trip: Amateurism was like all those other excuses for inaction, for not buying motors or home appliances or expensive holidays. Being poor but honest, hardworking if almost permanently borassic. Now I can afford to support the Arsenal, and Corinthian Casuals still play in chocolate and pink, but have long left the vaunted surrounds of the Oval. Now it's hard to even write about Arsenal. It's all so PN. Or Post-Nick. Hornby, of sacred memory.

Dads doing their best. On January 30, 1965, my father went north to Peterborough to bury his father, my grandad, a distant fob-watch figure with a second wife that I wasn't allowed to call 'Gran', even though she soaked me in kindness and cooked some awesome stews in the kitchen of their Knights Hill bungalow. I looked up the date, because it happened to be the day that Arsenal played the Posh in a fourth-round Cup-tie (which they lost, like so many in those fallow years, poorly and against inferior opposition). I can't believe that it happened, what I asked him as he made to go: we knew about Grandad, even though we hadn't seen him in ages and knew he was in some hospital or home; but what made me tell Dad that he should stop off on the way back and watch Arsenal, I don't know. Dad never hit me, any clouts came from Mum, who only went berserk over that 'c' word long before I knew what it meant. But now he looked at me fit to kill. Never had we seemed so far apart, me the cocky sixth-former already looking down on the Beatles, preferring Miles and Ellington, early Dylan and blues. Him, about to bury a man who had never taken him to any kind of football match: a brutal taskmaster who'd fought bare-knuckle for drink-money on Streatham Common and returned from the First World War so shattered that he'd become a local bully. Though I didn't find out until much, much later, my own father grew up to the sounds of his mother being beaten while he and his brothers cowered in the outside toilet, locked there by an older sister for safety's sake. Even later in life, I found out about the awful void that no funeral service could ever plug, that, when these brave, loving women perished in the same bombing raid, my father hadn't seen them for six months. A daft row with that same father had driven him back to barracks; then they died and his grief remains petrified and frozen like a corpse buried in mountain ice, forever silent. He'd never said goodbye.

That look he gave me that day, when he had to bury a man he neither knew nor loved, no longer fills me with dread or shame, but the quiet recognition that comes with the experiences we can't dodge; anyway, we've buried enough hatchets since. How little do we ever really know about the people who love us the best, or how much they try to do to ensure that our lives will be an improvement on their own? I still look out for the Casuals in the smallest print of Sunday, and when Palace got to their Wembley Cup Final it was me who bought Dad his Palace rosette which he wore throughout the game, but still impassive as ever in the armchair, some faded shadow of his own rough dad. In fact, it was me who cried over that Mark Hughes equalizer. Mind you, in an ironic half-time interlude, Dad did admit that Palace's centre-forward Ian Wright might have been good enough to grace the Arsenal side of 1933. Sorry, Dad. Next season, of course, we had him.

Steve Grant's first story appeared in the *Time Out Book of London Short Stories*. 'Casuals' is only his second. Born in 1947 and now executive editor of *Time Out*, he writes extensively about arts and entertainment. He has written and broadcast about football for the *Morning Star*, the *Sunday Times* and LBC radio. He has been an Arsenal supporter longer than he can remember.

Iain Sinclair

Hardball

The harder I gunned the engine, the worse the wheels spun. I could hear them coming, thrashing through the reeds, calling to me, my name. I couldn't see a thing. The screen was fogged with my panicking breath. I had no idea how to start the windscreen wipers. I was a walker, not a driver. I'd watched the Pole from the passenger's seat, that's all I had to go on. His eccentricity. The way he swore in Polish, spat out of the window. 'Shit on your Arsenal. Shit on beards, Communist wanking bastards. Curly boys, arse-fuckers.' That's what it sounded like. Then he would cross himself.

I put my heel to the pedal. Useless. There was smoke coming from the wheels. I was more likely to end up in the river than to find the track across the marshes. What did the Pole do when we were caught on black ice? He fetched out a sack of ashes that he kept among all the other rubbish in the back. He spread grit and clinker around the wheels. He kicked at the thick tread. 'Lazy wanking bastards.' And it always worked.

I listened. The fog had closed everything down. I couldn't hear them any more. I chanced it, opened the door. Crept around to the rear of the van. Night sounds were distorted. A weasel crunching a mouse's skull was amplified into a collision of icebergs. My heart was an animal trying to claw its way out of my chest. Any movement, any sigh in the reeds, was a forest fire.

There were two sacks. I had to make my choice by

touch. One was tied at the neck with string. It was lumpy with hard round shapes – footballs? The other was slippery, a bin bag. I tore at it with my nails. Ripped it, as if it were the Pole's cheek. I felt the stuff trickle out into my hands. I tasted it. Ash. I dragged the split sack from the van and heaped what I could around the wheels. All of it, all of the sharp bits, the coal splinters, the powder that was as soft as icing sugar. As dream cocaine.

Now they were calling again. It was the kid's voice, turning my name into a joke. He was caught in the undergrowth, blaspheming and yelping like a bitch, then breaking into song. A maniac. I liked him. I'd probably regret it afterwards if I had to stave in his head.

A spade, I'd definitely need a spade. To hold them off or to dig myself out. I fumbled once more through the junk the Pole kept in his van. What the hell did he want with bundles of umbrellas, women's shoes, paperback books he couldn't read, tyres he'd never fit on to a pram? A pickaxe, a broom, a rake. I got my hand on the spade. Left the doors open, rushed back, while there was still time. One last try. The kid was out there, further off. It sounded like he'd blundered into one of the ponds. He was cursing a blue streak. Out of it for the moment, problems of his own.

I heaved myself back into the driver's seat. Gripped the wheel. Deep breaths. Took the clammy grey air down into my lungs, held it like a draw. The pitch of terror was easing. It was going to be all right. I visualized the wheels biting, the van moving off. No lights, pushing a clear track through the reeds. Hurtling recklessly towards the sodium necklace marking the road that skirted the industrial estate. That's why none of the street names had been in my tattered *A–Z*. They were new, optimistic, part of the redevelopment, the low buildings, the units that would all, one day, be occupied and busy. I saw the future, prosperity. I'd get a real job, a wife. I might even learn to drive.

The Pole, who was waiting quietly in the passenger seat, reached across for the keys; switched the engine off, took the keys from the ignition. He wound down his window, spat. 'Fucking Georgi Greyhead Graham, Communist wanking bastard, thief.' Then he patted my knee.

The Pole had never been one for conversation. I worked with him, on the marshes, for three years and got nothing more than grunted orders – recipes for white lime, the number of goalposts required, ritual anathemas on Arsenal, leftists, homosexuals. We didn't see many Afro-Caribbeans among the dog fanciers and coarse-range golfers who patronized the grasslands on weekdays. Which was just as well. Bouncing along in the trailer, behind his tractor, we got used to the way he would come to an unexpected halt. 'Shvartzer!' The cursing would continue until he'd worked up enough of a thirst to dig the vodka bottle out from the inside pouch of the mildewed greatcoat he wore, winter and summer, over a leather waistcoat and a couple of rancid sweaters. Cap, muffler, fingerless gloves.

We always worked three handed. There were over two hundred pitches to be marked out, a task that was as eternal as the painting of the Forth Bridge. Get to the finish and then start again. I loved the pure geometry of it. I pictured the patterns as they might be seen from the air. White mandalas decorating the green. I loved the width of the skies. Once we'd begun for the day, there was plenty of space to avoid each other. I would see the Pole on the horizon, sitting in the tractor cab, arms folded. Unless I needed to refill my roller, I kept clear of the man, his aura of unquenchable spite.

Iain Sinclair

The casuals who made up the team never stayed long.
Two or three weeks was average. The Pole ignored
them. Wouldn't answer if they spoke to him, took out
a copy of the *Radio Times* and covered his face with it.
He didn't have a radio, or a television set, I knew that
much. 'Television whore bastard, no good. Eyes, head.'
He gestured with two fingers pressed against his eyeballs. He had found the magazine in the tractor when
he inherited the job, after one of the wars. Most of the
casuals learnt to respect his whims – before they found
themselves trying to paint white lines that had the con-
sistency of bone porridge. Before he rolled a crossbar
out of the trailer on to an unprotected foot. Some of
these gypos and vagrants were crazier than he was:
snackers on dog turds, skeletal naturists, baby faces who
licked pus from freshly squeezed blackheads while
boasting of the hits they'd got away with, sheep rapists,
grass bulimics, hairtrigger millennialists. White trash
too weird to be housed in prisons or asylums. They
couldn't take the marshes. The first teabreak and
they were gone. They'd trot into the bushes to enjoy a
crap, the more sensitive of them, and never be seen
again.

But the kid was a sticker. As well as a speed freak.
You could hear him rabbiting from the other side of
Epping Forest. Football mad. Chased the Hammers up
and down the length of the country. Which was why,
like me, it pissed him off to have to work on Saturdays
and Sundays. Opening up the changing rooms, cleaning the filth that the amateurs left behind: mud, plas-
ters, shampoo sachets, embrocation, even condoms
floating in the trough. What did they get up to? Had
they saved the knotted rubbers as a macho boast? Or
did a win excite them so much they shot off in an
orgy of mutual congratulation? The Pole wouldn't have
anything to do with it. Too many black athletes. Too

much backchat. He drank fiercely in his tractor, waiting until we were ready to take down the goalposts.

My grouse was that I couldn't play myself. I was a loner, never part of a team, never in thrall to the whistle. Night football was just my way of coming to an understanding with the magnitude of London, seeing it as an anthology of green scraps, fragmented meadows, wastelots, school yards. I cruised as a serial five-a-sider. I'd go anywhere. Set off at random, hop a bus, or simply walk until I was exhausted, in a direction that I'd never before attempted. Scuffed trainers, baggy jeans, ready for it. I was a three-and-in, headers and volleys freelancer. I pocketed change (lost it frequently) on park challenges. I'd grown up learning to control a wet tennis ball, shooting at a chalked goal, never losing possession – even to another member of my own team. Elbows out, eyes down, no headers, no percentage play, no long punts into space. A Sunday league kick-about or a pub challenge on proper turf gave me agoraphobia. I could do anything with the ball except pass it.

I scored games against black kids turned off the astroturf in Caledonian Park. We dodged traffic for a Brewery Road shoot-out. I cardiac-arrested a trio of retired Scottish postmen on London Fields, clattered their superior skills. I played as a mercenary for a Kurdish mob in an afterhours playground at the back of Ridley Road Market. I kicked lumps out of middle-class pretenders in Regent's Park. I made up the numbers on Tooting Common. I took a few quid off a heritage film crew in Charlton Park. Through these contacts, nameless encounters, I mapped the city, the shape of its energy patterns.

When the weather turned, and the speed freak was still with us – Julian Dicks crop, mouthy, sweat-ringed Ribena shirt – the Pole started to take the tractor, in

the lunch break, down to a strip of grass between the
canal and the Hackney Stadium, the dog track. He'd
open his *Radio Times* and leave us to it. But, it just so
happened, that he had a sack of footballs in the trailer.
He let us find them, and, in boredom, use them. Three
and in (except that the kid refused ever to come out)
against a roughcast wall. An ugly place. The wall in
slabs, razorwire above it, on which flapping kites of
plastic, wingless birds, signalled the breeze. Earth
mounds from the stadium's renovation backed up to
the wall, and, beyond the mounds, rows of seven-
lamped light towers. It was obviously a favoured site for
the Pole. And you could see why. Even the Alsatians
that various sullen members of the underclass exercised
along the perimeter made him feel at home.

The kid fancied himself as a goalie. Dog shit didn't
deter him. He flung himself about in wild abandon,
climbed reeking on to the trailer. Indoors, he'd have
been unbearable. If I got five shots in succession past
him, I won a slug of vodka. If he saved three on the trot,
it was his turn at the bottle. Half-pissed, we returned to
our white lines. Mine meandered into crazed calligra-
phy, oval pitches, no corners. I got slower and slower
and finally bunked off to doze under the poplars. The
kid did his wiz and, pin-eyed, scorched the grass like
an Exocet. Tramlines that ran for half a mile. Pitches
divided up like chessboards. You could hear him rabbiting on. He swore, against all evidence, against the
yelping of hounds, that Orient played in the Hackney
Stadium. He'd been there, seen them. Had a trial, been
offered terms. He could have been a five-grand-a-week
man, trading wisecracks with Barry Hearn. He could
have followed the former manager to Forest. He was
like every politician you've ever heard of, like David
Frost. They could all have been pros. Orient were bollocks. It was the Hammers or nothing.

Hardball

At the end of the afternoon, when the Pole picked us up, he surprised me. He gestured that he had something he wanted us to see. He fumbled beneath the leather waistcoat and retrieved a yellow packet. Photographs, murky, taken at night, football stadia. Highbury, Loftus Road, the Den, the Valley, Upton Park – even Craven Cottage seen from across the river, as well as from Bishop's Park. They weren't bad. They looked gaunt and sinister, floodlights fogging. Broken-down people's palaces. Tarted-up leisure and entertainment facilities. Symbols of exclusion. The Pole's album was like the proposal for a Channel Four documentary. He lacked White Hart Lane to hook the desktop fantasists.

Apparently, and this was the biggest shock of them all, the kid had been helping him, taking him around. The speed freak wasn't bothered about getting into the game, if it didn't involve the Hammers. He'd happily play one-on-one, against the car-park wall, with some local urchin, uphold the honour of Plaistow and Forest Gate. There was always a wager which the Pole supervised. He didn't explain, not then, what the stake would be.

'Who do you support?' I asked.

'Football shit. Arsenal wankers.' Only the grounds interested him, the architecture of enclosure, the baying mob. The dogs, the security cameras. The columns of floodlights. Not for nothing had the partisans of Allende been massacred inside a football stadium. Hadn't the Parisian Jews been rounded up in such a place to wait for transport? The Pole wanted to feed on bad karma, the malign passion of the crowd. He would lurk in the shadows and concentrate all that latent mayhem into his camera. Unwatched football was his metaphor of chaos. He didn't need to see the Christians torn apart by lions. It was much more subtle to listen in the deserted street outside, to interpret every nuance that emanated from the trapped punters. Foiled orgasms of sound. Then pick some ragamuffin who nobody would miss to play against his feral gladiator.

I agreed to meet them outside White Hart Lane, at the back of the East Stand. The next evening game, an eight o'clock kick-off, happened to be against Manchester United. Insanity. The way the purity of proletarian Saturday afternoons, one time for all, has been shafted by market forces. The crowd reduced to a rabble of high-profile extras. Extras who pay royally for the privilege of dubbing background noise on to a TV special.

A bleak, damp evening in the long post-Christmas lull. I walked there, up the Lea Valley, past the marshes, Springfield Park and the old sewage farm. Nowhere open, nowhere to get a drink to lift the choking poultice of oily air. A Scotch egg and a black coffee from a petrol station was the best I could do. I was in an evil mood by the time I found them, parked up in a dirty blue van.

The Pole was eating cold cabbage from a chipped mug, washing it down with the usual draughts of vodka. The kid was chewing on a pig's foot, wiping the grease into his lank hair. A consumptive Presley imitator. The foot was a gesture at grossness. He couldn't hack it. No appetite. Dry lips. Curd at the corners of his mouth. Thirsty for a hit of cola sugar, a tooth-rotting suck at a sticky can. He dropped the nibbled hoof out of the window. Even the rats refused to take the bait. The mindless vandalism was a provocation aimed at the supposed cultural bias of the Tottenham supporters, a fatty compass tossed derisively in the direction of Stamford Hill. Spurs, as far as he was concerned, were the pits. The acceptable face of football, football for tourists from Hampstead, broadsheet dickheads, flabby essayists hymning Gazza as a cock on legs. Football as a cash cow,

a way of laundering sweatshop slush funds, insurance
barbecues. Sugar by name, salt by nature. The kid
ranted like a decommissioned poet.

The game had been in progress for about half an
hour when I found them. Even the technicians hanging
about in their caravans seemed to think they'd got it
right for once. The crowd were going mad, wave after
wave of ecstatic roars, an opera of the masses. Thick
vine clusters of electric cable ran from the TV vans,
over the wall, into the stadium. The electrification of
the unwashed. Not a star in the sky, warm air pushing
in from the south, hurting the indignant gloom of the
Lea Valley, the trading estates, the night-flashing railway, the dead streets with their boarded-up shops. Football turned Tottenham into Belfast. And the entire
country, and probably most of Europe and Asia (bets
down), were hooked on this, plugged into this unlikely
confrontation. Tottenham were stuffing United. Chris
Armstrong, the Crystal Palace charger, the recreational
puffer, had glanced in a header that was worthy of
Klinsmann. Hallucinatory madness. Kids were ghosting
out of the gloom to peek at the monitors. It was easy
to use their excitement to set up a game, a challenge.

There's a carpet pitch behind a fence in the lee of
the stadium, lights of its own, a parasitical facility. The
lights weren't enough to turn night into day, they
spilled a sort of laboratory glow at the corners of the
field. The illumination enjoyed by brain-wired beagles.
We would be in our element. The flash of the Pole's
camera would fuse our spastic actions with the larger
drama on the other side of the great white cliff.

Most of the glue-sniffers and night casuals had drifted
away from the pitch towards the circle of OB vans. They
were hooked on the big match. They wanted to see the
plutocrats of Man U come unstuck. Our yids and wops
can stuff yours: that was the message. The two that were

left, supposed brothers, were unreconstructed dysfunks, ambulant basket cases. A safe bet for the Pole. He wandered over with his bottle and a shuffle of paper to set up the challenge. A penalty shoot-out. First to reach five goals. One player as the nominated goalkeeper and the other as the shooter.

The speed freak pulled on the gloves (motorcycle gauntlets) and jumped up and down, leaking gusts of white smoke. 'Yes yes yes.' He clapped his hands together. He couldn't wait to showcase his ineptitude. I couldn't afford to miss. I knew that something more than a couple of quid, and a free hit at the vodka bottle, was involved. The Pole had his arm around the kid's shoulder. The kid was mouthing his usual stream-of-consciousness rubbish. Mexicans, Indians, Mayans, sun-worshippers, snake god cannibals. Jungle bunnies with chipped profiles and a winner-takes-all attitude to life. These Mayans, apparently, saw football as a fate game. They played with their victims' skulls. The geometry of the court reflected a demonic cosmology. I had a bad feeling about this. Every touch of the ball was prophetic. If I hit the back of the net, so would Spurs, so would England, so would the white races, so would the order of angels. If I failed . . . Heads would surely roll.

I failed. For my first shot I concentrated on placement, not pace. I feinted left, then hit it low towards the right-hand corner. The goalkeeper bluffed me. He wasn't a mover. Stood like a funerary mute, arms hanging awkwardly, until I put toe to leather. Then he sprung, anticipated me, read the flight. Tipped it, effortlessly, around the corner. Their penalty taker, a rickety beanpole who could barely stand erect without his callipers, didn't bother with a run-up; smashed the ball, with no backlift, straight through the kid's arms. There was no way back. But we had to carry on to the death.

I blasted shots two and three safely into the top-left corner. The same way twice, fooling nobody. The spider-monkey guessed right both times, but couldn't hold them. Their second attempt rocketed down off the post and in. The third, by some miracle, was saved. Keep diving the wrong way and sooner or later, by accident, you'll get it right.

The Pole went back to the van, fetching a black bag that, he said, contained a couple of bottles for the winners. Spurs must have tucked away their third goal, Armstrong's kneeling header, as I scored ours: top-left corner again. I felt like praying. I would have been down there crawling if I could, duplicating the position of the Tottenham striker.

Could the speed freak take it to the wire? Not on his own. But the Pole had moved around directly behind the posts and his unblinking glare, red-eyed in the sodium-puddled darkness, threw the thin streak's concentration. He ballooned it gently into the kid's grateful grasp. See him dance and cavort. 'Come on you Irons.' He jigged and punched the air. He tried to embrace the Pole. Shove his tongue down his throat.

I pushed my luck with the final shot, tried for my lucky corner, and had the keeper fingertip it on to the bar. Their last effort was a formality, depositing kid and ball, together, in a tangle in the corner of the net.

I was all for shaking hands, calling it an honourable draw, three apiece, and home – when the roar of the fourth Spurs goal overwhelmed us. News of madness. An adrenalin hit that was not to be denied. All or nothing. The Pole was playing with the neck of his bag. His big fists clenching and unclenching. Now the problem was the quantity of electronic interference in the air. Commentators blathering about upsets. Action replays. Slo-mo distortions. Real time fractured and tormented. World Cups recalled. I kept seeing Waddle punting it high, wide and handsome. We were wired. In a mind game, we were bound to be losers: the kid with his free associating meltdown of West Ham mythology and misunderstood Mayan blood rituals, his arcane pulp images of terror, and my own crippling sense of psychogeography. His racist bile, my singular attitude towards landscape. Too much memory. We were too easily accessed. The other pair existed only in the present. Autistic innocents. Drooling but functional.

We tossed for first kick. They took it. A mishit trickled through the kid's legs. He was frozen in a drama of self-sacrifice. It was more dramatic, at this juncture, to lose heroically. Who remembers the man who hits the winning goal? But who can forget the goalkeeper's fantastic error? Gary Sprake fumbling it, or the backpedalling Seaman looped from the touchline?

I travelled behind the picture of my failure. I saw the ball sailing over the bar and into the road. I heard it thump against the roof of the van. That was what the story needed and that was what I did. The full Waddle impersonation. The bandy-legged slouch. The loser's sleepwalking approach. The scoop.

The Pole handed over cash and bottles and we walked in silence to the van. We had to get away before the real match terminated and celebrating thousands rushed out into the streets to get home to have their triumph confirmed on *Match of the Day*. To have Alan Hansen put the damper on it.

I was never much good at directions, but when the van went off the road – to avoid the worst of the traffic – and took the track through the reed beds, across the marshes, I knew we weren't heading for Hackney. The kid was in the back, blowing his bubbles, and swilling firewater. The Pole drove in silence. I couldn't see much. The fog mixed with smoke and the damp night to seal us off. When we stopped, I couldn't have guessed where we were. On the edge of the river or at the centre of a swamp. The Pole told the kid to get out and start a fire. Sat beside me, the windows wound up, headlights off, listening to the kid stumble about, whimpering that he was cold and wet, and couldn't find any dry wood. The Pole left the keys in the car and swung himself out to take control.

That's when I decided to make my run for it. When I started the engine and juddered off, blind, in the direction the van was already facing. I didn't know anything about gears, but it worked. I was moving, reeds thrashing across the windscreen. Voices behind me. It went well until the wheels stuck in the mud at the edge of the black river. Until they spun and screamed and the Pole caught up with me, claimed his forfeit.

Icy cold. Turning slowly through the water, the tangle of weeds, a taste of iron and powdered aspirin. Blood clogging to silt. Spinning over and over. Tunnels of light splintering ahead of me. I hadn't thought the Lea was so deep. But I knew everything now, knew that the ashes I had been spreading so cavalierly around the wheels of the van were the ashes of men. Victims. Sacrifices. I could feel the light but not see it. I tried to scrape off the lily pads that were covering my eyes. Scratch the caul from my face. I had no face. Those were not footballs in the Pole's sack. They went with the rest of his collection. One hard thing hidden away for each night-stadium photographed. I could hear the kid chanting 'come on you Irons' as he rolled my head through the fire, as he prepared it for the place it would always occupy.

Former parks gardener Iain Sinclair has published three novels – *White Chappell, Scarlet Tracings, Downriver* and *Radon Daughters* – as well as numerous essays and reviews. In all his work he disregards convention and reinvents language to spectacular effect. He constantly prowls the borderland between history and myth, with a particular interest in London. In the 1970s he ran Albion Village Press, publishing Brian Catling and Chris Torrance, as well as several collections of his own poetry, two of which are now in print again – *Lud Heat & Suicide Bridge* – in a single volume, from Vintage.

Nicholas Royle

Referee's Report

Imagine the job description: you're to run around in the mud on a Saturday afternoon and accept the malicious abuse of up to 40,000 people for ninety minutes plus injury time. Pay negligible. You wouldn't get many takers. 'Who's the bastard in the black?' crowds used to sing. For some reason 'Who's the bastard in the green?' hasn't quite caught on, but referees have not necessarily become any more popular since they changed the colour of their shirts; after all, a football chant predicated upon a particular shirt colour, in an age when shirt colours change faster than traffic lights, may not be such a good idea.

In short, why would anybody in his or her right mind do it? Most people would rather hit themselves in the face with an axe – a fine first strike by M John Harrison, who understands fully that when I ask for a story about football what I really want is a story about real life. He's used the language of one to write about the other and has ended up writing about both. Right out of left field. Christopher Kenworthy is a crafty all-rounder, a Steve Lomas figure who battles hard then out of the blue produces something totally unexpected – such as using a Don Howe quote from the TV coverage of World Cup USA '94 for his title and failing to make any reference to it in his text. Pick that one out. Irvine Welsh, Scottish midfield dynamo – his writing comes straight from the terraces, in a land where they still have them. But

question marks hover over his chemical status and his
persistent foul language, and it's as well to bring him
off before he gets sent off – and so on comes plucky
debutant Tim Lawler. You'd never guess that playwright
Lawler's hymn to 'Manchester's Other Association Football team' was written in Bangkok, *by a Spurs supporter.*
SF master Steve Baxter delivers a well-struck volley that
will surprise anybody whose knowledge of the life of
H. G. Wells is as poor as mine was. Maureen Freely mixes
it up with Germans and Turks on the Greek island of
Naxos, where a melting pot can all too easily become a
cauldron; it's a good job it's 'More Than Just a Game'.
Sunday-league football likewise, as Tim Pears shows in
his non-fiction account of how he spends his weekends.
Most fans' idea of football hell may be a wet Wednesday
night in Grimsby watching Wimbledon reserves, but
Conrad Williams's is of a never-ending penalty shoot-out
after an unresolved FA Cup Final. Nicholas Lezard's first
fictional foray is a bold reverse run down the left into
inversion-theory territory – and funnier than, say, Jimmy
Hill and Terry Venables tearing each other's throats out
on air. Commentators, of course, speak an entirely different language, one which I hoped would be satirized by
at least one contributor to this book – and now over to
Glyn Maxwell at Wembley. In Steve Grant's distillation
of memory and invention, personal glory and collective
tragedy coincide on a cold February night in 1958. It's
been said (by Luke Jennings in *ES Magazine*) that the
novelist Peter Ackroyd knows London's 'dark alleys and
darker secrets . . . better than any other living writer'.
Surely no better than Iain Sinclair, whose poems, stories,
novels and other speculations have excavated the myth
and mystery of the capital and reinvented it to spectacular effect. Read 'Hardball' and you'll never play Sunday-
league on Hackney Marshes, or knock about at the back
of White Hart Lane again.

Referee's Report

The second half kicks off with Graham Joyce's trip
back in time to Highfield Road – a sort of Goalkeeper's
Fear of Dietmar Bruck's Liverwurst – and continues with
Geoff Nicholson's leap into the future, to 2010, and the
unexpected participation in the World Cup of twenty-
two aliens who bear a striking resemblance to a world-
famous footballer. Geoff Dyer brings us back down to
earth with his inch-perfect kick-about in a Parisian playground, and Mark Timlin has his regular private eye Nick
Sharman getting into deep water as temporary body-
guard to the 'Wonder Boy'. Michael Marshall Smith's
'Sorted' stays in the world of professional players,
although there's not a ball in sight – or not of the FIFA-
approved variety anyway. Liz Jensen's jilted 'Mum' may
experience an epiphany in the games room, but *oral sex*!
She'll have to come off (before she can be charged with
bringing the game into disrepute) and make way for
youngster James Miller. Still playing for the Under-21s,
Miller reveals there's more to 'Scoring' than goals. Mark
Morris does what he does best – draws a bead on tough,
streetwise Yorkshire youth (must be all those years spent
supporting Leeds United). In Kim Newman's strangely
believable alternative history we meet a new incarnation
of one of our best-loved – and most despised – story-
tellers. Luton Town fan John Hegley peers into football's
crystal ball and comes up with a hat-trick of new poems,
while Simon Ings goes to Brazil's Maracanã stadium and
comes back with a tale in the tradition of Latin America's
magic realists. And in time added on for stoppages,
Christopher Fowler celebrates the real magic of the
game and those who go to watch it. This book is for those
people and many others as well.

It's for overgrown boys who play on Sunday mornings
yelling 'Push up, push up!' in the hope of an offside
decision despite the lack of a linesman; it's for insecure
defenders who crowd into opposing teams' penalty areas

161

for corners just because they like the attention; and it's
for referees everywhere (even Alan Wilkie, whose dubi-
ous penalty awarded to Manchester United at Old Trafford last season put paid to Manchester City's FA Cup
run). It's for every kid who's ever had to knock on a
neighbour's front door and plead 'Can we have our ball
back, please?' It's even for that overgrown schoolboy
(there's one in every amateur team) who during the
warm-up, instead of tapping the ball to another player,
will tee himself up and blast it miles past the keeper – and
then not go and fetch it.

There are a few people it's not for. It's not for the
cheats, the bullies or the few who still shout racist abuse.
It's not for those who fought and won the battle to make
us pay extra to watch live football on TV. Nor is it for
those 'supporters' who leave games five minutes before
the end in order to get home more quickly – there's a
video to be made consisting of all the last-minute goals
never seen by those miserable bastards. Several of them
sit in front of me at Maine Road and I think they should
take a large part of the blame for City's relegation to
Division One.

In short, this is a book of excellent new stories by some
of the best writers in the country, and it's for anyone who
likes the sound of that.

Graham Joyce

A Tip From Bobby Moore

I was seduced by Jimmy Hill when I was eleven years old. All it took was for him to wave a packet of crisps and a bottle of Vimto and I would wait behind the Main Stand after a match at Highfield Road until he was ready to receive me. He had a lot of other schoolboys like that. Hundreds. Possibly thousands. It's difficult not to resent him for it.

In fact on the particular day he succeeded in binding my heart to the fortunes of Coventry City FC there were hundreds of other boys jostling for Vimto and favours at one of Jimmy Hill's sub-legendary pop 'n' crisps parties. The simple idea was that all boys under the age of fourteen should wait behind after a game, whereupon they would meet the players, who would readily sign autographs. Pop and crisps were offered to keep the kids quiet immediately after the final whistle, while the players frolicked in the showers and played Hunt The Bar Of Soap or whatever it is that professional footballers do for so long in the changing room after a game.

After this agonizing delay, we were trooped single file into what I now realize was a social club, behind the bar of which all of the players were presented, red-faced and with gleaming wet hair. Attired in suits, they were thinner and of shorter stature than one had always imagined, and each had a slightly glazed and unfocused look. Every one of them had a fag on as they giggled to each other and scrawled utterly illegible signatures on the pages of pristine autograph books laid before them by boys stunned into silence by the eerie proximity of these seraphim of the kick-and-rush.

It may be necessary to point out (I don't assume everyone to be a statistician of Coventry's days in the lower divisions) that the Sky Blues were in the hunt for promotion from the old Third Division. There slouched Ronnie Rees, the Welsh Wizard, burping into George Hudson's ear; there teetered Ernie Machin, laughing like a drain at something no one else could understand; John Sillett kept hiccuping and repeating the word 'Archie' in a falsetto while leaning heavily on diminutive Willie Humphries. Of course I never realized at the time, but these Olympians, these gladiators, these only a little lower than angels, were pissed. (Or at least, that's how an admittedly imperfect memory reports it to me.) Pissed? They were *slaughtered.* Every man-jack amongst them.

How often have you wished you could return as an adult to right an injustice to some moment in time when you were a helplessly tongue-tied child? The moment came at the end of the line when skipper–thug George Curtis finished scratching his cross and my pristine autograph book was snatched up by Jimmy Hill. Now every other inebriated dimwit Coventry City player had grasped the imperative of having each to sign their name on a fresh page. Not Jimmy Hill, who carelessly, one might say imperiously, laid his signature in a dreadful tangle with the moniker of the aforementioned George Curtis.

'Hey! HEY! FANNY HILL! Get a grip! Don't you realize this child spent TWO WEEKS' pocket money on that sad little autograph book? Don't you understand how IMPORTANT these things are to a small boy? Now get back here and write your name out PROPERLY!'

I still have the autographs, somewhere. The result

looks like two team-mates from a Sunday league colliding as they race for the same ball. But the fiendish scheme worked. The pact was accomplished. The slightly satanic-looking Jimmy Hill, complete with trim, Mephistophelean beard, had brandished a contract which we signed if not in blood then in Dandelion & Burdock. Our loyalty had been secured for decades to come.

Moreover, on the way out, my Uncle Harold, waiting for me behind the stands, pointed to an elderly figure in a cloth cap. The man had a small dog on a lead and was talking quietly with the club chairman. 'Chief scout,' said my Uncle Harold, knocking out his rosewood pipe into the bowl of his hand. 'The one who goes round the schools.'

Chief scout? Round the schools? This was crucial information. I tried, unsuccessfully, to steal another look at the said chief scout, but a ruck of bodies interposed and anyway it was time to go. I swiftly reported what I'd learned to my team-mates in the Keresley Newlands primary school team the following Saturday morning, after we'd beaten Holbrooks Junior 10–0. 'He's got a little dog. On a lead.'

'I saw a bloke with a dog, watching the game,' said Keith Randle, our centre-forward who had just scored a double hat-trick. Keith Randle had a long, blond fringe he was perpetually flicking from his eyes.

'Did he have a cloth cap?'

'No. His dog was an Alsatian.'

'Naw. That's not him.'

But the word had been enough. The fact was that I'd managed, inexplicably, to communicate the idea that Coventry's chief scout had somehow *indicated* to *me personally* that he *might* be coming to watch one of our games. Everyone was so taken with the idea that I unreservedly believed it myself.

And we had the team to impress. Our last four results

had been 9–1, 11–0, 14–0, 7–1 and today 10–0. Even as team goalkeeper it was possible for me to play without touching the ball for the entire game and still garner great personal kudos from these sweeping victories. I don't know why we used to win by such margins; perhaps our mining-village team was a bit beefier and somewhat thuggish in a way that intimidated a lot of eleven-year-olds, but these statistics are the facts. At that time the Coventry education authorities ran a primary schools' challenge shield tournament and, after our school retained the trophy for the seventh consecutive year, we were ruled inadmissible for all subsequent years the competition was staged. This appalling injustice would not be tolerated in the Premier League should Liverpool or Coventry City prove seven-times champions but, as I say, these are the facts.

We'd already progressed to the quarter-finals of the above competition and were scheduled to face, away from home on a fine evening after classes, a school with the bizarre name of Our Lady Of The Assumption.

'Catholics,' said Keith Randle, flicking his fringe. 'Left-footers.'

I thought for a while about the footballing implications of this, before checking back on the subject.

'I'm not sure,' said Keith. Flick.

We changed in the same shower room as the opposition, eyeing each other furtively. Little lads slapped muscle rub on their chubby thighs in imitation of the pros. The air was charged with Sloane's Liniment and high expectation. They looked a tall, gangly crew, and a lot of them seemed to have excessive overbites, which we thought might have something to do with their Catholicism. Then their captain, a particularly goofy character, came across and asked us to identify our 'skipper'. We pointed to Mick Carpenter, captain by dint of being team hard-case.

A Tip From Bobby Moore

'Welcome to Our Lady.' The boy offered a hand that wanted shaking. 'Here's to a good game, and may the best side win.'

Mick Carpenter stared at him with cloudless, unblinking blue eyes. We were all arrested in the act of pulling on shirts and tying bootlaces. For a moment it seemed as if Mick was going to reject the outstretched hand, but finally he offered his own, solemnly shaking hands without saying a word. The boy coloured and went back to his cohorts. Mick Carpenter glanced round at the rest of us. I must admit, we hated all that sporting shit.

It was an unexpected struggle. By half-time we were leading 2–1, and in the shock of having to do something I was playing out of my skin. I'd read that England goalkeeper Gordon Banks had said that all keepers are crazy, and I tried my best to live up to this. What I lacked in gymnastic skills I tried to make up for by being prepared to fling myself at anyone's feet, whatever the risk, and this I did that evening. I tipped one shot over the bar, palmed another round the post. We weren't used to this.

Shortly into the second half they pulled level, and after that they piled on the pressure. They were set to give us a pasting and suddenly my team, who so confidently travelled around Coventry steamrollering all-comers, looked like frightened little boys. Then, when the opposition conceded a corner, I saw him.

There, on the touchline, chatting with our teacher. He was wearing a cloth cap. He had a small dog on a leash. I passed the word around. The idea that the chief scout for Coventry City was watching gave us extra impetus. Slowly we managed to resist the onslaught and hauled ourselves back into the game. The final whistle blew and we changed round immediately for a bout of extra time.

Back they came at us. Every single body was clustered

in our own penalty area and we spent fifteen minutes frantically scrambling, scooping, heading and clearing balls off the line. Shot after shot. Outrageously, the home referee–teacher, anxious to see his boys press the advantage, allowed the game to run on five or six minutes after the agreed time. Our own teacher was protesting from the touchline, to no avail. Then came the opposing captain stepping round every lunging tackle we could offer, until he was through, with only me to beat.

So I poleaxed him.

The boy went down with a groan, I gathered the ball, and gave it the old-fashioned bounce-bounce-boot as if everything was normal. The referee stood inches away, looking deep into my eyes. He was agonizing over his decision, the silver whistle trembling between his lips.

Albert Camus said that everything he knew about morality in life he'd learned from football. Camus knew what he was talking about. The referee understood perfectly well he'd shamefully abused his authority and that he'd stepped beyond the bounds of all sporting decency by ignoring the clock. Precisely because of that, he was in no position to award what under any other conditions would have been a clear penalty. He had one last opportunity to vouchsafe a sliver of his tattered integrity. He blew the whistle, not for a penalty, but for full-time. A replay would be necessary.

In the excitement we had forgotten about the chief scout. I quizzed our teacher Mr Shipley about him.

'Chief scout? What are you on about?'

'The man with the dog.'

'Oh, that was the school caretaker.'

Meanwhile Coventry City were closing in on promotion, and the pop and crisps party had infected me with the autograph-hunting virus. It may seem pointless to some to duplicate autographs already collected. But no, the biro scribbles secured that afternoon somehow lacked authenticity; they were too easily come by, no suffering had gone into the collecting. And a true fan had to suffer.

I'd discovered that if I caught the eleven o'clock bus into Coventry on a Saturday morning when there was no school fixture, I would be first in the turnstile queue outside the Spion Kop. Thus admitted, I could race to position myself at the exact centre behind the goal, in line with the penalty spot. Odd really, when much of the game would be spent gazing at the goalkeeper's back, and with the opposite end almost entirely obscured from view, but it's pointless trying to explain these things. Still, it wasn't enough having arrived at the game four hours before the kick-off. I wasn't entirely satisfied until I'd waited behind at the stadium sometimes up to two hours after the final whistle. Autograph hunting. Which is how I came to be in the toilets with Dietmar Bruck.

I had it on good authority that if you waited for long enough behind the Main Stand after the game, players would emerge. What they didn't tell me was that you had to wait long enough for them to down seven or eight pints, and there was nothing to do while waiting, except to lurk.

Lurking is a very dull activity. There might be another sad eleven-year-old around, similarly lurking, but the time is not passed in cheerful conversation about the day's result or in the exchange of fascinating football statistics, since this boy is a rival. Footballers tend to dash off autographs on the hoof. They snatch up a book, scribbling in it on the trot, not returning it before having travelled a distance roughly equivalent to the diameter of the centre circle. A boy has to look sharp, offer the book ahead of the moving target in a well-timed pass, stay with the flow and be ready to trap the return, all in a single clean action. Often only one signature is on offer and, when the pressure to get an autograph is on, I've seen boys falter, fumble and even go down in a sorry heap. The big occasion gets to them.

That evening had been just such an occasion, and I'd missed at least half a dozen of the team through poor timing. The evening grew darker, and the other boys began to trickle away, convinced that everyone had gone, when I saw a shadow emerge from a side door. There was just enough light for me to realize it was Dietmar Bruck, City's Danzig-born German half-back (yes, half-back, these were the days when a packet of Woodbines was a shilling, or whatever). Dietmar Bruck skipped across the yard and entered a dank outbuilding for some inscrutable purpose. I followed him.

Once inside I realized the building was a simple urinal. Dietmar Bruck, pissing heartily against the black-painted trough, farted briefly and seemed slightly startled to discover this small shadow at his side, book and pen sullenly offered. An expression of exasperation crossed the German footballer's face.

'Not now, son,' he managed to say after an uncomfortable pause. 'I've got my hands full.'

Memory, like language, is apt to transmute, but imperfect recollection of the event coupled with race-stereotyping has left with me an abiding image, after those words, of myself peering at the fat, pink-grey *liverwurst* in his large hands as he declined to sign my book. I waited. And waited. Dietmar Bruck seemed to go on pissing *for ever*. Finally he zipped up, turned and found a brass tap under which he could wash his hands. It didn't work. Still shaking his head he took the book from me and signed his name.

We could now both go home.

The school team continued to do well. We punished Our Lady Of The Assumption in the replay a thumping

5–1, and it felt good. In another game, against timorous Brent Croft Junior, Keith Randle came close to a triple hat-trick in a genocidal 14–0 victory, and even then Mr Shipley blew the whistle ten minutes early to stop the other boys from getting too depressed.

Meanwhile the chief scout continued to overlook us. 'There he is!' said Keith Randle during the Brent Croft game, but although the man had a dog, he had no cloth cap. Similarly Mick Carpenter's, 'Is that him?' had us all excited for a moment, but this time although a cloth cap was in place, there was no dog.

For the semi-final we drew the appalling Brent Croft again, who had sneaked through the first round on a bye and who had passed through the quarter-finals by default when their opposition had mysteriously failed to turn up. Our place in the final was secure.

Then Mick Carpenter, Keith Randle and a couple of the others discovered smoking and Woodpecker cider. At first I resisted. I recalled dire warnings from Jimmy Greaves and England captain Bobby Moore in the pages of my schoolboy comics. They fronted strip cartoons in which feeble-looking squirts comfortably duffed up six-foot bullies. They were able to do this, according to Jimmy Greaves, because the bullies smoked cigarettes whereas the squirts, surprisingly pugnacious and quicker to the punch, didn't.

'Take a tip from me,' I told my team-mates, quoting Bobby Moore verbatim, 'the best way to stop smoking is never to start.'

We were skulking under the canal bridge at the time. Mick Carpenter was sharing round a packet of communally purchased Woodbines. Mick and the others gave me the exact same look they'd given the sporting captain of Our Lady Of The Assumption. I took the proffered snout and accepted a light from Keith Randle. We all smoked at least one cigarette that evening, while some of the team smoked two – and despite this we still won our next match 7–0.

The end of the football season was approaching. Coventry City looked set for promotion to the Second Division, and the spring weather was unseasonably warm. So warm that Roy Stokes and Mick Carpenter had the bright idea of the team camping out in Roy's back garden the night before our walkover semi-final against Brent Croft. Roy's parents owned two tents and had approved the idea when Roy had cunningly explained that it would build team morale and the evening would be spent talking tactics. Seven out of the eleven managed to get permission from their parents. Meanwhile there would be cigarettes. There would be cider. There was even talk of girls.

Roy Stokes' father insisted we settle by ten o'clock that evening. We bedded down, under blankets safety-pinned together, and waited until the lights went out in the Stokes' household. Then we cracked open the smuggled cider and the Woodbines. Everyone had produced at least one two-pint bottle. Even though Deborah Cook and Jane Spencer from school were supposed to put in an appearance, all talk of girls proved luxurious. We sat up talking in hushed tones, smoked the cigarettes down to their butts and drained the cider bottles dry.

About three in the morning everyone was still wide awake and starting to feel peckish. Roy decided to make a raid on the fridge inside the house. Keith Randle went with him, but all they came back with was a pound-and-a-half of raw pork sausage.

'You can't eat raw sausage!' someone protested.

'Course you can!' retorted Keith Randle, severing a link and taking a generous bite. He flicked his fringe. 'Lovely stuff.'

Terence Harper clowned around with one of the

links, holding it to his groin, reminding me unpleasantly of Dietmar Bruck. But eventually we polished off the links of pork sausage, and I must say it didn't seem to taste too badly. Until about two hours later when we all tasted it again. Every soldier in the troop was as sick as a dog. Roy Stokes was terrified that his folks would find out about the cider and the fags. Vomiting into the hedgerows we hid the empty bottles, and with our football kit at the ready we left the Stokes' household before anyone else was awake.

Green-faced we arrived at the school desperately early for the ten o'clock kick-off.

'It'll wear off,' promised Keith Randle.

'Don't let anyone find out,' fretted Roy Stokes.

'I'll personally chin anyone who throws up in front of Shipley,' warned Mick Carpenter.

The school caretaker unlocked the changing room for us and we got outside and on to the pitch before Shipley arrived. Supposedly there to warm up we clustered in the goalmouth shivering and hugging ourselves. Keith Randle took a stab at a practice ball and promptly vomited over the penalty spot. At last the rest of the team arrived and Shipley flagged us over for a pre-match pep talk.

He eyed us strangely. Shipley had never seen us so subdued. 'I can see you're nervous, lads, but don't let it get to you. This is just one game like all the others. Now get out there and take no prisoners.'

It was a shambles. We had four good players. All the campers were wincing at every tackle, failing to chase, unable to strike the ball with force. Shipley, refereeing, shook his head in exasperation. It was a good thing Brent Croft were so utterly useless. Most of the ineffectual play took place around the centre circle. Then the inevitable happened just before half-time. A long ball came our way out of the ruck. A Brent Croft forward came chasing after it. Mick Carpenter stepped up to wallop the ball back again, but something stopped him in his tracks. Looking like a man who has just remembered leaving a gas tap running unlit, he froze, standing stock-still as their forward nipped by him and slapped the ball past me into the back of the net.

They went wild. They were delirious; punching the air and foaming at the mouth. I bent to pick the ball out of the net. I knew what had happened: Mick Carpenter had shat himself in mid-stride. He was already shuffling off to the changing rooms with as much dignity as he could muster. Shipley called after him, but getting no answer, he simply restarted the game.

'What the hell is the matter with you all?' Shipley wanted to know at half-time. We were so terrified of him finding out about the booze and fags no one dared hint that we were a team of invalids. 'And where have you been?' he demanded of Mick Carpenter when he came trotting back in dripping wet shorts rinsed out under a tap.

Mick looked up at him with those cloudless blue eyes. 'Toilet.'

The second half was hardly any better. A shot from a Brent Croft winger hit me slap in the belly and I instantly puked up, over their inside-right as it happened; Keith Randle spent most of the time languishing near the corner flag; Roy Stokes headed the ball and had to steady himself against the goal post for a moment or two; and Mick Carpenter trotted off to the changing rooms on two further occasions. Only two individual goals from little Jack Manning, whose mother had refused him permission to join the camping group, won us passage to the final round.

It was as I staggered off the pitch behind the others that a little dog snapped at my ankles, causing me to vomit freely again, narrowly missing a pair of highly polished, brown, adult shoes. I glanced from the dog to its leash to its owner. I knew that dog. I knew that cloth cap. The chief scout regarded me steadily, with eyes that were stormy black holes.

Shipley ranted in the dressing room, about how we'd have to do better in the final and how he was particularly disappointed with our performance. 'I don't know whether to tell you this, lads. But I went to particular trouble to get someone to come and watch you today. *Particular* trouble.'

We all looked at the floor, or at our muddy bootlaces.

We went on to win the shield, a narrow 2–0 victory over Limbrick Wood, and Coventry City won promotion to the Second Division, so I suppose everything worked out. What can I say? That if the chief scout had seen me play better I would have gone on to become a professional footballer? In which case I would by now be running a pub, which is what most ex-footballers seem to do.

All I know is that some small light faded after that season, even if I continued to be a devotee of the beautiful game. I stopped collecting autographs from men in urinals, and I quickly saw through Jimmy Hill's pop and crisps parties, even if, some thirty years later, I retain an abject and tiresome need to follow the mixed fortunes of Coventry City FC.

On balance, I believe it might have been better to have taken a tip from Bobby Moore.

Graham Joyce enjoys the occasional Sunday morning kick-about with a bunch of ex-offenders, kids with learning difficulties, and the chronically unskilled, known as the Victoria Park Strollers. The author of five novels – *Dreamside, Dark Sister, House of Lost Dreams, Requiem* and *The Tooth Fairy* – he teaches creative writing at Nottingham Trent University. Born in 1954 in Keresley, near Coventry, he now lives in Leicester.

Geoff Nicholson

The Visiting Side

If there was one thing more than any other that changed the complexion of the 2010 World Cup, it was the arrival on earth of a group of aliens from the distant planet Keya just six months before the start of the finals.

I was a jobbing journalist at the time and I'd been given the assignment of covering the World Cup. It was a job for which I had no great enthusiasm and I was having a couple of weeks' holiday in Cornwall to do some reading round the subject, and more importantly to steel myself for the task ahead. It was my luck, good or bad, I'm not sure which, that the aliens landed in Cornwall too, on a school football pitch a few miles outside Newquay, where I was staying.

I knew something was wrong straight away. The sudden presence of military hardware on the roads, in the sky, off the coast, suggested something serious was going on, but I had no idea what, so like any good journalist I stayed put, continued to read about the exploits of Pelé and Eusebio, and waited for someone to call a press conference.

You may well ask what I was doing reporting on the World Cup at all. Why was someone like me, short of stature, short of breath, infinitely lacking in match skills and the highly specialized vocabulary of football, why was I chosen by my paper to write about soccer's biggest prize? It's a good question and one I often asked myself. I regularly asked it of my editor too, and he said he needed someone who wasn't a sports buff, who knew nothing about soccer and would therefore have an oblique and unusual take on the sport. I gritted my teeth and said OK. Hell, I was supposed to be a professional, wasn't I?

It wasn't quite true to say that I knew nothing about football. The truth was that school had taught me more than I had ever wanted to know. I knew what football was all about. It was about standing in the cold and the rain, praying for the final whistle. It was about being the last person picked for every team. It was about mis-kicking the ball, slicing it and watching it go past your goalkeeper for an own goal. Then it was about being shouted at by the rest of the team. I'd heard the lot. I was called a wussie. I was called a big girl's blouse. It was regularly said that I couldn't control my own bollocks if they weren't screwed on.

Then there were the changing rooms and the showers, a final chance for the football stars of the school to flick you with a wet towel and make jokes about the size of your knob. Oh sure, it was character building. I learned a great deal about the sporting mind, about fair play and team spirit. I learned that it didn't matter whether you won or lost, so long as you had some poor bastard to blame, and usually that was me. So yes, my take on soccer was oblique, but I was sure I was not alone in this. I suspected there were millions like me. I thought this was going to be my audience, the people like me, the losers, the scorers of own goals.

So I did my research, read the histories and the record books, and got ready for the World Cup. I was planning to write some cynical, jaundiced pieces about the absurdity of grown men kicking a ball around a patch of grass and occasionally kissing each other, about the viciousness and stupidity of football fans and players, about the dangers of nationalism inherent in the World Cup, that sort of stuff. But then the Keyans arrived and the job changed out of all recognition.

I well remember our call to that first press conference. We made our way to a school assembly hall a couple of miles out of town. Security was phenomenally tight and there were many grey-suited men from the Ministry of Defence. We were ready for the worst – nuclear leakage, escaped germ warfare – but the men in the grey suits looked quite jaunty and one of them finally said he had some good news for the world. We had made contact with an alien life form, or rather they had made contact with us, and in a couple of minutes he would introduce us.

First they showed us the 'space ship', a thing that resembled nothing so much as a 1960s single-decker bus. It had a few futuristic touches, no wheels for example, and a series of wicked-looking fins, and it turned out to be made from materials unknown to science, but there was something very warm and unthreatening about aliens who travelled in such retro style.

Then we met the aliens. I don't know what we were all expecting – creatures with more than the usual number of arms, legs, eyes or heads – but a curtain was pulled back and a lone figure appeared, who looked a lot like Bobby Charlton. Not exactly like him, you understand, he was rather taller and with the stature of a serious body-builder, but the face was uncannily similar, and that too was reassuring. And then more and more aliens appeared on the stage, twenty-two in all, and they all looked awesomely similar, to Bobby Charlton and to each other. The only noticeable difference was that their skin was a kind of glossy, metallic green.

Of course there were people who said these guys were fakes, that they weren't aliens at all but the results of a sinister genetic programme, or maybe twenty-two Russians or Islamic fundamentalists who'd had plastic surgery to make them look acceptably English. Then, once they'd insinuated themselves into the British way of life they would no longer be the peace-loving aliens they were pretending to be, but would . . . well, it was never exactly clear what the specific horror was that they would perpetrate, but it was certainly going to be bad news.

And yet, it was clear to me and to the vast majority of people who saw them in the flesh, that these guys were the real thing. Despite their familiar faces, there was something so utterly alien, so completely other about them, that you simply had to believe they were from another planet. And I, for one, certainly believed them when they said they came in peace and wished us well.

We were surprised at the press conference to find that they spoke and understood English. They spoke it rather erratically, their vocabulary was small and they frequently fell into clichés. It was as though they'd learned their English by watching *Match of the Day*; and much later on they confirmed that this was precisely the case.

The Keyans tried hard to paint a picture of life on their planet, and they succeeded in portraying a place that resembled England in the nineteen fifties. It was a place of peace and prosperity. There was no violence, no crime, no poverty. They were big on family values and hard work, and they described courtship rituals that would have seemed tame by Doris Day's standards.

There were many who wanted to read some cosmic significance into the arrival of these aliens. Some people wanted to see them as gods and kept demanding a 'message' from them. The Keyans insisted that they had no message. They were not emissaries, not trained astronauts. They were not on any sort of mission. They were, they insisted, no more than tourists. They had got lost, strayed off the beaten space routes and had found themselves on earth. They were very happy to be here but they hadn't come to save us or warn us, or fulfil any of the other standard sci-fi plot devices.

There were those at the press conference who were immediately able to offer the aliens all sorts of earthly baubles, things like exclusive million-dollar newspaper deals, film deals, sponsorship contracts, book deals, their own chat show, the chance to perform in Vegas, but the aliens showed very little interest in any of this. They seemed reluctant to take anything from us. Surely, we men of earth said, there must be something you want, and the aliens looked embarrassed and sheepish and said, OK, if we really insisted, what they wanted above all else was to play in the 2010 World Cup finals.

It turned out there was no competitive sport on the planet Keya. They had some pretty tedious board games, and they occasionally indulged in variations of charades, but serious professional sport was unknown, and when a stray television signal showing an FA Cup Final had reached their planet it had been seized upon as something utterly exotic and compelling. They'd found a way of tuning in every week, and these twenty-two visitors from space had subsequently taught themselves to play soccer, and now they wanted to put themselves to the test.

Well, that caused quite a stir and the news conference ended in total disarray. The Keyans remained in hiding with the military and we all went back and wrote our stories. Next morning the sports pages were full of controversy. Alien planets were, by definition, not affiliated to FIFA, and some papers said they therefore could not possibly enter the World Cup. Less philo-sophically, others pointed out that the World Cup finals were fully organized and to add another team would cause administrative chaos. Nevertheless there was a groundswell of opinion that said we owed it to these plucky men from space to find a way of including them.

There was also the small problem of not knowing whether these guys could actually play football. In order to help their campaign for inclusion they started to play a series of exhibition matches against charity and celebrity elevens, and it soon became apparent that they could indeed play. Oh, not very expertly, of course, the sports reporters said; their ball control was patchy, their sense of tactics a little naïve. But even for their least-exciting matches they drew crowds of forty or fifty thousand spectators, and, when they drew 3–3 with a side of former Scottish internationals, the pressure for their inclusion became overwhelming.

It would be wrong to imply that all was completely sweetness and light for the aliens. Football is a game where supporters can hate each other simply because they come from the different parts of the same town. What price then the chances of hating a bunch of beings from another planet? The fans were not slow to express their sentiments. At Millwall they chanted, 'Fuck off back where you came from, you ugly green bastards,' and rather more wittily the Anfield Kop would sing operatic versions of the theme from the *Twilight Zone* every time a Keyan got the ball.

Others' suspicion was differently motivated. They said we shouldn't be playing ball with these guys at all. We didn't know them and we couldn't trust them and it was as simple as that. We should therefore treat them like any other group of illegal immigrants, that is either jail them or deport them. Maybe they had a few technological advantages over us, but they were still clearly inferior. If we started treating them like equals then before you knew it they'd be taking our jobs, stealing our women, moving in next door and bringing down house prices.

Even some of those who claimed, in theory, to be in favour of allowing the Keyans to play in the World Cup, said they wanted to be damn sure they knew what we were competing against. Maybe they had certain physical or physiological advantages over us that would make direct competition unfair. Perhaps they had giant lungs, or infinitely low pain thresholds. Maybe they were capable of teleportation or telekinesis, an ability to predict the future or the ability to read the thoughts of the opposition.

So the Keyans obligingly agreed to submit themselves to every test known to medical science: all kinds of rays and scans and probes, all kinds of psychological profiling. Various fluids and tissues were sampled. And at the end of all this, in a soundbite which has now become legendary, the official World Cup doctor said, 'They're the most human bunch of footballers I've ever come across.'

The only significant variation from human biology was the green pigment in the skin. Some spoilsports still said this might create an unfair advantage in that Keyan players might blend in with the grass and deceive opposing teams, but this was rightly regarded as insanity. And when the Keyans revealed their football strip, a mass of psychedelic tie-dye colours, not all of which you could be certain you'd ever seen before, you knew there was no way these guys were ever going to blend in with a football pitch.

For my part, as an avowed layman, I wrote a column in which I said there was no reason on earth or in the heavens why we shouldn't allow the Keyans to play in the World Cup. What were we so afraid of? I asked. Surely we weren't scared that these untutored guys from space were going to beat us? I got a certain amount of flack for that article, but it seemed I'd made an important point. The Keyans looked good but they didn't look too good. They looked like competitors but not remotely like world beaters. They weren't going to disgrace themselves, but neither were they going to disgrace anyone else. They looked like losers, and the World Cup needs losers. So, when some crummy little South American team was kicked out of the competition over allegations of match fixing and drugs, there was a gap in the fixtures and there could be no two ways about it, the Keyans were playing in the World Cup finals. Most of the world was pleased, and most sports commentators predicted a brave but early defeat.

Now, all the media agreed, it was time to get down to the real business of reporting the World Cup. The Keyans had been an amusing sideshow, a 'human'-interest story, but now came the real thing, the nitty gritty, the cut and thrust of what international sport was really all about. That was fine by me. I had become somewhat bored by the Keyans. For all their alienness and otherworldiness they were essentially a bunch of rather dull men. They were football players, for God's sake, as dumb and as inarticulate as any footballer on earth. They had nothing to say for themselves, and they didn't seem to be interested in anything that earth had to show. Offers came in from around the world, donating training facilities of unprecedented excellence, but they preferred to stay in Cornwall, conducting their training sessions at the Newquay school where they'd first landed.

Someone asked what they did for a good time, but the concept of 'good time' didn't seem to exist for them. All the Keyans did was train. They ran, they lifted weights, they tossed medicine balls. In fact they did it with such a humourless, measured obsessiveness that one newspaper, not mine, described them as 'Space Nerds'.

Geoff Nicholson

If I have become a sort of unofficial chronicler of the Keyans I owe it entirely to being in the right place at the right time: to being on holiday in Cornwall when they first landed, and then, more crucially, to being at the Dew Drop Inn in Stithians a few months later. I'd been sent to cover the training sessions of the Keyans, and having been bored to death I had retired to the pub for a long liquid session. I was not entirely alone, in fact I was in the company of a group of journalists, but they were sports journalists, and, as I have said, I'm not even remotely interested in sport. Consequently, after my companions had spent a couple of hours talking about great nil–nil draws of our time, I made my excuses and left.

As I stepped out of the pub I saw a battered white van parked in a dark corner of the car park, and there were three men sitting in it, passing a whisky bottle back and forth. The light wasn't good, but there really wasn't any doubting that these were three Keyans, breaking training for a night on the piss. That would have been interesting enough in itself, but it got even more interesting when a car swept into the car park and half a dozen Cornish lads, made violent and incomprehensible by scrumpy, staggered out. Having urinated and sworn at the world, they spotted the white van, saw the Bobby Charlton lookalikes inside and decided to have some primordial fun. They got the Keyans out of the van, verbally abused them, pushed them around a bit, and would no doubt have beaten them to a pulp given the chance.

But the chance didn't come. Without becoming angry or violent, without breaking into a sweat, without really having to move, one of the three Keyans, only one, adopted a sort of martial arts pose, and three seconds later the six scrumpy boys were laid out on the tarmac, bruised, bleeding, only intermittently conscious. I had never seen anything so fast, so ruthless, so efficient. It was over before it had started and the Keyans immediately got into their van and took off. I was left in no doubt about what I'd seen but it still seemed unbelievable.

And maybe that was why I didn't write the story. There were already countless tales circulating about the Keyans. Most of them were far more fanciful than the one I'd have written, but, even so, I didn't want to add to the mythology. Besides, if I'd been believed I'd only have got the guys into trouble, and at the time I had no desire to do that. I thought they deserved a break. It was surely significant that none of the six local lads went to the police or the newspapers, and I thought it was even more interesting that on the pitch, the Keyans had gained a great reputation for playing good, clean football and never ever retaliating.

About this time there came a backlash from certain political vested interests. A radical feminist group wanted to know why there were no women in the aliens' party. Humbly, one of the Keyans explained that was just the way it happened to be. They were on a lads' outing. They weren't claiming to be representative or even typical. Similarly, none of them was sexually aberrant or ethnically repressed, but they said sexual aberration and ethnic repression were unknown on their planet. It was accepted that the Keyans weren't actually lying, but those of a certain turn of mind said the boys were obviously dupes of an all-powerful regime that hid such matters from their general population.

It was a new twist on the 'problem' of the Keyans, but by then the World Cup had started and I soon found myself reporting on all the Keyans' games. It was all new to me but I like to think I soon got the hang of it. In the early games, I found myself writing the Keyans had no shortage of commitment but they often looked flat-footed and lacking that extra yard of pace. They scored some blinding goals, but they let in just as many soft ones. Then, in their final group matches, they began to show some authority. It was, against Somalia I seem to remember saying, good end-to-end stuff, and the Keyan forwards found the ability to take on defenders and go past them. In this match, and the one that followed against Portugal, they hit a rich seam of goal-scoring form and finished third in their group. They had earned a place in the last sixteen and the right to play Finland. The Scandinavians, it must be admitted, gave a lacklustre performance and never looked much like scoring. They left oceans of room on the flank and the Keyan centre-forward nodded in a late, floating cross that settled the match.

The Keyans had won and won with style. They played a brand of football that was all their own. They played with heart and bottle. There was no cynicism in their performances, no dreary so-called professionalism. When they got a one-goal lead they refused to shut the game down the way a more experienced and ruthless side would have.

After that, the quarter-final against Fiji was something of a disappointment. The Fijians played hard, uncultured football and nearly knocked the Keyans out of their stride. It was a scrappy, disjointed match and the Keyans only won thanks to a disputed penalty. However, all was forgiven come the semi-final against Serbia, which was a true classic, I wrote. The Keyans were inspired and played some of the most creative football of the tournament. Their work rate was high, they tackled hard, they attacked and counter-attacked. Their defence was often stretched but it never broke, and at the end of ninety minutes they were worthy 2–1 winners. Improbably, unbelievably, a team from another planet was in the Final of the World Cup, pitted against the might of Brazil. (Some things never change.)

The Keyans had been underdogs in every game they'd played, and Brazil were certainly favourites to win the Final, but it would have been a brave and a foolish man who'd have written off the aliens. Alas, as the world knows, it was not to be. The Keyans played good open football but they couldn't match the fire and deft skills of the Brazilians. It was as though they had shot their bolt in the semi-final and had exhausted themselves. They lost 2–0 in a Final that somehow failed to ignite, and afterwards, as the Brazilians did a lap of honour round the stadium, showing off the World Cup, there was something apologetic in their manner, as though they were sorry to have brought the Keyans' dreams to an end. For their part the Keyans were as cheerful and as sporting in defeat as they had been in victory, and the whole world loved them.

The Keyans finally and indisputably had the world at their feet. And you could easily argue that they were in a stronger position as gallant losers than they would have been as outright winners. They could undoubtedly have ruled the world, whether as sporting heroes, politicians, media stars, or figureheads for big business. It was then that the Keyans announced that they wanted to go home.

I for one thought their sense of timing was good. As a first encounter with alien life forms it had gone surprisingly well. The people of earth had acquitted themselves pretty well. None of the aliens had been mugged or shot or raped or blown up. I thought the Keyans had seen the best of us and were right to quit while they were ahead.

There were some crude attempts at coercion and emotional blackmail to make them stay, but in the end there was nothing anyone could do. The Keyans had every right to go home, and we as good hosts had to

speed them on their way. They said, more or less faceti-
ously, that they'd be back in four years' time.

And then a very odd thing happened: the Keyans
disappeared completely. You might think it odd that
twenty-two green men from outer space could slip so
completely from sight, but they did. There was to be
no farewell press conference, no final message and
bitter-sweet goodbyes. Months passed and, despite
major efforts by some so-called investigative journalists,
no trace was found. They had gone without trace, and
again I thought that way of doing things made a lot of
sense and had a lot of class.

That's when I found myself in the right place for the
third occasion. Having escaped the yoke of the World
Cup I was sent to Dover to report on a dock strike.
Almost as soon as I got there the dispute ended, but I
had no urge to hurry back and I spent the afternoon
driving along the coast sightseeing. And that was when
I rediscovered the Keyans.

They were in a campsite not far from Gravesend. It
was not one of the great beauty spots. There were a few
wrecked cars and abandoned caravans, and a passerby
might have thought this was just the base for a bunch
of impoverished travellers. However, the Keyans were
not doing any travelling. In fact they were working on
repairing their bus-like space ship. It seemed to have
been largely dismantled and they were each tinkering
with different bits of the mechanism. From the amount
of head-scratching and the lack of activity it was obvious
that little or no progress was being made. Finally one
of them said, 'This thing's fucked. Let's have a game
of football.'

The others needed no convincing. They arranged
themselves into two *ad hoc* elevens and began to play.
I thought it would be amusing to watch the World Cup
Finalists having a kick-about on a campsite, but I soon

realized it was far more than that. As I watched, I became increasingly amazed and disturbed.

Both these knock-about teams looked a hundred times better than the one that had so narrowly lost the World Cup. They started to make eighty-yard passes with pinpoint accuracy. They took throw-ins that sailed three-quarters of the length of the pitch. Their ball control was awesome, and when they got inside the eighteen-yard box they never did anything so prosaic as shoot for goal, they were only interested in scoring with scissor kicks and clever, clever back heelers. If two players jumped for a cross they leapt some fifteen or twenty feet in the air. Meanwhile the goalkeepers performed athletic saves and dives that defied gravity and belief.

And as they played, they talked and laughed, still in English I was pleased to hear, and I jotted down some of their comments in my reporter's notebook.

'Wales, what a bunch of wussies.'

'Finland, what a lot of big girls' blouses.'

'Brazil, they couldn't control their bollocks if they weren't screwed on.'

They were mocking the earth, and especially they were mocking our footballing talents, which they found pathetic and inept. In other circumstances I would have been happy to join in the mockery but it was different this time. I had been right all along. They were a bunch of crude, insensitive jocks, the kind I'd had a bellyful of at school.

Then a far more important realization came to me. These guys had been CHEATING all through the World Cup. Oh, they hadn't been breaking the rules of football on the pitch, but they'd been deceiving their opponents and the game's officials and, of course, the fans. Watching them play now it was obvious that they could have won the World Cup without breaking into a sweat, but they'd chosen not to. They'd chosen not to try. They'd just been toying with us, and clearly they'd only lost the Final because they'd wanted to. They'd thrown the match believing, perhaps rightly enough, that the world is full of people who prefer gallant defeat to effortless victory.

I left the campsite in a hurry, rang my editor and told him the situation, and by the time I got back to the office it was full of Cabinet Ministers and military top brass who listened to my story with great interest. Most of them said they'd been expecting something similar all along.

'If they'd cheat over something like football,' said some five-star general, 'what other forms of cheating might they be capable of. I suggest we don't wait to find out.'

And they didn't. Later that same day Nato forces surrounded the Keyans' hideout and hit them with all the weaponry at their disposal. It was a walkover, a massacre. The Keyans never knew what hit them and had no chance to fight back. The amount of ordnance used was enough to blow away whole armies of Keyans. It wasn't very sporting, perhaps, but when you come down to the things that really matter, like global security, then fair play doesn't really come into it.

Born in Sheffield and educated at the universities of Cambridge and Essex, Geoff Nicholson has published several novels, including *What We Did on Our Holidays*, *The Knot Garden*, *Still Life With Volkswagens*, *Hunters and Gatherers* and, most recently, *Footsucker*.

Geoff Dyer

Passage Thiéré

During the lunch-hour we played football in the play-ground at Passage Thiéré. We took our lunch late and the playground was never crowded. If other guys were around – the Algerians from the workshop on the corner always wanted to play but it was difficult for them to get away for any length of time – we played together, four- or five-a-side. If it was just the five of us from the warehouse we volleyed and headed the ball back and forth, making sure that the ball did not touch the ground, embroidering this basic task, whenever possible, with displays of individual skill: flicking the ball from foot to foot and on to a thigh before heading it to the next person; bringing the ball under control and restoring the flow of play following a miskick. We kept count of how many passes and headers we could string together without letting the ball touch the ground. Sometimes we settled into a rhythm that seemed likely to continue indefinitely until one of us fluffed a simple kick and we were back to square one and had to begin the count again. Alternatively one of us went in goal while the others crossed and headed or let fly with palm-stinging shots.

These bouts of lunch-time football made going to work something to look forward to rather than dread. After playing, especially if the weather was fine, we were reluctant to return to the warehouse, and sat against the graffiti-mottled wall, the sun dazzling our eyes, gulping

down water and chewing mouthfuls of bread and tomato, the minutes ticking by until, begrudgingly, like
troops returning to the front, we tramped back up Rue
de Lyon to work.

There was another incentive for playing: the women
who each day passed by, carrying books, talking or pushing bicycles. They were on their way back to offices or
to lectures at the university after their lunch-break, or
just strolling, eating ice cream when it was hot. Men
walked by too, but that was just an accident whereas
the women, we liked to think, came by deliberately. Just
a slight preference for this route back from the café
rather than another one, a simple suggestion by one
of a group of friends – 'Let's walk past the playground
at Thiéré' – which was always approved by the others.
No more than that. And even if it was not the consequence of any kind of preference, even if it was just a
shortcut that extended their lunch-break by five
minutes, we liked to think that they came by primarily
because of us. Certainly there were other places we
could have played football; even if they didn't come by
because of us, *we* played there because of them.

Luke noticed one woman in particular. She was tall
with a mass of black hair that fell below her shoulders.
One day, when he was over that side of the yard retrieving the ball, he smiled 'Hi', and she smiled back briefly
before walking on. Contained in that look there was
the seed of another meeting of eyes when, weeks later,
undressing each other for the first time, their eyes
flicked open at exactly the same moment. Luke watched
her walk away, wondering if she would look back. Her
legs were tanned, she was wearing tennis shoes, there
was something floaty about the way she walked, a light-
ness: a special quality which meant that if you were
walking behind her you could tell without even seeing
her face, just by her hair and the way she walked, that

she was beautiful. Luke watched her walk away. She didn't look back.

As we headed back to work, Luke said that the next time she came by we should kick the ball to that side of the playground so that he could talk to her. Thereafter, whenever we were playing and she walked past, the rest of us gestured to Luke to let him know she was there but kept passing the ball in the other direction, luring him away from her. Either that or we would eliminate him from the game completely, refusing to pass to him as he inched his way towards her side of the playground. Then, when she had walked past, *then* we would kick the ball over that way – 'Come on, Luke, now's your chance' – leaving him to retrieve the ball and gaze after her retreating form.

One day, though, after we had got Luke running round like a dog, Jean relented and floated an inch-perfect ball across the yard, landing a metre or two in front of her so that Luke could catch her eye, smile, kick the ball back and wait for her to draw near. When I next looked over he was speaking to her, hanging on to the wire diamonds. We only granted him a few seconds of repose before booting the ball over his way and shouting to him to kick it back, making her conscious of the way we were all standing around, watching and waiting while Luke trotted after the ball and curled it back to us. We let them have a couple of peaceful minutes and then Daniel blasted the ball over that way again, smacking it into the wire a couple of feet from her head like a cannonball. She jumped, Luke turned round and saw us all laughing like yobs while he was obviously trying to impress on her that he was not devoid of sensitivity and actually spent a great deal of time reading, maybe even dropping a hint that he was not without literary aspirations himself. And at the same time that he was annoyed about us louting up his chances you could see he also enjoyed it, the way that we imparted a hint of the ghetto to his wooing.

There was no sign of Lazare, the warehouse manager, when we got back to work, and so we sat with our feet up on the packing tables, eating sandwiches, gasping after sips of Orangina, crunching chips.

'Did you see Luke, after all that running around, legs buckling—'

'Breathing hard, unable to speak—'

'Coughing up blood – "Just let me get my breath back, you see I'm not like the others" – then BAM! the ball smacks into the fence about an inch from her face.'

'What she say, Luke?' Matthias asked. 'What she is like?'

'She's nice.'

'What is her name?'

'Nadine.'

'Oh Nadine! Horny name. And what does she do, horny Nadine?' Luke shook his head. Matthias belched and tossed his empty can, clattering into the bin. 'So what did you do, Luke?' I said.

'Ask her if she wanted to have a kick around?'

We would happily have spent the whole afternoon like that, grilling Luke about his attempted courtship, but ten minutes later we heard Lazare's decrepit Renault struggling through the gate and all leapt to our feet. By the time he walked in we were hard at it, as if we had been so busy packing orders that there had scarcely been time to grab a sandwich.

A few days later, when Nadine next passed by the playground, we decided to let Luke go over and talk quietly, without the ball thudding into the fence, like we were on our best behaviour. She was wearing a dress and a mauve cardigan so that we could not see her arms, which one day soon would be around his shoulders as he kissed her, which one day he would grip hard in his fists, shaking her, leaving ugly bruises on the same arms which one day, years later, would be around his neck again as he kissed her for the last time and left. I can still see them over there, separated by the fence, wondering what each other was like. She was holding some books in front of her. The sun flashed out from a cloud, the wire fence threw angles of shadow over her face. She held up a book for him to see and he bent towards her and conceded that he had never read Schopenhauer or Merleau-Ponty or whoever it was she was reading. Not that it mattered: the important thing about that book was that it served as an intermediary, a bridge between them. Luke watched her looking at him through the fence, sweat dripping from his hair, breathing hard. His sleeves were pushed up over his elbows, the veins stood out in his forearms. Strands of her hair breezed free. She fingered her hair back into place, over her ear, and he noticed her hands, her woman's hands holding the large book of philosophy.

They were running out of things to say. Luke asked if she would like to meet up sometime, if . . . His voice trailed off, he looked to the floor, at the sun-catching grit, making it as easy as possible for her to say, 'Well, that's difficult.' When he looked up again he saw her pausing, weighing things up, knowing the hurt a man has the power to inflict on you. But that pause was already giving way to a smile of assent.

She smiled at him and he looked into her eyes, which at that moment held all the promise of happiness the world can ever offer. He suggested Monday, which was no good for her.

'Wednesday, maybe . . .'

'Wednesday I have a dance class.'

'Oh . . .'

'I could meet you afterwards.'

'OK.'

'At nine?'

'Yes. Where is your class?'

'It's in Parmentier.'

'I could meet you in the Petit Centre. Do you know that?'

'Yes.' In the road a delivery truck was holding up traffic. Cars began honking. 'I should be going,' she said.

'They're not honking at you,' Luke said.

She smiled, made as if to leave. As she was going, he said, 'You will come, won't you?'

'Yes.'

Luke turned away from her and started walking back. Jean floated up the ball for him to volley, both feet off the ground, with all the force of his happiness, into the top corner of the segment of fence we called a goal.

'And the crowd go wild!' shouted Daniel.

I don't think Luke was ever happier than in the time that we spent working at the warehouse, playing football in the playground. And those first moments that he spent speaking with Nadine, making that first tentative arrangement, those were at the core, the epicentre of his happiness. In the months to come, as the weather improved and the days got longer, we played football not only at lunch but after work as well. Luke would play for as long as possible, leaving it until the last moment to run to meet Nadine.

A few weeks later I went with them to a party where I met Véronique, a friend of Nadine's. We began seeing each other and soon a symmetrical pattern was set that remained unchanged for many months. The four of us spent the evenings cooking dinner at Nadine's apart-ment, or getting high on the tiny balcony of my apart-ment with the view all the way down Rue de la Roquette, or just hanging out at the Petit Centre, the bar on Rue Moret that is probably not there now. The days got longer but they were never long enough to contain all the happiness we needed to cram into them. How different to now, when we have learned to measure out our happiness, distributing it evenly throughout the week so that there is enough to go round even though happiness is, precisely, an abundance, an overflowing, and even to think about rationing it is to settle for contentment – which anyone who has known real happiness rejects instinctively as the form despair takes in order to render itself bearable.

I am sounding like Luke now! Certainly if it had been possible to concentrate his life into one moment, when everything was poised between what had been and what was to come, when he was still nourished by his longings and not, as happened, defeated by them, it would have been during those months which can, in turn, be condensed into a single image of five young men playing football in the playground, one of them rushing over to talk to a woman with long black hair who is walking by. I said 'nourished by his longings' but that is misleading, and it is the image of us playing football in the playground that has made me realize why. The idyllic quality of those months came from the way that longing played no part in them; longing made itself felt only in the moment it became an act; only later, in retrospect, could you see the trail of desire leading up to the action that generated it, that was generated by it.

I think I understand now what happened to Luke, understand how, long after the age when *he* should have understood it, he was still aching after a possible future, some yet-to-be achieved ideal, some crowning moment of happiness; not realizing until much later – and this, I think, is what was so hard for him – that, far from being an intimation of the future, such a moment was actually a part of his past, was already a memory.

Geoff Dyer

Geoff Dyer's published works include the novels *The Colour of Memory* and *The Search*; *Ways of Telling*, a critical study of the work of John Berger; *The Missing of the Somme*, about the First World War; and *But Beautiful: A Book About Jazz*, which won a Somerset Maugham prize.

Mark Timlin

Wonder Boy

'Football is a game of two halves, Nick. You don't mind me calling you Nick, do you?'

'I don't mind,' I replied. I'd just finished telling him I didn't know much about the game. But I knew *that* much. I guessed we were starting with basics. Or maybe he always talked in seventies football commentator speak. He being the chairman of my local south London football team. A team that until recently had fallen upon hard times. Relegation from the Premier League to the First Division, then down to the Second, until almost single-handedly a young man had saved their bacon. Promotion back to the First Division, then the Premier League, was followed last season by victory in the FA Cup.

The chairman and I were sitting in his fancy office overlooking the pitch. He was behind a big, empty desk. I was on the other side, comfortable in a padded chair with a glass of Scotch in my hand.

'And it's not over till it's over,' he added.

Seventies football commentator speak I decided. 'Or the fat lady sings,' I ventured, trying to be one of the lads.

'That's American football,' he explained. 'Not that there's not a few fat ladies round here, because there are. But that's not why we're here. We're here because of Stan.'

The very bloke I was talking about. Stanley 'Stan the Man' MacNess. A nineteen-year-old superstar who'd joined the club just fifteen months before and had transformed the team from losers to winners, and picked up four or five England caps in the process.

'You must've heard of him,' said the chairman.

'I've heard of him,' I said.

'Every bugger's heard of him.'

The chairman was probably right. And not just about his skill on the field. Because of his antics, Stan had become a legend in the world of soccer. A legend as a boozer, dope head and womanizer, with the occasional foray into mild forms of crime like drunken driving, leaving the scene of an accident and, more seriously, several charges of causing an affray and ABH. None of the latter had come to anything. These days palms can be greased with ease when a Premier League football club is doing the greasing.

He was also apparently the most gifted footballer since George Best. Possibly the most gifted ever.

'He's the finest thing to happen to football for years,' the chairman went on. 'And he saved our bloody bacon last year.'

'So what's the problem?' I asked.

'He's in trouble again,' said the chairman.

'What kind of trouble?'

'Woman trouble. Some bird says he's got her in the club and her three older brothers reckon they're going to break his legs unless he makes an honest woman of her.'

'Not good.'

'Not for a professional footballer.'

'So buy them off.'

'They won't have it and nor will he. He says he never did the business with her, and it's a con.'

'Is it?'

'Don't fucking ask me.'

'Can't you send him away for a bit, till it all dies down?'

'Impossible. It's no secret he's up for transfer to United. Ten million quid we're getting for him. The biggest transfer fee in British soccer history. The first eight-figure transfer ever. I've got the papers here.' He patted his desk. 'They're going to be signed on Saturday after the match. He has to play.'

'But why are you selling him if he saved the club?'

'Simple. When we were doing badly we borrowed a lot of money to try and make a comeback. A *lot* of money. The interest alone is crippling. We need the cash to get ourselves straight. It's incredible. I spent a bloody fortune on dead legs who ponced around the park like hairdressers, and I found Stan out the back cleaning boots for them. And not one of them was good enough to lick his.' He shook his head in amazement. 'A famous man once said that football is not a matter of life and death, it's more important than that. So what we have here is a big problem, Nick. Come Saturday evening, with all the signatures on the transfer papers, we can send him up north out of the way. And to tell you the truth, after that I don't give a shit what happens to him. They can break his sodding legs and his arms once he's off our payroll.' I imagined that although he was a football genius, Stan was the reason that the chairman was losing his hair fast, and that he'd be happier with the cash the boy was going to generate. 'After that he's some other poor sod's problem. But till then we need to keep him in one piece. It's Thursday now, so that's only two nights and a day. You get him here early on Saturday and he'll be fine with us. Till then, Christ knows what kind of trouble he could get into.'

'Not so fast,' I said. 'I'm on my own. Why not bring in a big security firm, with people on shifts? That way you'll be sure he's safe.'

'He won't have it. Says it cramps his style. But he's heard of you. Read about you in the papers. You're local, like him, and he wants to meet you. It's you or no one. And frankly I'd rather it was you. Two nights and a day. And when the papers are signed you get a cheque for three grand. I can't let him stay at his flat because of these threats, so I've booked you both into a suite at the Gatwick International Hotel by the airport. It's out of the way, but you can be there in half an hour ... sooner, the way he drives.'

'I'm not sleeping with him,' I said.

'A suite with two bedrooms,' the chairman said dryly.

'Well, if I'm the only option . . .'

'You are.'

And I could do with the cash, I thought. 'OK,' I said. 'It's a deal.'

'Starting now. Have you got a car with you?'

'Yeah. It's in the car park.'

'What is it?'

'A beaten-up silver Beemer.'

'Give me the keys. I'll get it put in the players' car park, out of the way. You'll be driving with Stan tonight, God help you.'

'I don't have a clean shirt or anything.'

'There're shops at the hotel. It's five star. Charge anything you need to the room. We'll pick up the tab. Just look after the boy.'

'I'll do my best.'

'He's in the Green Room waiting for you. I'll show you the way.'

And he did.

The Green Room was painted red and blue, the club's colours. But who said that anyone ever had to be totally literal.

Stan the Man was sitting on a long sofa eating a Big Mac and sucking on a shake. 'Stan,' said the chairman.

'This is Nick Sharman. Nick Sharman, Stan MacNess.'

Stan got up, dumped the remains of his late lunch into a bin, and came over, mitten extended. 'Great, man,' he said as we shook. 'I've seen your picture in the papers.'

'I've seen yours too,' I said. 'Good to meet you.'

'Are we gonna have a good time tonight. A right laugh.'

'An early night, Stan, I think,' said the chairman warily. 'Big match on Saturday.'

'Piece of piss, Den,' said Stan in reply. 'Piece of piss, mate. Anyway, there's always tomorrow to recover.'

Standing up, Stan was smaller than you'd've guessed from the TV or news photographs. Thin and wiry, with long, floppy brown hair, he was amazingly young, and dressed in a suit that screamed top-of-the-range Bond Street, with a button-down shirt and tiny black shoes to protect his ten-million-pound feet. He looked exactly like the guitarist in Oasis who my daughter is apparently in love with, plays their records all day at home, and made me promise to watch on *Top Of The Pops*.

The chairman sighed. 'Right, you know where you're going. Any problems call me on my mobile night or day.' He handed me a pasteboard card with an 0831 number printed on it. 'Stan, you're excused training tomorrow, but be here for the tactics meeting, Saturday at ten. Nick, you're looking after a valuable boy. Make sure he comes to no harm.' And with that he left me and Stan MacNess to get acquainted.

'Fancy a night up west?' said Stan as soon as the door had closed behind the chairman.

'I think not, Stan,' I said. 'Too dangerous. Too much temptation. How about going to the hotel, a spot of dinner and *EastEnders*?'

'Fuck's sake. Do me a favour, willya. I always watch the omnibus on Sunday.'

I tried to hide a smile. 'All right. No *EastEnders*. But we go to the hotel, OK. I'm trying to earn out of this, and you can do me a favour.'

Stan was a south London boy and I hoped that the reference to earning would bring out the best in him, and it did.

'OK,' he said. 'The hotel it is. But I tell you one thing, Nick. Since I got me picture in the papers I can start a party going anywhere. And I reckon a hotel's as good a place as any. Specially when we can charge everything to the old firm.'

We left the Green Room and he led me down a set of corridors and out into the players' car park. One car dominated the lot, and it wasn't my old BMW. Parked in one corner like a great white shark in a lake full of minnows was a Greenwood G350SC Chevrolet Corvette. Only this great white was painted pillar-box red, and even standing still it looked like it was going at a hundred miles an hour.

'Fucking hell,' I said. 'Is that what I think it is?'

'Depends what you think it is,' said Stan proudly.

'A Greenwood,' I replied.

'Yeah. How did you know that?'

'Saw one in a magazine a while back and fell in love. Where the hell did you get it?'

'A sweetener from United. Right colours, see. My old man always wanted a Yank. He died a couple of years back, poor old sod. Never saw me play except for the school. This is my way of remembering him.'

'What about insurance?' I asked as I walked round the motor, admiring its lines.

'Fuck knows. The club pays that too. Something tells me, with my record, it would be in five figures.'

'And they trust you with it? With your record and all.'

'If they want me, the car comes as part of the package.

I think the way they figure it I'll lose my licence soon anyway. I've got nine points now. Three more and it's goodbye Corvette for a bit. But shit. Let's enjoy it while we've got it.'

He worked the alarm and door locks from the gizmo on his key ring and we climbed aboard. What a fucking motor. I won't bore you any more, but just let me say it was the dog's bollocks and then some.

He started it up with a roar like a randy lion who's just walked into a lion's knocking shop, snicked the lever into first, dropped out the clutch and the motor took off with a scream of rubber and a fishtail across the tarmac. Then he had to slam on the brakes, which took another month's rubber off the tyres, in order to stop by the barrier, work the machine with the card on the dash and, before the barrier was an inch higher, took off again across the visitors' car park and out into the street where he neither looked left nor right before doing the turn.

'Nice,' I said. 'Or at least it is when the G-Force stops.'

'Good motor or what? Nought to sixty in three point seven seconds.'

'Yeah, but do you have to do it *every* time?'

He laughed out loud at that and overtook a bus on a blind bend. I closed my eyes.

When I opened them again I said, 'Tell me about this bird.'

'Linda Homan. I thought she was all right, but she's just a bitch like the rest of them.'

'It's not your baby?'

'Is it fuck. Listen, Nick, I gotta bit of a confession to make. All the old bollocks you read about in the papers is just that. Bollocks. If all the stories you read about five days in a love nest with page-three girl Carol was true I'd be dead by now. And the drugs and boozin'. I own up I do get up to some larkins, but fuck me, any tart with big knockers or some scumbag who once sold me an eighth of dope can use my name to get a few quid out of the papers, and they print it like it was gospel.'

'Sue 'em,' I said.

'Do you think I want to waste my time and money sitting in court all day for the next ten years? Screw 'em. It goes with the territory. The papers think I'm right stupid. But I ain't. I ain't trying to be flash with you, but do you know how much I earn?'

I shook my head.

'Right now, about twelve grand a week. A sodding *week*. My old man never made that much any year. And in the end he was on the sick and copped about fifty nicker a week. He was a good bloke. But I watched the poor fucker die in front of my eyes. Then I went on a YTS to the club, doing all the shitty work they could throw my way. I got a game on the first Friday afternoon and all that changed sharpish. I was in the juniors that Saturday, reserves midweek, and first team the next Saturday. Now I'm on a ten-million-quid transfer. I get a tenth of that, plus a signing-on fee and first-team bonuses and winning bonuses and fuck knows what else bonuses. I'm a rich boy, and if I spent like a sailor on his first night's leave till it killed me, I couldn't spend it all. But I don't. Do you know what paper I read every day?'

I shook my head again.

'In the glove box.'

I opened it. Inside was the familiar pink newsprint of the *Financial Times*.

'That's my paper,' he said. 'I ain't no mug. I've invested a lot. Good investments. Blue chip. If this only lasts another year I'll never need do any work again if I live to be ninety. If it lasts another ten, then I'm going to be in that list of the richest people in the country before long. But I don't take the fucking *Daily Sport* into the khazi with me to be one of the lads. I ain't one of the lads. I am the lad.'

He shut up then and we shot through Croydon on to the A23, then the motorway, and we were drawing up outside the Gatwick International Hotel only twenty-something minutes after we'd left the stadium. The chairman had been right.

We checked in, and the girl behind the reception desk got all flustered when she realized the identity of one of her guests. We'd been booked in as Mr Smith and Mr Jones, so the whole process took about fifteen minutes longer than it should have. But eventually we found ourselves in the penthouse suite with a tip-top view of the main runway at Gatwick, two bedrooms with *en suite* bathrooms, a sitting room, a basket of fruit, a big bouquet of flowers and two bottles of champagne, which Stan dived straight into, courtesy of the management.

'Why don't you pay Linda Homan off? Get her off your back,' I asked.

'I ain't payin' nothin', or letting anyone else pay for me. They're taking the piss. Listen. I met her at the ground. The whole family follows the team. She seemed nice. I asked her out, but her brothers, Johnny, Terry and Barry never let us alone. I never had a chance to give her a goodnight kiss, let alone put her in the family way. In the end I had to knock it on the head. She understood. She was as pissed off with them as I was. But I've got a reputation. And you know what that's like.'

I certainly did. 'OK, mate,' I said. 'So what's the plan?'

'Bit of nosebag,' he said, 'then a booze. Whaddya say?'

'Sounds all right to me, Stan.'

'You gonna change?'

'Got nothing to change into, mate. I need a shirt for tomorrow, a toothbrush and some shaving gear. You do the business, I'll go to the shop and meet you back here.'

Which is precisely what happened, and I returned within twenty minutes with a mid-blue Oxford cotton button-down shirt, a pair of boxer shorts, a pair of cotton/wool mix socks, a razor, foam, toothbrush and paste, all courtesy of the old firm, as Stan would have it.

When I got back Stan had destroyed the first bottle of bubbly, showered and changed into tight black leather jeans, boots and a big white shirt with frills down the front. He looked more like a pop star than ever.

'Poofy, or what?' he said. 'Ambiguous. Gets the birds at it.'

There was definitely more to this boy than met the eye.

We went down to the cocktail bar, which at that hour contained only one solitary drinker at the bar and what looked like the remains of a sales conference sitting round one of the large round tables at the back. Three blokes in identical grey suits, and two blondes who could have been sisters, in navy blue suits with short skirts. One had a white blouse, the other pale blue. They clocked us when we came in and obviously recognized Stan.

We went up to the bar, where the barman recognized him too and added more than the usual amount of hard liquor to the pair of brightly coloured cocktails that Stan insisted on ordering. 'Where's the action?' he said to the barman when our drinks were safely in front of us.

'This is it.'

'Gets a bit lively later?'

'Could do.'

'It fucking better.'

We drank our drinks and went into the restaurant.

The food was OK. Usual stuff. Steaks with all the trimmings. Stan looked happy as a couple of bottles of fifty-nicker red wine went down with our meals, followed by coffee and several brandies. And, early as it was, I could feel myself beginning to lighten up. Not a good sign. Could lead to mayhem later, but as that was what my charge obviously wanted, so be it.

After we'd eaten we went back into the bar, which was a little fuller. The party we'd seen earlier were still at their table, but now, like us, were a little the worse for wear. Stan and I went up to the counter, and he insisted on another round of brandies. As we were waiting one of the blondes came up beside us to order some drinks. Stan gave her a big smile and she smiled back.

'How do?' he said.

'Fine,' she replied. 'Aren't you—?'

'Who?'

'Stan MacNess, the footballer. Jim says you are.'

'Who's Jim?'

She turned her head towards her friends, who were watching her.

'He's over there, from my office.'

'Your boyfriend?'

'God no. He's from marketing.'

'Is that good?'

She made a face.

'Have a drink,' said Stan.

'I'm with them.'

'Get them over. We'll all have a drink.'

'I'll ask them.'

She went back over to the table and said something. They all looked at each other, came to some agreement, then stood up and came over. 'Hello,' said Stan. 'I'm

Stan. This is my mate Nick. We're up for a good time. Whaddya say?'

They all seemed to be up for it, especially when Stan called for a couple of bottles of good champagne, and I realized that somehow or other there were going to be tears before bedtime.

And I was right.

You see Jim fancied Trisha. That was the name of the girl we'd spoken to at the bar. The other blonde was called Gail. Then there was Jim, Martin and Peter. I'd been right. All five of them had been down for some kind of conference and were going back the next day. And Trisha fancied Stan. She was the younger of the two women by about ten years, and I reckoned Gail was no more than thirty.

Now Jim not only fancied Trisha, but he resented her fancying Stan, he was well on the way to being seriously drunk, and thought he was a football expert.

Especially on how overpaid professional footballers were.

I thought his attitude was crass to say the least, especially as he managed to shift at least thirty nicker's worth of Stan's, or rather the old firm's, champagne during the next hour.

And the more champagne he drank, the more lippy he got, and you could tell the other four were well pissed off, but not as pissed off as Stan.

He was trying to chat-up Trisha, and old Gail was getting to look better and better to me with every glass, until Jim went too far.

He started on about all the old football stars like Matthews, Best, Greaves and Venables, etc., etc., etc., and how the footballers of the nineties wouldn't have a chance against them, until Stan looked away from Trisha's limpid eyes, took a coin from his pocket and tossed it into Jim's lap.

'What's that for?' he asked.

'It's ten pence,' said Stan. 'Why don't you give someone a call who might give a shit?'

'What do you mean?' said Jim.

'I mean I wish you'd shut up and fuck off,' said Stan.
'And stay fucked off.' And he went back to talking to
Trisha.

So Jim gets up, grabs a champagne bottle by the neck,
and is about to commit serious mayhem to ten million
quid's worth of footballer, when I lean forward, duck
under his arm, grab his bollocks in my right hand and
twist and squeeze them so tightly that he screams, drops
the bottle, which bounces off my back, and he hits the
Wilton, doubled up in pain.

'I'd've sorted him,' said Stan from his seat.

'Sure you would,' I said. 'But it's my job.'

After that things got a bit fraught, with Jim threatening to call the police, which only the intervention of
the barman, Trisha, Gail and a bunch of other patrons
of the bar who'd seen the whole incident, prevented.
Even so, Martin and Pete weren't so friendly after that,
and only the fact that they thought we might be a bit
dangerous prevented a punch-up big time.

Eventually, they helped Jim off to his room, and as
they left, Martin said to the women, 'You coming?'

Trisha would have none of it. All the stardom and
violence and booze had obviously got her juices flowing,
and she wanted to stay.

'I'll stay with her,' said Gail, which was exactly what
I wanted her to say.

All the stardom and violence and booze had got my
juices working too.

After they'd gone Stan suggested we'd all be more
comfortable in our suite and we all agreed.

Once up there we raided the cornucopia that was
the mini bar, and after that one thing led to another,

which I won't elaborate on here, but concluded with Trisha ending up in Stan's bedroom and Gail in mine.

Oh *l'amour*.

But it's been my experience that just when you think things are going well, you really should start looking out for razor blades in your scrambled eggs, and the shit really hit the fan on Friday morning.

I can never sleep in strange beds, so I woke up early with a mouth like an unwashed jockstrap, and a head that felt as if it had been run over by a bus. I left Gail where she was, snoring like a train, called for coffee from room service then hit the shower and was drying myself when the waiter brought it and the papers that Stan and I had ordered the previous evening. *Financial Times* for him, *Telegraph* for me. Very middle class. The geezer who brought the tray gave me a funny look but I took no notice as I swallowed the first cup whole.

Both our mobile phones were sitting on the coffee table together, where we'd left them, and at seven-ten exactly they both trilled simultaneously. I almost dropped the cup then picked up my phone in one shaking hand and answered it. It was the chairman. 'Have you seen the papers?' he said in a voice that broke into a squeak.

'Sort of,' I said, and looked at the front page of the *Telegraph* that I'd dropped on to the floor after a brief scan. 'Bosnia, rail privatization, law and order, the usual.'

'The tabloids,' he screamed. 'The tabs.'

'No. We're too high class for that.'

'Then get them. I'll call you back in fifteen minutes.' And he cut me off.

With a sense of impending doom I dressed quickly and went downstairs and picked up the *Mirror*, *Sun* and *Star* and saw what he meant. I'M UP THE DUFF BY STAN

THE MAN read the headline in the *Sun*, and that pretty well summed up all the coverage. The 'I' in question was Linda Homan, and it looked like she'd had a field day talking to the press.

I took the papers back to the suite and gave Stan a knock. He was tucked up snug and warm with Trisha. I chucked the papers on to his bed and after one glance at the headlines he was wide awake. 'Better get rid of her,' I said. 'The chairman wants a word.' And I backed out and shut the door behind me.

Trisha came stumbling out of the bedroom a couple of minutes later, which had given me time to wake Gail and get her partially dressed. Both gave me sheepish grins and left the suite. I gave Gail a kiss and promised to use the number she'd scrawled on the dressing-table mirror in bright pink lipstick. Thirty seconds after they'd gone, Stan came into the room in one of the courtesy towelling robes supplied by the hotel, carrying the linens in his hand. 'Fuck, shit,' he said. 'That silly cow. Now look what she's done.'

'The beans have been well and truly spilled,' I remarked.

'Fucking lies, man,' he said. 'What do these people want?'

'Don't ask me. Your chairman should be ringing back in a minute. Maybe he knows.'

'I need coffee first,' said Stan, so I poured him a cup, added milk and sugar and he swallowed it in one gulp. As he put the cup down his mobile rang.

Stan picked it up. 'Yeah, it's me,' he said. He paused. 'I've seen them.' And that was about all he did say as I heard the sound of the chairman's raised voice from where I was standing.

When the one-sided conversation was over Stan handed the phone to me. 'He wants to talk to you,' he said.

I took it off him and said, 'Sharman.'

'This is a right fuck-up,' said the chairman. 'Look, get him out of there. Take him somewhere out of the way. We'll talk later,' and he cut me off. I hadn't said another word. I switched off the phone, put it back on the table and poured myself more coffee.

'He's not pleased,' said Stan.

Understatement of the day so far, I thought.

'We're out of here,' I said.

Stan's phone rang again and he picked it up and switched it on. 'No comment,' he said, and lobbed it at the wall where it smashed into a dozen pieces.

'They don't make phones like they used to,' he said, and laughed. After a few seconds I joined in.

We packed our stuff then pissed off. Stan was well aware that there were moles at the club and knew that before long the place would be besieged by reporters and photographers. In fact one or two were hanging around in the lobby when we checked out, and I had to play tough before we could get into the motor and away. A couple of cars followed us, but they were no match for the Corvette and we lost them on the motorway before Stan came off it just ahead of Coulsdon, on to some back roads that led us through the suburbs then on to the South Circular and round to my flat. It was the only place I could think of to go. Home sweet home.

'Excuse the mess,' I said as I let us in. 'I wasn't expecting visitors.'

'You should see my place,' he replied, as he sat down and I put the kettle on.

'What now?' I asked.

'Can we hang around here for a bit?'

'Sure.'

'Then tonight I want to go see the Homans.'

'Are you sure?'

He nodded. 'Sure I'm sure. It's the only way I can sort this out, and I know exactly where they always are on Friday nights.'

'Where?'

'A pub called The Fallen Angel in Dulwich. Know it?'

I shook my head.

'It's their local. They always get in there on Fridays. There's three of them, like I said. One's big, that's Johnny. One's medium sized, that's Terry. And one's a right little sod, that's Barry. He's the one to watch. Fucking mental. Always ready to take anyone on. Specially if they're bigger than him, and nearly everyone is. He was in the SAS, so don't say I didn't warn you.'

Fucking hell, I thought. I wish I still had a gun.

The Fallen Angel was a big old boozer, but far enough off the beaten track to be one where the regulars ruled and passing trade was unusual. Stan parked the Chevy outside at five-to-nine.

As you can imagine, we hadn't let the chairman in on our plan.

'Are you sure about this?' I asked again as we left the motor.

'It's the only way to get it sorted,' he said. 'And remember, watch the little one.'

We pushed open the doors to the saloon bar. A nearby church clock struck nine. It would have been more apposite if it had been high noon.

The place was about a quarter full and the fashion police would've had a field day. There were plenty of shell suits and white stiletto heels as the glitterati of East Dulwich celebrated the onset of another weekend of *Blind Date* and lottery fever.

In the far corner sat a little posse of punters who turned round as one at our entrance. There were three young blokes, a girl who I guessed to be in her late teens but who could pass for older, and one middle-aged woman who was trying desperately to pass for younger.

'That's them. The old tart's the mum,' said Stan as we made for the bar, where a huge Persian cat wearing a red and blue striped ribbon bow round its throat sat between two of the beer pumps in defiance of every public health ordinance in the land. As I politely asked for two pints of lager I could feel several pairs of eyes boring into my back. When we'd been served I turned round in time to see the three young geezers heading our way. Just like Stan had said, the small one had a glint of mayhem in his eyes. He was the one to watch.

'What the fuck are you doing here?' demanded the big one, who must have been Johnny.

'I've come to clear up this mess,' replied Stan.

'The only mess you'll clear up is your blood on the floor,' said the little one, Barry by all accounts.

'I just want to speak to Linda,' said Stan, looking over at the girl in the corner.

'No fucking chance,' said the middle-sized one, who by a simple matter of elimination had to be Terry.

'It can't hurt,' I said mildly.

'Who the fuck are you?' demanded Terry. 'And what's it got to do with you?'

'Just a mate,' I said.

'You look like something the dog sicked up,' said Barry dismissively.

How to make friends and influence people.

Then Johnny had a brain wave. 'You're the fucking minder,' he said.

'The minder,' said Barry. 'Fuck me. The club must be hard up.'

'Cheers,' I said.

'Linda,' Stan shouted across the room. 'Why are you lying? You know nothing happened.'

She looked ashamed.

'I . . . I . . .' she stammered.

'You leave her alone, you bastard,' the middle-aged woman said.

'Yeah, leave her alone,' said Barry. 'We told you what would happen if we saw you.'

Shit! I thought. Bad things were about to happen, Stan was going to lose his mobility, his livelihood and his transfer, and I was about to lose my three grand and the rest of my already precarious reputation.

As the three brothers advanced with intent towards us I looked round, my eyes skidded across to the fat Persian then back, and I grabbed it by the scruff of the neck, picked it up and shouted. 'Stop! Or I'll kill the cat.'

A terrible hush fell over the bar as I held up the huge moggie like a trophy. I brushed past the Homan brothers and went over to the two women. I sat next to Linda and said, 'You don't want me to hurt it, do you?'

She shook her head. 'It's a him,' she said. 'Mungo. He's old.'

Fuck me, I thought. Mungo. Like in *Mary, Mungo and Midge* that I used to watch on TV with my daughter, and I felt ashamed. But at least it had stopped the fight before it started.

I popped the cat on to her lap and she stroked him. 'Then tell the truth,' I said.

She looked at me, her mum, her brothers and Stan, and dissolved into tears. The big cat jumped down as she threw herself at her mother and started to cry. 'I didn't want him to go,' she sobbed. 'The club won't be the same.'

'Are you really pregnant?' I asked.

She shook her head as mascara-stained tears rolled down her cheeks.

'You two didn't ever . . .' I went on.

She shook her head again.

I looked over at the three brothers and shrugged.

'You silly cow,' said Johnny.

'I didn't mean to cause all this trouble.' Linda again. 'I just thought that you'd make him stay if you thought I was having his baby. Then he wouldn't go to United. I only did it for the club . . .'

'We could have done him,' said Terry. 'Seriously.'

'And his mate,' said Barry.

Thank God for Mungo, I thought. 'No worries,' I said. 'It's all sorted now.'

Barry came over to the table, leant on it, and he still had that look of mayhem in his eyes. He stared straight into mine and said, 'Fancy a drop of short?'

Stan played on Saturday afternoon and scored twice. Once with a header he converted from a corner kick, and once from the penalty spot. He signed the transfer papers at six o'clock, got his money, moved up north and bought a penthouse loft apartment overlooking the old ship canal, and the last time I heard from him he was going out with a page-three girl. Some things never change. I watched the game from the directors' box with the entire Homan family and we cheered the team to victory, and at two minutes past six I got a cheque for three grand from the chairman, who looked about as relieved as any man I've ever seen.

I still see the Homans now and then when I pop into The Fallen Angel for a pint, and when I do I always take Mungo a little bit of smoked salmon, or some other little treat that cats like, to thank him for saving my bacon that night.

If there were an annual award for the-most-entertaining-crime-writer-to-have-around-at-a-literary-convention,

Wonder Boy

Mark Timlin would win it every year. His hugely successful south London detective novels featuring private eye
Nick Sharman have been adapted by World Productions
for Carlton Television.

Michael Marshall Smith

Sorted

All right. Here it is.

Friday night – lads' night out. Down 'Club Bastard'; owner's a big fan, what can I say. Beautiful. Everything on tap. Something to drink. Something to snort. Something to shag. Sorted.

Roll up about ten; fucking photographers outside. No, love them, actually. You got to. Helped put us where we are, know what I mean? Stand outside, with the lads – in our top Armani coats. Flash flash flash. Questions: what about that penalty, eh? What about the ref? Are we going to win the FA Cup?

Course we fucking are.

Inside, rows of shag; take your pick. Bottle blonde, extra tits, legs up to their arses. Lovely. Stand at the bar, lads together – like fucking kings. Free bubbly? Yeah, I should think so, mate – just give us the fucking bottle.

Who've we got? Ted Stupid. Man in goal – safe. Top lad. Kevin Legg – out on the left. Goes like the clappers – excellent. Paul Tosser; solid at the back. Try to get past him – seven types of shit kicked out of your shins. Ha ha ha ha ha. No, seriously; great little player, great skills.

And me. Gavin Mate. Fucking midfield general, innit.

Do we dance? Do we fuck. No need, mate. Stand there in a circle and the fucking club dances around us. Big laughs – Ted sticks his hand down some shag's top. Lobs her tit out – signs it. Excellent. Some cunt tries to muscle in – boyfriend. Paul elbows the twat in the face; end of problem. Great skills. Great little player.

Go behind the bar; help ourselves. Barman gets shirty; bunch of arse. *We can do what we fucking like.* Owner comes down – pour him a drink, he's fucking loving it. Flash flash, more pictures. Great on the back page. No fucking problem.

One o'clock, Kev's pissed as a twat – Paul's chewing face with some top black shag. I'm caning it with Ted at a table in the corner. Hundred notes of charlie up each nostril by then – fucking flying. Then:

See this shag, other side of the room. Red mini, no top to speak of. Gypsy skin, Bambi eyes. And an arse to fucking die for. Suzy all over again: I'm thinking – right. That's me fucking sorted. Go over, bit of chat. She's loving it. Put in half an hour's worth – time to go. Give the nod to the lads; later – yeah, cheers.

Flash flash out the front so slip out the back; I'm fucking Gavin Mate, I am. Shag's wetting itself – ten seconds of fame, innit. Limo pulls up, pile in. More charlie, obviously. Roll up the fifty, cut the rocks. Show her how it's done. Excellent. Tweak a nipple, just for a giggle. She's going to go off like a fucking rocket.

Back to the flat. Get more bubbly down her then think why fucking bother? – it's in the bag. Get on the pitch, blue satin sheets. She's wriggling like a pig in a tin. Another line, I dump the Paul Smith and then it's game on.

Fuck her. Fuck her again. And then;

Hang on. Start again.

Gavin Mate. Midfield supremo. But not always, obviously.

Eighteen. Tipped up at the gate. You going to give me an apprenticeship, or what? Guy takes the piss until I show him what I've got.

Silky skills.

Team's going nowhere – that's the whole fucking point. Said that one man can't make a team; proved what a bunch of twats they are. Straight in the As: slow start – playing with wankers, aren't I. Couple of games, goals slotted in. Crowd loves it. Owner thinks 'Hang on – could have a winner here': stumps up for some decent players. Kevin Legg. Ted Stupid. Suddenly we're a fucking team. End of first season – promotion, thanks very much. Gavin Mate the hero of the hour. Course I fucking am.

Meanwhile, outside world; it's a performance, innit. Got the lads out on the prowl – flash flash, people talking. Bought top suits. Oh yeah. And bearing – made old Eubanks look like a twat. Not difficult, of course. Joking – Chris and I are mates. Serious. He's the only loser I go round with. Ha ha ha ha ha.

Couple of seasons, build the rep and up the ladder. Receipts through the roof; owner's like a pig in shit. Going lovely. Manager knows I'm top lad. Paul Tosser joins the back – World War Three on a stick. Night life. Shag on tap. Fun to be had; up the nose and up the arse. Money in buckets. Cheers.

Dodgy moment; some slag from the *Sun* starts nosing into where Gavin Mate comes from. Can't have that; had a word. Slag never works again. Sorted. Manager's not going to let anyone piss off Gavin Mate – too fucking important. Gets the goals. Gets the press.

Meet the untouchables.

Now. This season. Premiership's in the bag. Just the FA to play for. We going to win it?

Course we fucking are. I'm Gavin Mate, I am.

Leave the shag in the bedroom; go for some bubbly. Thirsty now. She's saying come back; begging for it. Course you got to oblige.

Sorted

Give Ted a call first; getting his knob polished by a couple of teenies. Hear the girls laughing in the background – he's fucking sorted. They're sisters, innit.

Shame about mine. Suzy was good value. Shame she had to go.

Back in the bedroom, give one to the shag again. She falls asleep after. Finish the bubbly, go for some more. Sit in the kitchen a while. Know it's going to happen.

Nothing I can do about it. Artist, I am. Artist of the pitch. Got to do what I fucking feel like.

Top plan. Find a way of getting away with it. Stop being poncey Nigel Smith, lose the accent, fuck the past; find a way of getting sorted. Off the parents – car crash – shame Suzy had to go too. Probably her fault though, if you think about it; shouldn't have let me watch her. I'd give her one now, if she was alive. Slag. But she isn't. Probably give her one anyway.

Disappeared for a while – Middle East. No one's going to find the ones out there. Then back, Gavin Mate, and a knock on the right door. Goals. Welcome to the untouchables.

Finish the bottle, raring to go. Pissed as a twat, good news; more fun that way. Back in the bedroom, tape the shag's mouth up. Then break the bubbly bottle and have some fun. Manager'll sort it during the game tomorrow: get back here, be like it never happened.

Are we going to win? Course we are.

Nice one.

Although he professes to have little interest in football, Michael Marshall Smith always seems to know the form – who's going up, who's going down – as if he gets Ceefax in his head. His first story to be accepted for publication was 'The Dark Land', which lent its title to the anthology in which it appeared, *Darklands*. His first

Michael Marshall Smith

two stories won awards, as did his first novel, *Only Forward*. His second novel, *Spares*, is due from Harper-Collins in autumn 1996.

Liz Jensen

Sent Off

I'd been sent off, but I wasn't stupid. I took hostages.

We had the Family Bargain Suite: part of that Kost Kutter deal they offer. A Ye Olde, Ye-Ffyne-Shreddyde-Marmalade sort of place; the cradle of something, nestling in the heart of somewhere, rolling blah studded with traditional country blah, kissed by blah, peppered with wild blah, just a leisurely blah from, affording fine views of Blah, Blah, Blah. And for the kids: Marine World ahoy!

The fine views were of the car park, transformed by rain on the window into a cubist blur of forsythia bushes and Vauxhall Astras.

I knew what Gordon would be doing. He'd be sitting in front of the television watching the World Cup, with a beer, and one arm round Her. I can see his mouth moving, like a fish hunting amoeba, forming heartfelt words as he watches the graceless bovine shapes charging about the pitch. 'Just look at that. Do you know what that is? That's pure ballet, that is. Puuuure ballet.'

She smiles indulgently, runs her glossy nails through his hair. Is she aware of his dandruff? If she is, it's still too early in the relationship for her to care.

When I'd put the children to bed (Clark in the top bunk, Lulu in the bottom, plastic anti-bed-wetting sheets on both mattresses) I set to work on the bottle of wine I'd brought with me, an unusual-looking Bulgarian Rioja.

225

I never hit the drink alone, so I flicked on the television, carefully avoiding the pure ballet. I saw instead a sexy car, some sexy yoghurt, a tree falling in on a family's house, a new kind of gravy granule, specially formulated for the busy executive mum, a nerd dressed as a chicken, and a whole range of other commercials, seamlessly interspersed with an American movie. I had to keep the sound quite low, because of the kids; with that and the Rioja, I didn't follow it as well as I might have done, but I was nevertheless strangely gripped by the socio-medical storyline, in which a slag from the Bronx arrives on an island off the coast of Maine and sleeps with all the men except the doctor, so that eventually everyone but the doctor catches the herpes simplex virus. I nodded off at one point; when I woke up, the movie was nearing its climax, because a baby was critically ill, having caught herpes simplex from his mother while being born. In the end, the buck stops somewhere, and the doctor marries a woman who split up with her fiancé when he gave her the virus. ('Some engagement present,' she said.) I suppose the doctor still didn't get the herpes after he'd married her, though, because he could put her in a gynae chair with stirrups and check whether she was in remission or not, before they made love, but I'm just guessing there.

If not, 'Some wedding present,' she might have said.

The slag from the Bronx left – to become a nun? To defiantly and selfishly infect another island? I don't know to this day: I fell asleep in the chair again somewhere before the closing credits.

My road to hell has been paved with other peoples' good intentions. Gordon thought the Kost Kutter Weekend might cheer me up a bit, and take the edge off the pain of him dumping me.

No pain, no gain!

It's not the pain, actually. It's the humiliation that gets to me.

Among other things, according to Gordon, I'm unexciting in bed. 'Sexually disappointing,' he said, as though I'd once made extravagant promises about how I'd drive him wild with desire by performing unhygienic acts on his penis. Who in their right mind would do that?

But he has now met Her; she's less boring, obviously, and has an all-year tan, and is prepared to snuggle on the sofa beside him and undergo hours of pure ballet, and then throw hygiene and caution to the winds in bed. She's not from the Bronx, she's from Milton Keynes via Cheam, but there the contrast ends.

'Some anniversary present,' I'd like to have said to him, if I'd had the presence of mind, and if it had actually been our anniversary when he handed me the tickets and the brochure.

She's a travel agent.

When I woke up, it was the Open University; I watched a professor in a slate-blue cardie intoning reassuring things about gravity, and the Y Force Seven Theory. The carefully composed diagrams and the calm and reasoned presentation of a range of astrophysical phenomena seemed to re-humanize me in the way a sensitive and compassionate piece of broadcasting should. Cartoons followed, signalling dawn.

By breakfast time, I was quite numb.

I took the children out for the day, to visit Marine World, which is indoors, and partly underwater. They had giant rays that you were allowed to touch. Tentatively, I reached out to stroke one: the creature felt like an acrylic place-mat. Lulu wouldn't go anywhere near it; she held my hand tight, and we moved on.

It was Clark who spotted it first: a beautiful sea

anemone, attached to a rock, waving its tentacles. It was large and vulnerable-looking, and the same colours – goldy-yellowy-greeny-blue – as a scarf my mother used to have, which in turn matched the tweed trouser suit she wore to her second wedding. I stared at this anemone for ages, recalling the wedding, and the somewhat appalling marriage that followed, which was in some ways rather similar to my own marriage to Gordon, possibly, or perhaps probably. Then two lobsters sidled up, and the three crustacea began a sort of claw-waving discussion, which hid the anemone from view completely. I came to after that, only to become aware of a woman telling off Clark for dropping one of his sweet wrappers on a sea-horse.

I don't take kindly to other people verbally disciplining my children in my presence, so I whipped round and told the woman it wasn't as easy as she thought, being a one-parent family, and she glared back at me and said it wasn't a question of my family status, it was a question of 'the environment'. What's *that* when it's at home? She was wearing one of those Barbour jackets.

Today it's raining again, and we are in a puddle of shadows and scratched lino called the Games Room. The room smells of fish paste, crisps, Seven-Up, chocolate, celery, used baby-wipes.

'You should call it the Game Room, singular, not Games Room, plural,' I said to the manager this morning. He utterly missed the point, and chuckled, as though I'd made a joke, rather than a complaint about the fact that the only game in the Games Room is table football.

This is what happens when you cut corners, financially. Irony wins, and you find yourself playing a grotesque, bite-sized World Cup match with your son.

The football players are chipped. They're very old.

Probably from the sixties; they have smarmed sort of hair, and none of them is black. Apart from their shirts (my team blue, Clark's red), they all look the same; their faces are squarish, firm-jawed. I know these men; you see them on cereal packets. One, on Clark's team, is damaged; his forehead has been smashed in, in a crude frontal lobotomy.

He has already scored three goals.

We play another game, and my son thrashes me again. The whole thing is a stupid waste of time.

'You're crap at this, Mum,' Clark is saying. He's chewing on some blueberry-flavoured bubble-gum. 'You're just real crap.'

Ten-year-olds shouldn't use their pocket money to buy gum; nor should they use the word 'crap'. Especially not when their younger sister Lulu, asleep in her buggy, cocooned in a padded jumpsuit, might wake up at any moment and hear it.

Analysing it later, I realized that it was something about Clark's gum, and his use of the ugly word 'crap' in reference to me, that caused me to flip in the way I did.

Does 'flip' make it sound flippant? It wasn't. I lurched across, my hand raised to slap him, but the football table was between us, and instead I found myself shunting the heavy table towards him, like a bulldozer.

'Hey, Mum!'

He jumped out of the way, as I pushed the thing up against the wall with all my force, my mind on other things.

My mind on—

I had grabbed the handles. I was shoving them in and out, in and out. I was shaking the whole table. I could see the ball zig-zagging and ricocheting, and I could see my hands, and feel the frenzy in me. A strange silence roared in my head. The players whirred round on their poles, knocking at the ball upside down with their heads, scuddering and skidding backwards with their heels as I heaved and jolted the table about with my sudden strength, until—

YES!

Call it a weird miracle of aerodynamics, call it a fluke, call it idiot-savant instinct, call it pure ballet.

Or call it a bloody goal!

'Goal!' I screech. No one can take this away from me. I am filled with a crazy joy.

'GOAL! Goal! Gol-gol-gol-gol-gol-gol-goooooooooooo oooooooooooooooool!' I have heard a South American radio commentator doing this.

Lulu wakes up and watches me with round eyes. 'Goal!' I yell again. She smiles. She understands – in a way Clark clearly doesn't.

How can he, being male?

Yes, there *was* some weird epiphany. For several fractions of a second as I rocked there, shoving away at the handles and thwacking at the ball, in the instant I had scored that goal I had found myself not only playing the game almost properly, but having a tiny, ffyne-shreddyde understanding of what this thing football is about.

Later that night, when the children were in bed, I went back to the Games Room and sat in a plastic chair and stared at the football table. The herd of men was still and silent. Each row was at an odd angle, some tipped forwards, some backwards.

I think: this is what rigor mortis would look like, if two teams were to die on the pitch and be skewered on long pins.

Human kebabs.

I suppose they respect me now.

Sent Off

I slept. I dreamed I was on Sea-Horse Island, off the coast of Maine. I met a tall, thickset man in shorts. He had a terrible wound to his forehead. It was like melted wax, scarred over. It might have been a burn. He was clutching a fistful of baby-wipes. His face looked vaguely familiar. He led me outside. It was raining, so we went to shelter under a nylon net.

There I knelt down in front of him and pulled down his red shorts and parted my lips to take in the whole length of his hard acrylic, but he had no genitalia of any kind, so I just stayed kneeling there, open-mouthed, thinking Foul.

Born in Oxfordshire, Liz Jensen lives in south London. Her first novel, *Egg Dancing*, was published by Bloomsbury; she is currently putting the finishing touches to her second. She has also lived and worked in Hong Kong, Taiwan and France.

James Miller

Scoring

Getting through the school gates was always the hard part. Matt never knew whether it would be better if they ran, ducking down past the cars in the staff car park, or if they should stroll out casually, as if the headmaster himself had given them permission to bunk off games. It was a risky strategy. They had to pass the secretary's office, the staff room and the main entrance to the school, where teachers were always breezing in and out as if they didn't have classes to attend to.

'What do you think?' Matt said, turning to Phil. They were standing on the steps of a small outbuilding that led back to the changing room. Behind them they could hear Mr Simmons shouting at students to 'hurry up' and 'get their boots on'. There was the familiar smell of muddy showers, sweat and cheap deodorant.

Phil sighed, brushing back his long, floppy hair. 'I dunno. I reckon we just style it.'

'Just walk?'

'Yeah. We'll be cool. It's fine.'

'Oh . . . I dunno,' Matt shook his head, pursing his lips. 'I mean, after we got caught the last time, that was a fucking bad scene. I mean Mr Miles only let us off 'cause he likes me so much.'

'Yeah, he hates my guts, the wanker,' Phil laughed.

'I'm a prefect now. I'm meant to be responsible and shit like that. It's just that if we get caught again—'

'We're not going to get caught. Look, it's too late to

go on to the field now, and I left all my kit at home and I'm not wasting the afternoon pissing around this place. We're seventeen years old; I mean, Jesus Christ, I'm not—'

'Yeah, yeah, all right, Phil, I know what you mean, we've been here before.'

'We're here every fucking Thursday afternoon. You know it.'

'Yeah, that's true.' Matt paused, pulling his coat tight around his blazer. It was a freezing cold November afternoon, the morning's rain replaced by a bitter North wind. He could imagine how it would cut through his football top and freeze his fingers. He couldn't face another afternoon spent standing around on a muddy field whilst Mr Simmons would blow his whistle and shout 'offside' and other such crap at them. 'All right, let's go.'

They walked quickly across the car park, heads turned purposefully away from the school building. The school gates beckoned; Matt felt that momentary tingle of fear as they got closer, that some teacher would appear in front of them and demand to know what they were doing, and just where they thought they were going.

But nothing. They strolled through the gates and hurried down the main road towards the town centre.

'Easy man, so fucking easy,' laughed Phil.

'We going on to Jake's, then? Yeah?' Matt asked tentatively, casting one last glance back at the school. Just in case.

'I think so.'

'OK,' he muttered. 'Oh, look . . .'

'What is it?'

'I don't like going to Jake's.'

'Why not?'

'I just don't. He's such a dick, he really is . . . it's like . . . oh, you know.'

'Yeah? Well, you're going halves on this eighth with me, aren't you?'

'Yeah.'

'So you can come with me to get it.'

'I guess so . . .'

'So what's the problem?'

'Jake. He's a fucking dick.'

'But Jake's got the ganja.'

'Yeah I know. Look, I'm just saying—'

'I know you're just saying—'

'Well, good.'

'That's all right, then?'

'Yeah.'

They wandered down on to the High Street. Phil paused to light a fag. 'Look at that,' he said, gesturing at a gaudy tinsel snowflake several men were trying to hang from a streetlight. 'Christmas lights. It is still November, isn't it?'

'Twenty-ninth today.'

'Christmas lights. On the twenty-ninth. That's a disgrace. I just don't know what's happening to this country,' and he rolled his eyes back despairingly.

'Ten million years of Tory rule.'

'What?'

'That's what's happened.'

'Ten million years?'

'Feels like it. But anyway, this place is such a hole. I mean, does anything happen here?' It was Matt's usual complaint.

Phil hesitated, as if thinking deeply. Then he smiled, exhaling smoke. 'Not to sad fucks like you.'

Matt laughed. 'Yeah, fuck off.'

They walked on, past the W. H. Smiths, the Boots, the Woolworths. They hesitated outside Our Price. Matt glanced in. The shop seemed to be stocked entirely with copies of Mariah Carey's new album.

Scoring

'Fuck that. Let's just go and get some drugs,' muttered Phil, tugging Matt forward.

'Come on, "I want to get high . . . so high,"' he sang.

They fell silent for a while, walking faster, gradually leaving the town centre.

Here it comes thought Matt as they began to approach a new, surprisingly chic-looking café at the end of the High Street: *that's the place, that's where she works. Saturday mornings. That's where she is . . .* He was walking behind Phil and as they passed the café he slowed down even more. Phil, not noticing, pressed ahead, one hand steadying his scruffy canvas rucksack, the other moving fag to lips with almost religious determination.

Matt stared in through the steamed-up windows. There were a few people sitting around little tables, drinking coffee, maybe tea as well. He could see a couple of girls working behind the counter. A big menu chalked on a blackboard at the back.

'Matt!'

He turned around, looking over to Phil.

'What are you doing?'

'I'm just looking . . . I'm . . .' Matt muttered, blushing. *Sophie: 'I work at Orinoco's. Saturday mornings. Sometimes afternoons. The pay's shit, but they're all really nice. Come in one day. I'll do you my special cappuccino.' Sophie. So, so nice. Had she smiled as she said that? Did she mean it? Really?* He turned away. 'Yeah, I'm coming, hang on.'

'What's up, what is it?' asked Phil.

'Nothing.' Matt hesitated. He was never sure about telling Phil these things. They were best mates and Phil usually told him everything. But then sometimes Phil just laughed and told everybody else as well. 'No, it's where she works, that's all. I hadn't realized,' he added, trying to sound indifferent.

'She?'

'You know, Sophie.'

'Sophie Davidson?'

'No way! The one Steve pulled! Fuck off, I mean Sophie Kelly.' Matt cursed, shaking his head.

'Sophie Kelly? Oh, you mean Johnny's big sister.'

'Yeah, her.'

'Yeah, she is nice, yeah . . . You don't fancy her, do you?'

'Well . . .'

'Come on . . .'

'I dunno . . . I mean she's really nice, you know, as a person, I mean, I like her a lot. I was talking to her the other day, when I was waiting for the bus. She was there . . . she was reading Virginia Woolf.'

'Virginia Woolf. Oh, like, wow, you're in there,' Phil laughed.

'No . . . oh fuck off. You know what I mean.'

'Yeah, no, I do. So, yeah, anyway . . .'

'Well, we had a chat.'

'About Virginia Woolf?'

'No! Well, yes, at first. But no, about lots of things. I sat next to her on the bus. It was really cool. I've spoken to her before, but you know, by herself, I mean she's so nice.'

'And she works at Orinoco's?'

'Yeah. That's why I was looking at it. She said I should come in there some time. She said she'd do me a coffee.'

'For free?'

'Well . . . I dunno. I hope so. I was thinking about it; you know, I could just go in there, she'd be there. She could get me a coffee. We could have a chat. I could ask her what she was doing that evening. Or, like, I could come in about . . . half an hour, maybe, before she finishes for the morning, you know? And, like, ask her what she was doing afterwards. Will you stop smiling at me!' and he pushed a giggling Phil away. 'You see, if I could just talk to her again, properly, see what she's really like . . .' Matt paused, letting his words trail away. When he actually said it, like that, his whole plan, all his thoughts, sounded so stupid. When he said it he didn't even fancy her, not even slightly.

'Yeah . . . well, go for it,' said Phil, smirking.

'You reckon?'

'Yeah . . . and, if she says no, well . . . it'll be fucking funny anyway.'

'Oh, cheers.'

They were walking up to the north part of town, where Jake lived. The roads were quiet and tree-lined, all the houses hidden at the end of big driveways. The wind was stronger, bitterly cold and flecked with drizzle. Matt glanced at his watch. Back at school they wouldn't have even reached half-time yet. He could see Mr Simmons, charging up and down, mud splashed all over the back of his hairy, squat legs, bellowing 'kick the ball' at everybody. When he did play games Matt liked to stand around at the back. He had his own position, called 'Inner Defence', which basically involved keeping as far away from the ball as possible. Cricket in the summer was always better. There was never any risk of hypothermia and it was always easy to accidentally knock over the stumps when trying to bat. Fielding was best, though; he liked to wander as far away from the match as possible. Then lie down. It was another unique position. He called it 'Deep Fielding'.

But football wasn't important. 'Phil . . . Sophie. I just think . . . well, she is pretty, don't you think so?'

'Oh yeah, oh, she's fine, she's lovely. I snogged her at David Rickman's party last summer.'

'Did you?'

'Totally. Well, just a snog. I was pretty pissed. It was nice and all, a mistake at the time 'cause I was going out with Becky, but all the same . . . Where were you?'

'At home I imagine. I totally hate David Rickman.

But anyway, she said I should come in and have a coffee. Is that, like, encouraging? Do you think?'

'Well, it's not exactly the same as being invited *in* for coffee, but it's a start.'

Matt sighed. 'It would just be so nice, it really would. Girls, Phil, girls . . . why are there no girls in this fucking town?'

'There are, there are loads.'

'Well, I don't know them.'

'Well, make a fucking effort.'

'That's what I'm trying to do with Sophie. But you're not exactly helping.'

'Look,' said Phil. 'Nine months. In nine months we'll be at university. There are girls everywhere out there, you know, gagging for it. You won't fail. Neither of us will fail. Nine months from now, we'll both have smiles on our faces.'

'Yeah? Right.'

Matt sighed, looking away. He thought about it; he thought about how he'd do it, about what might happen. He'd have to stroll in, insouciantly, unconcerned. Not like he'd deliberately planned to go to Orinoco's but had just decided, casually, that he fancied a cup of coffee. He'd have to sit down, without looking to see if she was there. Then, hopefully, she'd come over. Then he could say *Oh, Sophie. Hi! How's it going? So this is where you work?* Something like that. And she'd make some comment and he could say *Does the offer for a cappuccino still stand?* Or maybe that was too cheesy. He wasn't sure what else he'd say. A joke of some sort, preferably funny, would probably be a good tactic. The importance was timing. Timing was everything. Timing and style.

'This is it,' said Phil. They stood outside the front of a big Victorian villa. Phil opened the gate and they scrunched up the gravel path.

Scoring

'Do you think he's in?' asked Matt.

'Probably. He'd better be. Are you going to ring the doorbell?'

'What?'

'Well, I don't want to!'

'Why not?'

'Because you're going to do it.'

'For fuck's sake.' And Matt reached out, pressing the bell. 'One day, Phil, one day I'm not going to do what you tell me,' he added, trying to sound annoyed. Phil just smirked.

The door was opened by a tall, middle-aged woman. She had a Margaret Thatcher hairstyle and a long Laura Ashley dress. Matt stood back. This was weird.

'Yes?' she asked.

'Um, hi. Is Jake in?' said Matt. It was an unwritten agreement between them that he always negotiated with parents. Phil claimed that having short hair and a prefect's tie was a good means of gaining their confidence.

'Jake . . . ?' the woman's voice trailed off, as if she'd never heard of him. For a moment Matt thought everything had gone wrong and was about to apologize nicely when she said, 'Jake, oh yes, he's upstairs. Just go on up.'

'Thanks.'

'Yeah, cheers.' They pressed past her. Phil led the way to a bedroom at the top of the house.

He knocked on the door. They could hear voices and a TV coming from inside the room. 'Yeah . . .' came the muffled reply.

'Jake?'

'Yeah?'

'It's Phil and Matt.'

'What . . . ?' There was a bit of scraping and a click as the door was unlocked. Jake peered round at them. 'Phil! All right, mate, come in, man, come in.'

The bedroom was large, but full of rubbish. Clothes and magazines and CDs were scattered all over the floor. There was a big poster of The Prodigy on one wall, *Natural Born Killers* on the other. A girl with dyed black hair wearing a streaky purple dress was sitting on the bed, her feet hanging over the edge, smoking a joint. She glanced at them both but didn't say anything. Then she looked back at the small TV in the corner of the room. Sky Sports: a football match. A team in red playing a team in blue. Matt assumed it must be some obscure European league match, filling in time before they could find something more interesting to show.

Jake stood in the middle of the room, looking sleepy, vaguely confused. He was tall and fat with floppy brown hair that never quite made it into dreadlocks. He was wearing faded combats and a *Reservoir Dogs* T-shirt.

'How goes, Phil? What have you been up to?' he said.

'Not much. School, shit like that. Bunking off games today, you know.' Matt slouched against the wall behind Phil. Jake usually ignored him, so he'd ignore Jake. He didn't care.

'You mean you have to do games?' laughed the girl on the bed.

'Yeah, fucking unbelievable, isn't it?' said Phil, squatting down on the floor.

'That's why I'm at college. No hassles, you know, no hassles at all,' said Jake. He still stood in the middle of the room, still looking rather confused and uncomfortable.

There was a small silence; the pleasantries over, business yet to be discussed. Everybody paused to look at the TV. A blue football player was running up to the goal. He deftly passed the ball to a blue striker. He kicked. The red goalkeeper started to move towards it. Then stopped. The ball rolled out, missing the goal.

Scoring

An enthusiastic fan grabbed it and threw it back on to the field.

'What was it that you wanted?' said Jake. The girl on the bed passed him the joint.

'An eighth.'

'Right, yeah, sure. Hang on.' He took a couple of heavy drags before passing it on to Phil.

'Cheers,' he whispered, taking it eagerly.

Jake rummaged around in a drawer. 'I only got solid, is that OK?'

'Yeah, fine,' muttered Phil, discreetly tapping ash on to the carpet. 'How much did you get?'

'Couple of ounces,' said Jake, smiling and looking generally pleased with himself. He gave Phil a small lump. 'I worked it out on my scales.'

'Yeah, looks OK,' he said, holding it up close and sniffing. 'Here, Matt.'

Matt took the eighth, then the remains of the joint. He sat down next to Phil. 'Looks fine,' he said, guessing completely.

'Fifteen, yeah?' asked Phil, digging in his pockets.

'That's right.'

'I've only got a fiver,' said Matt, giving it to Phil. 'I'll owe you two-fifty. Is that OK?'

'Sure.' He passed Jake the money. Jake sat down on the bed, putting his arm around the girl.

'Well, like, do you guys want to stay for a bit?'

'I dunno . . .' Matt began. He felt edgy in the house, stuck in the corner. He kept imagining Jake's weird mum knocking at the door and asking them if they wanted a cup of tea, or something. And he had an English essay to write.

'Yeah, cheers. Just for a bit,' answered Phil, pulling out a packet of Rizlas. He rolled a joint and began to smoke it. They watched football. A red player was given a yellow card for a nasty tackle. Phil passed the joint to Matt.

Jake started talking. 'The thing with football,' he said. 'I mean, the reason why I love it, you know, is because it's so tribal. That's what it is . . . tribes. Tribes of people, playing each other . . . and the supporters are also in the tribe. I mean, it's natural, tribes are natural. If you think about it, everything is like, a tribe, and football . . .' he paused, biting his fingernails. 'You see the thing with football is it's like an exaggeration of tribes, like an . . . an . . .'

'Amplification?' said Matt.

'What?' Jake hesitated, cocking his head at an odd angle as if he'd just been punched. 'No . . . not that, it's just . . . I mean, it gets you going. Football. Because it appeals to our tribal instincts. That's why it's fucking wicked, you see—'

The girl on the bed started to laugh. 'What the fuck are you talking about?' she said. 'You are one stoned fucker, Jake, you really are.'

'I'm just saying—' he protested.

'You're full of shit,' she continued, leaning over to kiss him.

Matt sighed, put the joint to his lips and inhaled deeply. He felt a bit better. The ball was being kicked pointlessly about the middle of the field.

'Has anyone scored yet?' he asked.

'No, man, no one's scored,' muttered Jake. 'No one ever fucking scores.'

Tell me about it he thought, taking a final drag before crushing the butt in an ashtray. *Sophie* . . . she had such beautiful eyes. That was it. They were so bright and shining. And she listened, she listened to what he said. Orinoco's . . . could he do it? *Hi, Sophie . . . which coffee do you recommend?*; *Hi, Sophie . . . come here often?* No, it was all terrible. There didn't ever seem to be anything he could do. He felt trapped. Trapped in school, in town, at home, in Jake's room. Everything was always

the same in the end. Life was nothing but failure; then
escape. Then more failure and more pain. And they
were bound to get in trouble for missing games this
week, again. They always missed games. He hated it
when Mr Miles shouted at him. What would he say this
time? *I felt really ill and went home? I was in the library? I
forgot my kit, you see? I hate games so I went and got stoned
instead, sorry . . . ?*

Phil leaned over. 'Let's go,' he whispered.

'Good move,' Matt replied.

Outside it was still cold, still almost raining. Matt
looked at his watch. At school the match would have
finished by now. They'd be warming frozen fingers on
radiators, buttoning up their shirts, pulling on their
ties. Mr Simmons would wander in and out, telling
people to get into the shower, that they should try
harder, do better. Matt saw him checking the register,
smiling to himself as he saw the big crosses by their
names. He was probably writing notes to Mr Miles at
this very moment. Still, it made morning assembly all
the more exciting; sitting through the prayers and
pointless readings, waiting to hear if their names were
going to be read out. Or, if they'd escaped again, for
another week.

Neither of them spoke much as they wandered back
into town, feeling tired, vaguely stoned. It was almost
dark and the Christmas lights had been switched on.
The High Street was choked with traffic. People hurried
home, wrapped in their coats, eyes on the ground.
Everybody looked harassed, depressed. Matt wondered
if Mr Simmons, or anybody else, really gave a toss
whether they did games or not. Probably not. He
remembered how, last year, he'd been playing a match,
and had suddenly found himself standing in front of
an exposed goal with the ball by his feet. It had been
a surprising moment. Somehow the goalkeeper had

been distracted and lost track of the ball. And the ball had been there, sitting in front of an open net! And Matt had been standing there, next to the ball. He remembered striking out, thinking *this is too good an opportunity, I just can't miss.* But, as he kicked, his boot had slipped loose: his foot just missed the ball; his boot sailed up, propelled by the enthusiasm of his swipe, and into the goal. The ball didn't move. Then someone else had kicked it away; and it was gone, and that was it. Matt wondered if such an experience somehow symbolized his entire life. Another failed opportunity. Another moment of pathetic vacillation, another dismal failure. He thought about telling Phil this. But no, Phil probably wouldn't understand.

They came to the bottom of Phil's road.

'Tomorrow night, my parents are out. Let's get fucked.'

'Your parents are out?' Matt asked.

'Definitely,' Phil replied emphatically.

'Oh, excellent. Tomorrow night.'

'Come round.'

'Yeah, wicked . . . See you later.'

Matt mooched up to the bus stop. There was nobody around, which meant he'd missed the early bus. He dropped his bag to the ground and leant against a streetlamp, shivering in the cold, watching the traffic driving past.

'Hey, Matt?' said a voice behind him.

He turned around.

'Sophie!'

'Hi.' She smiled, looked away, took a step back and smiled again, brushing her hair back behind her ears.

'How are you?' he asked, too surprised to feel embarrassed.

'OK. You?'

'Well . . . you know . . .' he sighed.

'Yeah . . .' she nodded, carefully placing her shoulder bag on the ground next to his. 'I get like that sometimes.' She looked at the ground.

Matt turned away, briefly glancing up the road; then, biting his lips, asked: 'Are you working Saturday?'

'In the morning. Yeah.' She shrugged sadly.

'What are you doing afterwards?'

She paused, looking at him searchingly for a moment.

'I don't know. Nothing.'

Matt hesitated: then, letting the words slip out of him, said, 'Well, look, do you fancy going for a coffee?'

And she smiled, and laughed. And he laughed too.

As football commentators are so fond of saying, James Miller is *still* only twenty, as if he's been twenty for three and a half years. His first short story to be accepted for publication, written when he was seventeen, appeared in *The Third Alternative*; other stories have found homes in *Last Rites and Resurrections* (TTA Press), *Time Out Net Books*, *Dark Terrors 2* (Gollancz) and *Dreams From the Strangers' Café*. Currently studying English Literature at Oxford, James Miller plans to be a full-time writer.

Mark Morris

The Shirt

'Wake up, you old fucker!'

The voice grabbed Potts by the lapels and hauled him up through the sludge of sleep. He surfaced gasping, disorientated, horribly defenceless. It was normally only his creaky old bladder that woke him in the night, but that had never shouted at him like this. Suddenly the familiar darkness of his room was no longer familiar, and a moment later neither was it darkness.

Light so blazing and so unexpected it felt like hot, fat needles, rammed through his eyeballs, searing his brain. For the first time since the War, Potts felt mortal fear. Although his head was burning with light, his heart was cold, and hatching like an egg. When he tried to breathe, pain sprang across his chest. Perhaps he was having another heart attack; if his doctor could be believed, the bout of indigestion he'd had five months ago had actually been a mild one. His doctor had told him then to stop smoking, but the minute he was out of the surgery Potts had had to have a cigarette to calm his nerves.

'Who's there?' he demanded, and was both alarmed and ashamed at the reediness of his voice. He heard hyenas cackling behind the juicy thump of his own blood in his ears. Then the torchlight danced away from his face and was extinguished, leaving an after-image: a bloated green whale floating in a sea of darkness.

'Who's there? Who's there?' The squeaky echo of his

words was evidently intended as mockery. As the green whale dissolved, Potts saw hulking black shapes moving on the black screen of his room. He raised a hand to shield his face from possible violence. 'What do you want?' he said.

'Your heart on a fucking plate.' The voice came at him like a torpedo, splitting the darkness. The hyenas cackled again.

'Please,' Potts said, 'I haven't got anything of value.'

'You mean you've *got* no fucking heart?'

'You mean you're a heartless cunt?' one of the other voices piped up.

More hyena noises. Potts tried to blink the darkness away. His eyes ached and his chest still hurt. When he breathed it was as if his ribs had been broken and were grinding together.

'Please,' he said, 'I'm an old man. I haven't got anything.'

'Shut it, you old fucker. Beaker, turn that fucking lamp on.'

Potts cringed as a patch of darkness bulged towards him. He tried to grab the edge of his blanket, a desperate, childish clutch at the most meagre of protective barriers, but his fingers seemed nerveless and he fumbled at fabric that felt lumpy, without edges.

Then there was a click and the lamp came on, a burst of mustard light that sent shadows flocking to the far corners of the room. Potts, squinting, saw the hyenas for the first time. Three of them. Big. Dark clothes. Black men.

No, not black men, he realized as the initial glare of the light, dingy though it was, subsided. White men wearing black balaclavas, scarves pulled tight over their noses and mouths and tied at the back so that only their eyes showed.

No, not even men, but boys. He saw it in the way

they moved and stood and held themselves, in their panther-like arrogance, their vicious naïvety. Sixteen, seventeen years old. Nothing but children, but bigger and stronger and more predatory than he had ever been. In the last ten or fifteen years, living on the estate had become like cowering in a cardboard box surrounded by prowling tigers. Now the tigers had found a way in.

'What you fucking looking at?' the biggest of the three, the one who had done most of the talking, said. His eyes were cold and grey, merciless, brimming with barely suppressed violence.

Potts averted his gaze, stared down at his frail, trembling, liver-spotted hands. 'Nothing,' he said.

'You hear that, Vash? He called you a nothing,' the boy who had turned on the lamp, the one called Beaker, said.

Potts tried to shake his head, but fear made his movements jerky, haphazard. 'No, I didn't, honestly.'

'Are you fucking arguing with me, you bald old cunt?'

'No, I—'

'Do you wanna fucking scrap?'

This time Potts was trembling so much he couldn't even speak. He gave another twitchy shake of the head. His heart and lungs felt as though they were being compressed into a smaller and smaller space.

'Hey, look at this fucking thing,' the third boy, the smallest of the three, said.

'What is it?'

'It's a fucking United shirt, what's it fucking look like?'

'That's not a United shirt, you twat,' Beaker said. 'It's yellow and blue, a bit like our old away kit.'

The smaller boy rolled his eyes. 'That's what our kit used to be like before Revie became the manager, you dumb fuck. It was him what changed it to all-white, 'cos he wanted Leeds to play like AC Milan or Real Madrid or somebody.'

'Fucking worked, didn't it?' said Vash. 'Fucking Champions twice under Revie.'

Potts tensed as Beaker approached the bed, but the boy was simply looking at the framed shirt on the wall above the headboard.

'Must be about a hundred years old,' he said.

'Oi, baldy,' said Vash, raising his voice as though Potts had dozed off, 'where'd you get that fucking shirt from?'

For the first time Potts felt a little of his fear seeping away and resentment pooling in the hollow it had left. It was as though the shirt, because it was from his youth, was giving him back a little of his strength from those long-gone days when he would never have believed he would ever become the victim he was now. It was his pride and joy, the shirt. Every time he looked at it it brought back memories of when Annie was alive and life was so full of promise, when if anything ever went wrong . . . well, there was always next season.

It was odd, but he hadn't given the shirt a thought since waking up; until the boys mentioned it he had completely forgotten it was there. Or maybe it wasn't *so* odd. His mind had been on other things, after all.

Now, though, he had to stop himself from blurting, 'You're not having it!' Instead he muttered, 'It's mine,' and was simultaneously gratified and alarmed to hear the defiance in his own voice.

'Really?' Vash snarled. 'And here's me thinking you're just looking after it for Tony fucking Yeboah.'

Beaker cackled, but the smaller boy frowned. Almost eagerly, he asked, 'Is it real or a replica?'

Potts looked up at him. It was the first time he had dared look any of the boys in the eye since Vash had asked him what he was fucking looking at. He saw now that the scarf tied around the boy's face was a United one, predominantly blue, with thin bands of yellow and white.

He cleared his throat, and in a voice that all at once was surprisingly loud in the small, stuffy room, he said, 'It's real.'

He saw Vash and Beaker exchange a glance. 'Must be worth a few quid,' Beaker said.

Potts shrugged and looked down at his hands again, trying not to show how fiercely the fires of both defiance and dismay were burning inside him now. Trying to sound casual, he said, 'I doubt it, not really.'

'Where did you get it from?' the smaller boy said. 'Did you buy it?'

Potts took a deep breath. 'No,' he said, 'it's mine. I mean . . . I used to wear it.'

'You used to play for Leeds?'

The note of awe in the boy's voice was so surprising that Potts' head snapped up.

He nodded slowly. 'Yes.'

'Fuck off,' said Vash. 'If you'd ever played for Leeds, you wouldn't be living in this fucking dump.'

Potts licked his paper-dry lips and even managed a smile. 'We weren't paid much in those days, not like they are now. We didn't have agents, we didn't get signing-on fees, none of that.'

'When did you play for 'em then?' said Beaker.

'Just after the war. 1946 to '52. Then I moved on. To Hull City. Retired in 1957.'

'What's your name?' Vash said.

'What's yours?'

'Don't get fucking smart!' Vash said, stepping forward.

'Oi, Vash, leave it,' said the smaller boy.

'Oh yeah? Or what will you do?'

'Nothing, I just . . . I just want to hear what he has to say.'

'Yeah, well, he shouldn't get fucking smart, should he? Just 'cos he played for Leeds don't mean he's God or nothing. He's still an old cunt. I'll still cut his fucking bollocks off if he pisses me about.'

'He wasn't pissing you about,' the smaller boy said placatingly.

'He didn't answer my fucking question, did he?' Vash said, and drew a hunting knife with a well-polished blade out of the pocket of his baggy black jeans.

Something in Potts' chest constricted, reawakening the pain that in the last couple of minutes had been easing slightly. Sparks danced in front of his eyes and he squeezed them closed, involuntarily hissing in a mouthful of air that made the remaining teeth he possessed throb with cold.

The smaller boy looked at Potts. 'You weren't pissing Vash about, were you, Mister?'

Potts shook his head, not trusting himself to speak.

'And you'll answer his question?'

Potts nodded.

'Go on, then,' Vash said, waggling the knife in the air so that light slid up and down the blade.

'My name's . . .' Potts began, then had to stop because all that emerged was a wheezy croak. Trying to suppress his blossoming panic, and the pain in his chest that seemed like a physical manifestation of it, he swallowed, licked his lips, which felt roughly equivalent to passing a Weetabix over two crusts of dry bread, and tried again. 'My . . . name's . . . Arthur Potts.'

Vash's voice was contemptuous. 'I've never fucking heard of you.'

Potts tried desperately to generate some saliva in his mouth, and wished that the burning ache in his chest would go away. Cold sweat was rolling off him.

'Maybe my grandad saw you play,' Beaker said. 'I could ask him.'

Potts nodded in what he hoped was an encouraging manner. Thankfully the pain in his chest was at last beginning to ebb a little.

'I think you're fucking bullshitting us,' Vash said.

Potts made himself speak. 'I'm not, really.'

'Prove it.'

'I can't. I've only got the shirt.'

'Haven't you got any medals or anything?' the smaller boy asked.

Potts shook his head. 'We never won anything when I was there. We weren't a bad side, but we never won anything.'

'Like now,' said Beaker, with a certain amount of melancholy.

'What do you mean?' said Vash. 'We won the Championship a few years ago.'

'That was fucking ages back. I wasn't even twelve then.'

'Yeah, well, we still won it, didn't we?'

'What position did you play?' the smaller boy said.

'Inside-right.' When they all looked blank, he explained, 'Up front. Just behind the centre-forward. The same sort of position as . . .' He tried to remember the name of the role's present incumbent, but his nerves had chased it from his mind '. . . you know, the tall, black lad.'

'Deano,' said the smaller boy.

'That's the feller. Good player.'

'Him and Yeboah. Fucking magic,' the boy said reverently.

'Score a lot o' goals, did you?' Beaker said.

Potts nodded. 'Quite a few.'

'How many?'

'Oh, I can't remember exactly. I'd usually get about

. . . fifteen or twenty a season. One season I think I got twenty-five.'

'What was it like playing in them days?' the smaller boy asked.

Potts looked at him. He was still the only one he dare look in the eyes. 'It was the same game it is now,' he said. 'The ball was heavier, and the crowds were bigger, and we weren't as fit as they are today, but football's football, isn't it?'

'What's it like running out on to the pitch at Elland Road?' Beaker asked, and now there was awe in his voice too.

Again, despite the situation, despite sitting in his bed in the dead of night surrounded by three teenage thugs who had broken into his house to rob him or worse, Potts smiled.

'It's like nothing on earth,' he said. 'You run down the tunnel and all you can hear are the studs clacking on the floor and your own heart thumping in your chest, and then you look up and there's this bright light and this patch of brilliant green below it, and it just gets bigger and bigger. And then you run out on to the pitch and the roar of the crowd hits you, and it's like a wall of noise. At first it's so loud that you think it's going to knock you over, and you're so proud that the crowd are making all that noise for you that you think the top of your head is going to fly off.'

He risked a look around. From what he could see of their eyes in the lamplight, the smaller boy and Beaker looked rapt. Even Vash looked as though he was trying not to be impressed.

Suddenly the smaller boy sat down on the end of his bed, and Potts was reminded absurdly of the children coming to sit on Julie Andrews' bed during the storm scene in *The Sound of Music*.

'So what's the best ground you've ever played on?' the boy said.

'Apart from Elland Road, you mean?'

The boy's eyes creased as he grinned and nodded.

'Oh, let me think. Goodison Park was always a nice place to play. They always had a very good pitch. And there was always a great atmosphere up in the North-East, at Newcastle and Sunderland. I once played in front of 73,000 people at Roker Park, you know.'

The smaller boy's eyes widened.

'You never,' breathed Beaker.

'I did. FA Cup semi-final against ... now was it Preston North End or Blackpool? Anyway, I remember we lost 3–2 in the end, but I scored our second equalizer. You should have heard the noise.'

'You can't fit 73,000 people inside a football ground,' said Vash almost resentfully, 'especially not Roker Park. I've been there, it's dead poxy.'

'Maybe not these days, but you could then. They didn't have all these safety regulations back then, you see. They just used to pack in as many people as possible.'

'So what's the biggest game you've ever played in?' Beaker asked.

'Probably that one. The semi-final.'

'Did you ever play for England?' the smaller boy asked.

The pain in Potts' chest was little more than a twinge now. He smiled. 'No, I was never that good.'

'What about Wembley?' Beaker said. 'Did you ever play there?'

'No, I'm afraid not. But I've been there to watch Leeds a few times. I was sent tickets by the club to see the '65, '70, '72 and '73 FA Cup Finals.'

'And you went to all of 'em?' the smaller boy said, awestruck.

Potts nodded. 'I wasn't going to waste my tickets, was I?'

'Liverpool, Chelsea, Arsenal, Sunderland,' Vash muttered.

Potts risked a glance at him, and was relieved to see he was no longer holding his knife.

'What about 'em?' Beaker said.

'That's who we played in the Cup Finals, you dim twat. Only won one of 'em, though.'

'Arsenal, 1972,' Potts said carefully. '1-0. Allan Clarke scored with a diving header from a Mick Jones cross.'

Vash nodded. 'Got it on video. Sound goal.'

'I wasn't even born last time we were in a Cup Final,' Beaker said glumly.

'We'll win summat this year,' the smaller boy said. 'Definite.'

'Hey, Mister, if we get in the Cup Final, will you get us all tickets?' said Beaker.

Potts licked his lips and looked down at his hands once again before replying, uncertain how far he could push.

'That depends, doesn't it?' he said at last.

'On what?'

'On what happens tonight.'

There was a silence. At first Potts didn't dare look at any of the boys, and then he became too nervous *not* to look at them. From what he could tell, just from looking at their eyes, Beaker and the smaller boy appeared a little shame-faced, but both were looking to Vash as if for guidance. Vash's eyes, fixed on Potts, were unreadable. Potts held Vash's gaze for a moment and then looked away. His stomach ached with tension.

Finally Vash said, 'Nothing's gonna happen.'

Potts was so relieved that he grinned and slumped forward. 'You mean it?'

Vash shrugged, looked at him a moment longer, then turned and walked out of the room without another word.

Beaker and the smaller boy looked at one another, as though uncertain what to do now that their leader had left. Beaker began backing towards the door. He pointed at Potts and said, 'You're sound, you are.' Then he fled.

Now Potts was left with the smaller boy whose name he didn't know. Slowly the boy got up from the bed and looked at Potts for a moment. Then he seemed to come to some decision, stepped forward and held out his hand. Potts looked at the hand, then he held out his own. They shook.

'Good to meet yer,' the boy said. He opened his hand and Potts released it. He began to back towards the door as Beaker had done. 'Sorry about . . . this. It won't happen again.'

He left.

For perhaps five minutes after the boys had gone, Potts remained where he was, listening. He heard nothing but silence. Finally he turned to look at the clock on his bedside table and saw that it was 4.20 a.m.

He pulled back his covers and swung his legs out of bed, then turned his head once more to look at the framed shirt on the wall above the headboard. He hoped that none of the boys would have the sense or the enthusiasm to check up on what he had told them, because of course it was all nonsense. As a matter of fact, he had astonished himself with his own inventiveness. He had made a conscious effort not to exaggerate too much because they would never have believed him. He had wanted to be a footballer when he was younger, had even gone for a trial with Leeds United once, but had never made the grade. All the same, even now he sometimes found himself daydreaming about the career he might have had, which was presumably why he had found it so easy to lie to the boys. In the end he had found a job as a carpet fitter and had contented himself with cheering United on from the terraces, until hooliganism got too bad in the mid-70s, since when he had watched the game only on television.

Suddenly, thinking of how he had outwitted the young thugs who had broken into his home he began to snigger, and then to laugh, and then to *shriek* with laughter. He couldn't stop himself, not even when the laughter became sobbing, not even when his legs buckled beneath him and he found himself lying on his bedroom floor, shaking uncontrollably.

He needed a cigarette. God, how he needed a cigarette. Still sobbing, he placed his hands on the floor and tried to lever himself up. He managed to get half-way before a pain, so massive he couldn't even cry out, tore into his chest. By the time his face hit the carpet, he was unconscious.

When he next became aware, he was moving through a dark tunnel, heading towards a bright light. He felt young again, his legs strong. He was surrounded by the clattering of studs. The light grew brighter; he felt it beckoning him, welcoming him, urging him on. As it engulfed him, the crowd began to chant his name.

You might think that a Leeds United season-ticket holder would have enough doom and gloom in his life without adding to it by writing horror fiction, but Mark Morris's fifth novel, *Mr Bad Face*, is due out in November 1996. His short story collection, *Close to the Bone*, was published in hardback by Piatkus but has not yet appeared in paperback. Born in Bolsover in 1963, Mark Morris now lives in Boston Spa with his wife, the artist Nel Whatmore, and their two children.

Kim Newman

The Germans Won

At the Enfield depot, off-shift crews let out a beery cheer. John clocked off just as an extra-time penalty put England into the World Cup Final in Los Angeles. The whistle blew and the cheer rose to an exultation.

The staff were watching the match on a colour telly bought especially. Four years ago, on the depot's Redif-fusion, the *Mondial* had seemed played in thick snow between teams fielding subtle variations of black, white and grey strip.

On screen now, Bobby Robson was chair-lifted across the pitch by jubilant supporters. The BBC commentator talked about how much better the game was now than when he was playing.

'Oor Bobby sits at God's right hand,' claimed Tommy, the Geordie driver on the 43 route. Tommy took football seriously, risking reprimand by wearing a Newcastle United scarf with his London Transport uniform. He patriotically switched to England for the duration of the World Cup.

'We used to think that way about Alf Ramsey,' muttered Stan, conductor on the 73. 'Till nineteen sixty-bloody-six.'

In the Final, England would face West Germany. Again.

John had been on the 134 route, the long haul from Brixton all the way to the Frozen North. He took off his ticket machine and cashed out with his supervisor, Jeffrey.

Every day, he thanked God for the GLC's Fares Fair policy, which had, since the early 1980s, made the sums so much easier. He had almost failed, all those years ago, the mental arithmetic test. He dreaded to think what would have become of him, and Norma, if he hadn't been able to go on the buses and get a job for life.

'Excellent, John,' purred Jeffrey, who liked to think himself a financial mastermind, as he weighed up the neat rolls of coins. 'Not a penny more, not a penny less.'

John was proud of his ability to keep track of change. Other conductors mistakenly accepted Irish 50p pieces or New York subway tokens, but he was scrupulous.

He took the roll of pound notes from his satchel and handed them over. A healthy wad. Regardless of policy, he could always make change for a £20 note on a 30p single from Tottenham Court Road to Muswell Hill.

Margi told him the urn was fresh-brewed and he took a mug of thick, sweet tea and a pasty. Norma would have gone to bed long ago, after the *Wednesday Play*; he might as well unwind with the other crews before going home to his council house in Gordon Hill. Snug, sound and rent-controlled, he thought of it as his council castle.

As the post-match discussion recapped England's four goals against Holland's two, most of the staff opened cans of Double Diamond. Stan, who had scooped the pool on the result, was generous with the bottle of Bell's he had won.

John resisted temptation: he didn't want to go home with whisky breath. He immediately regretted turning down Stan's kind offer. He felt a bit out of it with the other staff. They were matey, of course, but sometimes he felt he shared little with them. Once in a while, he thought the others were making fun of him and he was missing the joke.

In his satchel he found the book he was re-reading, *Phineas Redux.* Jeffrey clocked the Trollope immediately and sidled over, smirking. He knew the supervisor was about to tell him – for the fourth or fifth time – that he had once written a book.

He wondered if the crews thought he was in too tight with Jeffrey, brown-nosing. Actually, he wasn't sure if he really liked the supervisor. Jeffrey seemed to feel himself superior not only to staff under him but to the job as a whole.

'I wrote a book once, John,' Jeffrey said, as always. 'I made bad investments, found myself enormously in debt. I thought: I know, I can get out by writing a best-seller. You know, a real page-turner. Everyone I submitted the manuscript to sent it back with a form rejection. I expect they thought it was unpublishable crap. It probably was. Still, I wrote a book once. Not so different from your Trollope, John. Not so different at all.'

Jeffrey was still in debt, working at a job he looked down on, moving his money around in a variety of dodgy get-rich-quick schemes that always fell apart. He had invested in VHS video recorders and been wiped out by the success of Betamax. John couldn't understand Jeffrey's obvious desire to get out of London Transport. There was nothing better than helping the public, meeting people, travelling. Everyone had a smile for a bus conductor. Every route was an adventure.

He relished his pasty, home-baked at Marks & Spencer's this morning, warmed in Margi's trusty gas oven. Though the others might swig Bell's, he was content with a mug of Lipton's.

'How's the tea, love?' Margi asked.
'Warm and wet, that's what counts.'

On telly, Robson – face fringed with purple and green
thanks to slightly amateurish tuning – was cagey about
prospects for the trophy. He conceded that the West
Germans, having thrashed Brazil in their semi-final,
were favourites, but slyly hinted that there might be a
surprise or two coming. The interview was ended
prematurely by enthusiastic fans clamouring for the
beloved manager.

Stan, pleasantly glowing, reckoned England's
chances were pretty good. He was hopelessly optimistic,
a trait John envied. To groans, Stan produced statistics,
goal averages.

'Also, the German lads will be worried about what's
going on back home, with rioting along the Berlin Wall
and Russian tanks massing at the border. They'll be
thinking of their families.'

'It'd be a shame to win like that,' said John, who had
read John Pilger's sensitive analysis of the German crisis
in this morning's *Sun*. 'I'd be surprised if Robson
accepted the Cup under those circumstances. Honour
is more important than winning.'

The cheeriness lasted a while. Then Jeffrey said, 'Of
course, it'll be a different story in the Final. Like in
sixty-six. The Krauts might lose wars, but they win
World Cups.'

John remembered the 1966 World Cup. He had been
23, new to the buses. No grey in his hair. Bobby Moore's
boys were unconquerable, overwhelming all opposition.
People in the streets wore England scarfs and armbands
as if they were the insignia of a nascent totalitarian state.

During the host team's Cup run, John noticed something around him that he didn't like: an arrogance, a

xenophobia, a cruelty. It was sneering in the tub-thumping of commentators, politicians, union leaders, businessmen. Everything was adversarial, setting worker against boss, North against South, England against the world. There was even talk of troubles in Ulster.

Trollope would have been able to express it better than he could, but the initial success of Alf's commandos pricked something buried since the War. At the beginning of the Final, which he watched with his parents at the postman's house, English supporters chanted 'two world wars and one world cup', jeering as the Germans jogged on to the pitch at Wembley.

That wasn't the attitude. That wasn't the game.

He remembered thinking that if this was what England felt, then England deserved to lose. No matter how staunch Moore, the Charltons and the rest of the glory-covered team were, if the fans saw football as an excuse for expressing prejudice, then it wasn't worth winning.

Three–three by the whistle. Four–three to the Germans in extra time.

He felt like a traitor, but John thought the result was fair. And after that, something changed.

'You'll see,' Jeffrey announced, 'it'll all go pear-shaped in the Final. That's the trouble with bloody Britain. Never finishes the job. We're just not ruthless enough, too concerned with seeing the other fellow's point of view. Our players will feel so sorry for poor old Fritz, with his divided country falling under Commie tank-treads and 450 per cent inflation wiping out their wages. We'll let 'em have a couple of goals just so they feel better. And before you know it, some Kraut will be holding up the World Cup and blowing raspberries at us all.'

There was a lot of grumbling, but the supervisor was

capable of finding an excuse to fire anyone who argued with him.

'We'll lose. You know why? Because we like bloody losing. It makes us feel warm and fair-minded and decent. Remember in sixty-nine, when we tried power-sharing in Ulster rather than sending in the troops. Or eighty-two, when we had the *Belgrano* under our guns and let it sail back to port. It's as if nothing matters enough to us to fight for.'

'Oor Bobby won't let the lads lie back on the pitch,' said Tommy. 'England'll play to win, fair and square.'

'That's right, Geordie. Fair and square. If it's worth winning, then it's worth cheating for. Remember the last Final? In Italy.'

England had been in that too. Against Argentina. The final result found England losing two–one.

'The Argies put three of our blokes in hospital. And Maradona scored the winning goal with his hands while their midfield distracted the ref. Was that fair and square?'

'We don't play like that,' John said. 'If other people do, that's their problem. In the end, you'll see, it's better to be on the up and up, Jeffrey. Maradona may have won that match, but I very much doubt he's happy these days. I understand Argentine jails aren't very comfortable.'

'But we should have shelled the fuck out of the *Belgrano*.'

It wasn't just about football. In '66, with Wilson throwing his weight about and thinking of committing British soldiers to Vietnam, it had been about everything. The country was riding high and looking around for someone to trample. The Germans had tripped that up. Better it should happen at Wembley than on some battlefield.

That arrogance, the bossy brutality of the '60s, faded a bit afterwards with the arrival of the gentler 1970s. Wilson gave way in bad temper to Heath and the bridge-building policies which took the United Kingdom happily into Europe. Heath stayed in office long enough to open the Channel Tunnel and conduct John Lydon's Youth Orchestra in an all-Elgar promenade concert to celebrate the Queen's Silver Jubilee.

Subsequent prime ministers, Tory and Labour, were peacemakers not jingoists: Jim Callaghan, Denis Healey, Peter Walker, Chris Patten. Good blokes all. John, a born floater, had voted for the lot of them. Next year, for a change, he would give a woman a chance, and put Harriet Harman in Number Ten Downing Street. She had such a sympathetic face, and made a point of travelling everywhere on public transport.

It was true that England had never won the World Cup, but had played in four Finals since 1966 and never been knocked out before the semi-finals. The record was nothing to be ashamed of. West Germany, winners in '66, had collapsed in Mexico in '70 and not even qualified for '74 or '82.

In other countries – Holland or Spain – football was the focus of riots, violence, even mass murder. Families could enjoy British football every Saturday, either at thronging arenas up and down the country or on BBC1's *Match of the Day* after the news. Everyone said British football was the safest, most exciting in the world. And there was no chance of being under a petrol bomb if the away side lost. What with Berlusconi's satellite channel robbing Italian terrestrial viewers of their own league games, British football was even being screened to huge ratings in Italy.

'You're wrong, Jeffrey,' John piped up, courage swelling. 'There's nothing wrong with losing in a Final.

Being second best in the world means something.
There's nothing wrong with being top of League Division Two. There's nothing wrong with being honestly
second rate.'

'Second place is no place, John.'

'We always come second in the Eurovision Song Con-
test,' Stan muttered, spieling to break up the argument.
'It's because we always try to find a good group and get
them to do a good song. We never put in some crass
glitter bird like the Luxembourgers. All those la-la bing-
bang songs that sound the same in any language always
win. We should never have let Lennon and McCartney
write all our entries in the 1970s—'

'Show me a good loser, John, and I'll show you a
loser.'

Jeffrey made soft little fists. John knew he had to
argue, job or no job. This struck to the core of his
being. Every man can be pushed so far into a corner,
but there he will find the thing he truly believes.

'Results don't matter, Jeffrey,' said John. 'Playing the
game does. Life isn't results. When you die, they don't
calculate your goal average and judge whether you
should be promoted or relegated. Life is the game, the
process of the game, moment to moment. If you do
your best, no one can blame you. If you play fair, no
one can argue with you. Better to be a successful dust-
binman than a wash-out field marshal.'

A deadly, viperish calm fell on Jeffrey's face. Measur-
ing his words with venom, he said, 'Maybe that's why
you've been a bus conductor all your life, John.'

The staff fell silent. Only the telly – *Whistle Test*, with
John Peel – made a sound. Everyone looked at Jeffrey,
feeling the contempt of his words, trying to wipe out
the slight of what he had said from their minds.

John felt the others fall in behind him. Margi, who
always had a soft spot for him, held her rolling-pin like

a club. Tommy clapped a matey hand on his shoulder. Stan quietly turned off the telly and crossed his arms.

Tomorrow, Jeffrey would resign or request a transfer. He would not be able to keep working with these men and women. He could never be part of the crews.

'Jeffrey,' John said, pride in his backbone, 'there's nothing wrong with being a bus conductor.'

Kim Newman must bear some of the responsibility for this book, having suggested that it – or something like it – might not be such a bad idea. Newman published a frighteningly prescient soccer tale, 'SQPR', in *Interzone* magazine; this was later collected in *The Original Dr Shade and Other Stories*, one of his two collections. Brixton-born in 1959, he was brought up in Somerset and now lives in north London. He has published fourteen novels, six under his own name and eight as Jack Yeovil. In addition he reviews films for *Empire* and *Sight & Sound*.

John Hegley

Hat-trick

A Comparison of the On-form
Tony Yeboah and Yer Boa Constrictor

Neither is European in origin,
both are skilled at squeezing through
opponents' defences
but Tony Yeboah has got more legs.

John Hegley

Centre Forward-Looking

I've seen into the crystal ball
of football's future
and there are adverts on the shirts
which rearrange when the cameras
are on the player's advertising surface
for anything more than a second;
like those big billboards you see in three-
cornered strips which all twist round
to compose another picture.
The referee's a bionic robot
as are both linespeople
and they are as infallible as the TV
having radiophonic contact
with all cameras and instant-replay facilities
although the commentators have been removed
being adjudged by the robo-officials
to be a pain in the circuit.
Live spectators are a thing of the past,
the spell of the telly is iron-cast.
As has been suggested in our day
domestic television has the function of focusing
on the miked-up voice of the player of your choice
and very sensitive the system is too
not only picking up the soccer-speak
but also the guttural subtleties
of individual gobbing technique.
And to add to the feel of realness
supporters of the opposing side
are relayed from their homes into the system
where the subscriber can access them
for the purposes of virtual aggro.
A catalogue of chants are available
and you can log in your own suggestion
and have it chorally remastered on the spot.

Hat-trick

Surprisingly half-time oranges have been reintroduced
  in the
dressing room
as a concession to those who prefer
things the way they were.

John Hegley

Bristol City Versus Luton

I go to Bristol to see this match
with my Bristol based, big-faced school-day friend
we head for the home-team end,
he didn't get us tickets so I wonder if we'll get a seat.
He informs me that we will get a complete row of
    seats.
I think that he's joking – but no;
once settled within Ashton's Gate
there we are sat alongside a pride of fifty or so
unoccupied tip-uppences.
The away supporters' area
is also pretty bare of bottom
and you can see how the red
and white that City are wearing
is reflected in the chairing
to spell out 'Bristol City'.
Obviously the idea is that the effect is not visible
once the whole crowd has been allowed to roll in
and referring to the overall lack of interest and
    support
I pass comment that the arrangement of the letters
    ought
to say 'empty'.

If at some point during the 1980s and early '90s you
wanted to appear on stage but either lacked talent or
couldn't be bothered to learn a routine, and you happened to be a young bespectacled male, you had only
to sit in the front row at a John Hegley gig and he'd
volunteer you, without fail, to be Section C in 'Eddy Don't
Like Furniture' or to join the Brown Paper Bag Brothers
for a chorus of 'I'm In Love With a Brown Paper Bag'. If
you didn't want to be picked on, you took your glasses
off. It was as simple as that. Born in Newington Green,

Hat-trick

John Hegley moved to Luton at an early age. He has published several books of poems including *Glad to Wear Glasses*, *Can I Come Down Now, Dad?* and *Five Sugars, Please*.

Simon Ings

Sobras the Sacrifice

They call him Sobras – 'Scraps'. Because scraps are what's left.

When Scraps was eight—

No, look at this another way: Scraps is not yet born, and the pupa from which he will emerge is Jorge. Jorge it is who goes at eight years old to work in his uncle's tanning plant.

All day Jorge scrapes meat off the rotting hides, readies vast vats of caustic lyes and carries water, endless water, for vicious dyes and solvent baths, and his childhood is spent under a blistering equatorial sun and the crippling terror of anthrax.

Both his uncle and his father earned their carbuncles years before, and their faces and their hands are horribly mutilated. Jorge fears the scars more than death. Jorge thinks, Tele Globo will never turn their cameras on me, so disfigured. No matter what fine *jogador* I am.

Not that he stands a chance, not in this Pelé-proof shanty. The Cariocas and the Paulistas call the people of the Nordeste 'flatheads' and, for sure, that's no endearment. Besides, nobody's really wanted to give a black player a break since Barbosa let in Uruguay's winning goal in the 1950 World Cup.

Undeterred, Jorge plays barefoot in the sandy lots. Uncowed, Jorge dreams. Only *futebol* soothes his raw and blistered hands and calms his fears. Inane wank-

dream, supreme distraction, in Jorge's eyes *futebol* is the
very spoor of God.

When Jorge is nine his father gets a job in a cementation
plant in Niterói. The family – three boys and two girls
and an idiot mother, clowned by loose scaffolding in
their first year of matrimony – move to the Morro da
Esperança, into the cramped attic of a shack that smells
of wet mortar. There is no plaster, no flooring, and in
Jorge's room, no roof.

But Jorge doesn't care about the square of corrugated
tin lashed to the beams above his bed, wobbling, rusty
and serrated like the sword-blade of a gutter-rat Zeus.
Jorge doesn't care that his mother is howling in the
next room, convinced the cans she collects in return
for bread flee down the street and, if she catches them,
take root.

Jorge cares only that this is Rio, the home of the
Maracanã!

Jorge's father enrols Jorge in the junior team of a local
football club. It is a stake a poor father often places on
the future of his eldest son. If Jorge does well, the whole
family will benefit. And Jorge has skill, flair, determination and speed.

Jorge's father has none of these things. Instead he
loses three fingers in an industrial accident and gets
religion. Every Sunday he walks into a freshly painted
warehouse on the edge of town and hands half his
wages to Jesus in return for a promotion that never
comes.

Suddenly Jorge and his family are not just poor. They
are broke. Jorge can't even afford the bus fare to the
training ground. He is eleven years old. Old enough,
in this city of resourceful beggar children, to stop the
turn-around.

Old enough to say to his father, Not that life for me. Not tanning, cementation and wreckage and death.

No!

Futebol!

Old enough, when his dad tries to beat him, to take to the street and rob chemists' stores, mug tourists, face off kids weaker than him. True, the girl trawling the Copacabana, the *pivete* with the razor-blade who cuts off his ear, sets him back: he misses one training session.

So Jorge, unsupported and alone, beats and blunders his way through his apprenticeship and earns a transfer to the Vasco junior team. He promises to become the fastest striker in the city, which is the same as to say, the world. Rumours fill the city, earning Jorge a new name. The Cariocas, obsessed with *orixas* and the spirits of animals, christen him Potro, 'the Foal'.

In his first game at the Maracanã, one hundred thousand people come to watch the Foal play. Jorge, turning his head to one side to hide the ragged stump of his ear, puffs out his chest and promises the longed-for cameras of Tele Globo a show to remember.

Even his mother is happy, gathering cans from the concrete terraces. Cans that lie still and patient in her grasp and, soothed by the Foal's magic, have no will to flee.

Four minutes into the second half, with the score 2–1 to Vasco, Fluminense's elderly winger mistimes his tackle and splits Jorge's shinbone into equal halves.

Jorge lies on his back and stares up into a sky made blind-spot black by flaring floodlights. A green dragon-fly hovers over his head, his good fairy, perhaps, bidding him a reluctant farewell. On this hot night, its wings are twin scythes of green ice—

Then it is gone.

A spot of rain falls on his brow. Jorge thinks, dully: another christening.

The Vasco crowd is howling. They are stamping and screaming their love and concern for this new boy, this tough kid with the speed of an angel, this new Bebeto, this home-grown Bebe Chorao, this Foal.

But down there, sprawled in the magic circle of the holy green, something untoward is happening. The raindrop scours Jorge's brow with a line of fire, blessing him in the name of a deep, dark faith.

Not the Catholicism of his youth. Not his father's Pentecostal bread tomorrow. Not the ragtag remnants of Macumba, nor even Carnaval.

No.

Something else.

Surgeons at the General Hospital set Jorge's shinbone badly. Jorge accepts the punishment. (Faster than Bebeto, he'd bragged, and craftier than Pelé!) His manager, blind to the Foal's hubris, only laughs at the boy's remorse, and pays for corrective surgery.

But the publicity surrounding Jorge's crippling accident kills the Foal as surely as a vet's bolt-gun. An independent witness corroborates a keen-eyed chemist's allegations, and Jorge is imprisoned on charges of armed robbery. The prison doctors have few drugs with which to treat the arthritic pain in his mis-set leg, pain that worsens terribly in damp weather. And it rains and it rains and it rains.

(In his cell, Jorge tells the story of how, when it first rained during a game, the spillwater ran straight off the concrete awning of the newly built Maracanã, flooding the dugouts and drowning two sets of managers, press agents and reserves.)

*　　*　　*

Jorge is released from prison some years later. His brothers and sisters are all grown up and have left Rio for the Minas Gerais. His father has been dead a year, immolated with his mother in a suicide pact of her own devising. Jorge recalls Dario Jose dos Santos's mother: the madness and dreadful burning that birthed Brazil's greatest striker of the modern era. He wonders if his own mother knew about this; was her self-demolition some sort of tribute? A rite, to give Jorge some of dos Santos's diabolical power?

Fearing *futebol*'s further vengeance, Jorge stays away from the Maracanã. Without a trade, he's marking time washing windscreens on the Avenida Borges de Medeiros. The air is sickly sweet with gasohol and heavy with moisture. Jorge's leg is on fire.

Across the road, Vasco's juniors run by in full strip: their second circuit round the Lagoa. Jorge cannot help but grin through teeth snapped and broken in prison beatings. He wishes he could join them. Just for one lap! Just for old times' sake! The lights change and he doesn't notice.

A nervous tourist in a rented Gol runs over his good foot.

Months pass. Winter comes, with rain. Beneath a pewter sky, girls in drenched Vasco zebra-stripes dance about the mirrored pavements, swaying to the bass beat of massed *surdos* within the Maracanã, a quarter-mile away. The rain stops but the clouds aren't spent; they hang there solid and unbroken, tinged with green as evening comes.

Evening – and the midweek match. Jorge ponders: how long since he watched *futebol*?

Too long! Forget the bitter past, he thinks, enjoy the game! So he slops through the swimming streets on crooked leg and metal foot to the concrete ramps of the Maracanã. Vasco are playing Fluminense and Jorge, feeling no bitterness, buys a ticket and ascends. He hobbles round the oval and picks a tunnel at random. It brings him out on the fringes of the Vasco crowd. The place is nearly empty: barely twenty thousand people, clustered into opposing camps across a stadium built for two hundred thousand.

Here there are no railings, fences or safety guards, but only concrete stairs with seats marked out in yellow paint, as in some monstrous amphitheatre. There is nothing, in short, to distract your eye from that hallowed green rectangle, that perverse altar-top.

The greenish sky grows more jewel-like as the light fails. The stadium lights flare up around the concrete canopy, and dragonflies spark and wheel in the glare. The teams emerge, gaudy and lusty as the transvestite priests of the Macumba, and the roar of the crowd drowns the rattle of *tamburins* and *pandeiros*.

Confused and elated, Jorge surges forward. Perhaps he thinks to greet his old *companheiros*. Perhaps the dragonfly is his good fairy, his *orixa*, come to recover for him his fortunes and his flesh. Whatever the reason, Jorge elbows forward, misses his step, falls and cuts his remaining ear on a jagged bottle-stub.

Two weeks later Jorge lies in the General Hospital on the brink of death. Only a total plasma transfusion stops the septicaemia from killing him. Even so, his ear, gone gangrenous, will have to be removed.

Months pass. Jorge is back in the Maracanã again. It isn't *futebol* that draws him here now. He'd happily not hear another 'Gooooooooooooolllllll!', nor ever see another fan's flag tug at its bamboo tether. Only necessity draws him in. For the poorest of the poor and the lamest of the lame there is very little work, and for these the Maracanã at least offers a living: roasting chestnuts in an oven made out of old catering tins, or selling coffee from a steel water-heater strapped across your chest. Children hawk bagfuls of unpleasant foamy wafers or collect cans for recycling: every fifty cans buys a loaf of bread. Old men buy cans of drink in the booths downstairs and mark them up for a crowd thirsty with Samba and adrenalin.

It is a blisteringly hot night in December, and Jorge is busy filling a tiny paper cone with bad coffee from a water-heater strapped to his chest. A fellow Vasco supporter – enthused by the team's wholly undeserved 3–0 lead over Flamengo – lets off the customary firework. He could not have timed it better: it makes a beeline for Scraps's face and plugs his left eye, searing it beyond repair. Scraps topples, and scalding, syrupy coffee scours his throat and chin and cheeks.

Of course the Maracanã houses other businesses. Shady occupations. And Jorge, who cannot now lift or carry or even walk much when it is wet, must muscle into this scene as best he can if he is to make a crust.

The Maracanã is a miniature city. It has its trades and occupations, bosses and workers, laws and law-breakers. For a while Scraps – they are starting to call him Scraps – prospers. But his misfortunes have confused him and made him careless, and so one day he breaks those brutal Maracanã laws, selling his bad sulphate under the nose of a *bicheiro* and his mob. They punish him, as they must, lopping off his nose with a cabbage knife.

Returning some weeks later, bitterly reduced, Scraps hunts for – well, scraps. Finding a half-empty packet of foamy wafers, he guzzles the lot. The last one lodges in his gullet. He tries to force it down. He retches. He tries to cough it up. He drools, and passes out in a corner where the overalled policemen and the stewards never look. A cleaner finds him the next morning, quivering and retching, the concrete beneath his head spotted with blood. He is taken to the hospital.

The porters recognize Scraps instantly. They cheer him into theatre.

Scraps has no money for the barber, so he hacks off his hair as best he can with a blunt razor blade, wiping the blood out of his eyes with a careless hand.

On the terraces, Vasco are losing to Fluminense, 2–1, the tension is unbearable and Scraps, his gag reflex permanently damaged by his night-long battle with the *futebol* wafer, retches and drools on to the heads of the seated spectators beneath.

He doesn't care which team wins. He, alone of all the people here, truly appreciates the irrelevance of a final score.

When it is all over, Sobras, whose name means Scraps, climbs the terraces and kneels at the foot of the top step. There is a puddle in the concrete there, and in it he studies the reflection of his head. Featureless now: a bald ball of leather, cured and tanned by sunlight and time and two gallons of boiling coffee, its remaining eye tiny and black like a valve. Gently he lays down his head on the stone step and waits for his dragonfly to come. The game's insect god with its twin scythes of green ice.

Once his head is off, the children of the Morro da Esperança can have it for a football.

Simon Ings has published three novels with Harper-Collins. His short fiction has appeared in *Critical Quarterly, Omni, New Worlds* and other magazines and anthologies. He enjoys collaborating and working in various media – with M John Harrison he wrote a story,

Simon Ings

'The Dead', which appeared in *The Sun Rises Red*, *Interzone* and *Best New Horror 4*; with director Simon Pummell, who contributed graphics to Ings' most recent novel *Hotwire*, he is engaged on a number of film projects; and with Nicholas Royle (that's your editor) he wrote and performed *Station2Station*, a commission for the Bath Literature Festival, with musical accompaniment by Billy Jenkins and the Voice of God Collective with Fun Horns.

Christopher Fowler

Permanent Fixtures

No man is an island, but quite a few are peninsulas. I guess if you really hate people, it's easy to cut yourself off. You move into the countryside, never go to the cinema or a football match, avoid casual arrangements, lock yourself away. But it won't make you a happier person. A friend of mine called Paula told me this story over lunch the other day, and I'm still not sure if all of it's true, although she swears it is.

In 1972 Paula upset her entire family by marrying a man they all felt to be unsuitable for her. She was nineteen years old, an only child who had just moved to north London from the kind of small Hertfordshire village where everyone knows everyone else's business and doesn't approve of it. She knew nothing of city life and very little about men. Kenneth was her first boyfriend, and the courtship lasted just four months. They were married in a registry office in Islington, and no one was allowed to throw confetti because of the litter laws. The ceremony was reluctantly attended by Paula's father, who barely bothered to conceal his disappointment and left immediately after the photographs were taken. Paula's mother telephoned during the reception to wish her well, but turned the call into a catalogue of complaints, and only spoke to her daughter on one further occasion before she died of a stroke seven months later.

Kenneth Stanford was thirty-one. He drove a Ford

Corsair, collected Miles Davis and Buddy Rich record-
ings, worked in a town planning office and promised
to love Paula for ever. He decided he had enough
money saved to buy a house, and carefully chose where
he wanted to live. The location he picked was in Avenell
Road, Highbury, right opposite the gate of the Arsenal
football ground. He had supported the Gunners since
he was a kid, and had recently bought himself a seat
there.

In typical London style the area hid its surprises well,
for who would have thought that such an immense
stadium could be tucked so invisibly behind the rows
of little houses? In an equally odd arrangement, famous
film stars and directors often visited the road to check
on their feature prints at the nearby Metrocolor film-
processing labs, but the child who ventured to suggest
that he just saw Mel Gibson passing the fish shop usually
received a cuff about the head for lying.

So it was that Paula moved into a damp Victorian
two-floor terraced house in the shadow of a great
stadium. She became pregnant twice in quick succession, and saw very little of her husband, who worked
late, spent his nights drinking at Ronnie Scott's and his
weekends attending football matches with his mates. In
accordance with the social etiquette of the day he never
introduced his wife to his friends: the people he met
at the jazz club to whom he wished to appear cool; or
the people he met on the terraces to whom he wished
to appear laddish.

Paula had no interest in football. She regarded the
red and white hordes who periodically trooped past her
bay window as some kind of natural phenomenon, like
a plague of frogs. She learned not to invite friends over
for lunch on Saturday afternoons. She grew used to
being segregated from fans in the Arsenal Tube station,
watching guiltily as they were herded into the separate

tunnel of their rat-run. She became accustomed to the
closed-off streets, the suspended parking bays, the
colour-co-ordinated families, the makeshift souvenir
stalls selling booklets, flags, scarves, T-shirts and rattles,
the neighbours who ran out into the road to collect
the horse-droppings from the mounted police for their
gardens, or who turned the fronts of their houses into
tea and sandwich shops. The fans were just another
vexatious and slightly mysterious part of life, like
wondering why garages sell charcoal briquettes in winter or why Rolf Harris never gets any older.

So she lived with the sharp smell of frying onions
and beefburgers, the nights being lit as bright as day,
the packets of chips chucked over her gate, the cans
of Special Brew left on her front windowsill, the local
supermarkets bumping up their prices on Saturdays,
the Scots boys for whom her bedraggled front garden
held eerie allure as a urinal, the spontaneous outbursts
of singing, the great endless flow of generally good-
natured people. She accepted it all as something that
came with the house, a permanent fixture, like having
a pylon in the garden.

Eventually she rather liked it. She liked watching
fathers pass by with their hands on the shoulders of
their sons. She had given birth to two beautiful daughters. It was no coincidence that Kenneth's interest in
football and marriage ebbed from this point. Soon he
became indifferent to the point of vanishing altogether,
and Paula raised her children alone. He let her keep
the house, which was falling into disrepair, and moved
into the more spaciously appointed Westbourne Grove
residence of a sometime nightclub singer who appreciated his record collection.

And through the years Paula watched from her
window as the great red and white sea trudged back and
forth. It seemed strange that such a vast cross-section of

humanity could remain so placid, but there was rarely any trouble in the street. A grudge match against Tottenham Hotspur would occasionally create a small explosive pocket of anger ending with shouts and the sound of broken bottles, and on one late summer afternoon somebody slipped a hand through her open bay window to steal the handbag she had foolishly left lying on a chair, but such incidents were spaced far apart across the seasons.

The girls grew tall, developing in a curious way that mixed coarse humour with immaculate behaviour. By the age of ten they were already growing familiar with the works of Lewis Carroll and Conan Doyle, but also knew the words to popular songs like 'You're Going Home In The Back Of An Ambulance' and 'My Old Man Said "Be An Arsenal Fan", I said "Fuck Off, Bollocks, You're A Cunt".' They weren't really fans, but so much of their lives had been played out before the audience that ebbed around the house, they knew more about the Arsenal and its people than seasoned veterans.

Times remained hard for Paula and her children. Her maintenance cheques had to be extracted with threats. She feared the future. One Saturday afternoon she sat in her front garden in the slanting autumn sunlight and cried a little. The girls were both out with friends, and she was feeling alone and saddened by the knowledge that she would one day lose them, when a grinning young man called at her from the ocean of people shuffling past, 'Hey, cheer up, missus, can't be that bad, come along with us and have a laugh!' and she smiled and wiped her eyes and got up, and got on.

After that, she never felt alone on Saturdays.

But she met a man, a red-headed minicab driver seven years her junior, called Malcolm, and in her desperation to overlook his faults she ignored his worst;

his disrespect for everything except her sexuality. After the first time he hit her, he apologized for hours and even cried, then quoted the Bible, and treated her nicely for several weeks.

The girls stayed out of his way. He was infuriated by the creativity of their swearing (something they did naturally as a consequence of where they lived) and forced them to attend services at a bleak little Baptist church near his cab office in Holloway, although they only managed to go three times. It seemed to Paula that he stared at her girls too hard, sometimes with dead-eyed hatred, and sometimes with a little too much liking. He was an unhappy man, embittered by his lot in life, yet he could be kind and supportive, and she needed him, and the affair drifted on long enough for him to be given his own front-door key.

But there came a time when she wanted it back, and she wanted him out. She knew that he looked upon the three of them as godless and doomed. He nagged at Paula to be a better mother. He complained that she was disorganized, forgetful, useless, a lousy house-keeper. He worked nights and slept days, forcing her to creep around and hold her breath each time she dropped something. He warned the girls against form-ing undesirable friendships after school, then enforced the warning with a curfew. He did not approve of Paula's friends, who were Caribbean and Greek and Indian and nothing at all like the suburban couples his parents invited over for barbecues. Little by little the house in Avenell Road became a prison with limited visiting hours. During the day its atmosphere was sepul-chral, colder and quieter than the street outside.

Then the new season began. The Gunners played well and ascended the league table, swelling the gate and filling the streets with more fans than ever before. There was to be a midweek charity match for a beloved

285

retiring player. By half past six that Wednesday evening the tide of fans had risen to a deluge. Gillespie Road and Plimsoll Road were at a standstill. The floodlights had given the backstreets the brightness of Las Vegas. Malcolm strode about the living room shouting, and Paula became frightened that he would smack her again. He was annoyed that she had allowed Caroline to bring friends to the house while he was trying to sleep. She knew he took 'jellies' – Temazepam – to sleep, and suspected that this addiction was the cause of his mood-swings, but she could not bring herself to discuss the matter with him.

'If I don't sleep I can't work, and that means no fucking money for any of us, do you understand?'

'I don't take anything from you,' she complained. 'I provide for the girls.' To cut a long story short, she asked for the front-door key back and he refused to return it. Paula's older daughter was away on a school trip, and Caroline, the younger one, was hovering by the kitchen door chewing a fingernail, listening to the escalating row. When she heard the screech of furniture shifting and something – a vase? – knocked over, then silence, she ran into the room to find her mother sitting on the floor with a look of surprise on her face, as if she had just slipped over while learning to ice-skate.

When Malcolm advanced on her again she yelped and scuttled into the hall like a frightened dog, and Caroline was ashamed of her mother's cowardly behaviour. '. . . fucking kill you,' she heard him say, and now he had something in his hand, a poker she thought, but by this time Caroline had opened the front door and was calling out for help. He said something about 'everyone knowing our business' and made to hit Paula because she was embarrassing him, but Caroline pulled her mother through the door into the front garden and stared desperately into the relentless crowds.

Which must have helped because there he was right in front of them, the grinning young man in his red and white scarf, him or someone very much like him, calling out 'Oi, you wanna hand? Is he botherin' you?', and Paula must have looked grateful because here were outstretched hands, dozens of hands, lifting her and her daughter over the garden wall and into the crowd, over the heads of so many fathers and sons, cresting the human surf faster and faster, bearing them away from danger on the same surf that turned to crash against her attacker, to push him back, and the more Malcolm tried to struggle the more they pinned him down, so that it appeared as if he had been thrown into a boiling river with his clothes stuffed full of rocks.

Paula and her daughter were borne aloft by the living wave, away into the beating heart of the maelstrom. The crowd was singing as it worked to protect them. It was then that she saw she had entirely misunderstood the football match. The centre of this mighty organism was not the pitch, not the game itself, but the surrounding weight of life in the stands, in the streets, a force that made her dizzy with its strength and vitality. Yet the centre was as hushed and calm as the eye of a hurricane, and it was here that the crowd set them down. Watching the men, women and children dividing around them like a living wall she momentarily felt part of something much larger. She somehow connected with the grander scheme for the first time in her life.

Of course, the crowd had also connected with Malcolm, or to be more accurate had connected with his collarbone, his left ankle, his skull and four of his ribs. Paula tells me that this is why she now goes to football, to experience that incredible moment when the crowd becomes a single powerful creature, when for a split second it feels as though anything in the world is poss-ible just by voicing your desire.

She tries to tell me that here is something mystic, deep-rooted and inexplicable, but I point out the simple truth: When you have so many thousand people all concentrating on one man's ability to plant a ball in the back of a net, you harness an energy that can shift the world from its axis.

Paula's children can tell you what life is really like. It smells of frying onions, and will beat the shit out of you if you resist it.

One of the busiest and most prolific writers of his gener-ation, Christopher Fowler remains completely unaffec-ted by the success that atter,ds the publication of his novels and their development into big-budget movies. He has published six novels and four collections of short stories and somehow still finds time to run the Creative Partnership, his Soho-based film promotion company. Although his characters are often to be found engaged in running battles on rooftops or destroying entire com-muter towns and generally having a big, exciting, out-rageous time of it, occasionally Chris Fowler comes right back down to earth and tells a simple tale of great emotional depth and power, such as the above.